AUTHOR	CLASS
CHRISTIE. A	F

TITLE First act.	No
	18302602

FIRST ACT

Anne Christie

PIATKUS

Copyright © 1983 by Anne Christie

First published in Great Britain in 1983 by
Judy Piatkus (Publishers) Limited of Loughton, Essex

Typeset by Phoenix Photosetting, Chatham
Printed and bound by Mackays of Chatham Limited

ISBN 0 86188 216 4

Christie, Anne
  First Act.
  I. Title –
  823'.914[F]   PR6053.H/

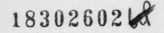

Will the gentle reader please note that
in fact this is a fiction.

In memory of Jack Ronder

Chapter 1

There were two wedding cakes, but only one bridal pair. The groom, Ben, was a full-blooded Lithuanian Jew, tall, thin, dark, third generation immigrant to Scotland. Thirty-five years old, he'd been eating bacon since his voice broke, but his mother had still not acknowledged the fact. He was supposed to marry a nice little Yiddishe girl, but I wasn't. I was a Shiksa, largish, blonde and twenty, with one blue eye and one brown eye, and although I wasn't Jewish, I wasn't a total disaster either. For one thing, I was upper class, lapsed, poor, but definitely upper. For another, I was half-Swedish, and Sweden was only a beigel-jump from Lithuania. And anyway, I'd never been christened.

Ben's mother, Mrs Mandel, was, of course, at the wedding, encased in hat, gloves and handbag, smiling but tearful, and secretly thinking she'd soon have him back in his own little room after this particular wedding-nonsense was finished.

When our intention to marry had been announced, Mrs Mandel had asked Ben if I'd turn. 'To what' he'd said, 'I've not been in a synagogue for twenty years.' My own mother, not bearing the thought that she was losing her youngest child so soon, clutched my arm

1

several times during the day's festivities. She was the Swedish half of me, tense, gaunt, and loving. Neither of our fathers was still alive.

Of the two wedding cakes lit by the Edinburgh summer sun, one was a Swedish Spetkakka – a great yellow cone made with three dozen eggs built up into a complicated Baroque pattern, like a golden Tower of Babel. The other cake was just a wedding cake, white, square and two-storeyed, horse-shoed and silver-slippered. We had two cakes because there were two of us getting married, for in those days in Edinburgh even emancipated thinkers married each other. It was even before the first Russian spaceman had caused wonder and excitement by orbiting the earth.

Mrs Mandel dubiously bit into a mushroom sandwich. 'It's good,' she said, surprised. I blinked through the champagne haze at the penguin suits and florid hats, guffaws and teeth, Swedish anecdotes and Jewish recipes. 'My God,' I thought, 'I'm married.'

'Aye,' said my friend Pete glumly by my side, 'you've gone and done it now,' and he winked.

When I was five I had been on a sunny doorstep with a six-year-old boy who drew a large grinning face on the stone step with white chalk. Fascinated I watched as he showed me and told me that was how to draw a face. I took the chalk and drew teeth on the great curved mouth, and was filled with excitement as the drawing changed and reappeared under my hand. It was magic, and I knew that this was what I must do with my life.

'I love you,' said Ben.

Two years ago he'd said that for the first time, and then my heart had clunked. I did love him, but I didn't want the responsibility of him. After meals and theatres, films and long goodnights, he would say, 'When

2

are we getting married?' And I would remain silent, paralysed, and an uneasy voice within me would whisper, 'Remember, you want to be a famous painter.'

'Yes,' said my fellow students – the ones who were only going to be teachers. 'No,' said a London painter friend, 'For God's sake go and live with him, but don't marry him.' And here I was, all geared up, roses in hair, flowers in hand, white lace dress, and I still wanted to be a painter more than anything in the world.

I looked across the coloured hubbub of guests at Ben. I was holding my enormous striped cat in my arms, where it lay dozing, like a huge stuffed piece of Fairisle knitting. Ben was miming a combine-harvester to my Uncle Lionel. He was my husband now, this beautiful and brilliant man; he met my glance and smiled, and I crossed my eyes at him.

Ben wrote plays. He also taught science at school, but most of his days and half his nights were spent at the typewriter. One of my reasons for loving him was my total faith in his talent. And after all Ben had said, 'I will only marry you if you go on painting all your life.'

'I shan't ever stop working,' I had announced at the engagement tea at Mrs Mandel's. The Mandel ladies had dropped stitches and spilt tea, and there had been a horrified silence before they remonstrated in a chorus of disbelief. But Mrs Mandel had given me a big bottle of Jewish cooking oil. She had given it impulsively, and I had been thrilled. My fellow student, Pete, at Art College the next day, had looked more serious than usual, and rubbed his chin thoughtfully.

'Here, fellie,' he said, 'that's fantastic of her; that's your acceptance into the tribe – she's telling you it's O.K. to cook for her son. It's a symbolic ritual you've just gone through.'

3

O.K. to cook for her son? O.K. to be domestically in thrall? I wondered.

Even the day before the wedding Ben's mother said, 'Don't you worry, you'll see. You'll not want to paint once you're married.' She made it sound like a definite ultimatum.

The actual marriage had taken place three hours ago in a dark brown Victorian registry office. The two small family groups sat nervously in a stark waiting-room with a black mantelpiece and an empty grate. There was my mother, my brother Charlie, Scottish uncles and Swedish aunts, and at the end of my row my vastly pregnant friend, Cordelia.

Ben was represented by his mother, his sister Rachel and husband, various aunts, and a lone uncle, Reuben, who had made a lot of money in Liverpool, selling clocks and china animals to the masses.

Ben flashed a sickly white-twitched smile at me. He looked wonderfully handsome and desirable – yet vulnerable. The pregnant Cordelia clutched her bulge sideways beside me and muttered out of the corner of her mouth, 'You can still escape if you want to, they haven't locked the door.'

I nodded sagely. 'I know, but don't you think it's time he proposed?'

Cordelia snorted, and I hoped she was wearing two pairs of pants – her bladder being weak at the best of times. The snort turned into a paroxysm when the dark brown door at the back of the room was thrust open and a little fat Scotsman in a brown suit stood and glared stiffly at the assembled company, nostrils quivering like a rabbit's.

'No smoking.'

He pointed to a blank white card sitting on the mantelpiece.

4

'You have turned that notice to the wall!'

'What notice?' asked Mrs Mandel querulously.

'We certainly have not!'

'We didn't even see it!'

The fat little man goose-stepped to the mantelpiece and lifted the card, knuckles white, ears scarlet. He turned it round, and the reverse side read 'No Smoking by Order', in large black print.

'Kindly put those cigarettes out at once!'

Mrs Mandel glared, hand clutching heart, flower-decked hat quivering. My own mother exhaled almost invisibly from a last long draw, and sat with her cigarette held tensely behind her left buttock. Ben watched the argument with a big pussycat smile. I grasped Cordelia's arm firmly to stop her from hitting the little man with an orchid. Then my Uncle Lionel, normally obsessively shy and agricultural, stood up in his striped trousers and slightly green pre-1914 tailcoat, and took charge in an awkward but decidedly military way. Like naughty children the smokers exterminated their cigarettes in the empty grate. Uncle Lionel apologised to the little man, who, breathing heavily, retreated to the door, where he paused and said:

'You may all enter now.'

We stood up, and I saw that Cordelia was trembling all over, her posy of flowers was rattling.

'You've got stage fright,' I said.

'I know,' she gulped. 'This is it. There's no retreat.'

'Come on,' I said. 'I'm not scared.'

We entered, and were married quite quietly and simply. The plain civic ceremony was adequate, bereft as it was of prayers, song or promises. Ben didn't drop the ring; we each responded firmly and surely, and very much enjoyed the kiss at the end. (Although I distinctly heard Ben's mother moaning as we kissed.) The registrar had to tap Ben on the shoulder in order to offer his official congratulations. The mothers both wept, my own for my going, Mrs Mandel for my coming. The men were back-slapping and hearty. Then the registrar called for a witness; he looked piercingly at the obviously pregnant Cordelia, and, offering her the pen with the tips of his fingers, said, 'Miss Mac-Naughton will you kindly sign the book,' with a chilling emphasis on the word 'Miss'. Cordelia, who was an old married lady of almost twenty, froze, glared furiously at him, took the pen, signed the book, and whisked her great bulk away, seething with insult and still clutching her orchid like a truncheon, as the registrar watched her sepulchrally.

The reception was held back at my home. An elderly acquaintance of Mrs Mandel's, Auntie Emma, climbed over several guests, barking their shins in the process, in her effort to be the first person to see the young couple's wedding presents. One present she didn't see was a duet for piano which was donated by a very serious young composer, who had written the piece specially to celebrate the marriage. Two of the more musical guests performed the piece as part of the celebrations, and since the performers had been celebrating for some time, and the piano had not been tuned since the bride's early decision to become a painter, the music sounded unusual and also frightened the cat, who leapt from the bride's arms and fled, leaving his imprint on the trifle and thereafter on the lap of Skinny Hazel Ochiltree who made a disgusted face towards Ben.

Once, all of fifteen years before, Ben had kissed Hazel Ochiltree in the oblivion of a student party, and since that time she felt that she had part-ownership in all his affairs. She rose now to confront Ben with a ten-doney smile. 'That cat. . .' she began, but Ben was

already cornered into trout-fishing and the marketing
of sugar-beet with my Uncle Lionel. Uncle Lionel had
a purple face and an orange moustache to match his
whisky, and he was not happy at social gatherings. He
missed his boots and tractor, and manfully muttered
'Jolly good' as often as he could. His wife, Aunt Mabel,
was now lecturing beside him on some awful people
who pronounced jodphurs 'joddpers' and not 'joad-
pores' as they ought to be pronounced. She had been
born on a regimental march to the hills south of Simla,
and was a sternly handsome figure of a woman, not
unlike Queen Victoria.

Lionel's only daughter, Louise, tall and pop-eyed,
joined the group; I was surprised to see her in a dress
and hat, and not even a riding-hat. I wondered if
Louise's jodphurs were standing alone and upright in
her room, and felt fleetingly sorry for them.

I picked up the cat again; Ben appeared beside me
and we touched arms.

'I love you.'

'I love you.'

We were interrupted by Marcus Thomson, a dashing
BBC radio producer who sometimes employed Ben for
script-writing. We both liked Marcus, except when he
was pompous, and today he was a little. The occasion,
and the acquisition of a purple velvet waistcoat, had
rendered him for once over-avuncular and self-import-
ant. I half-listened for a time, as he and Ben spoke of
scribes and scripts, until I realised that a large striped
cat, a bridal bouquet, and a champagne-glass is too
much to carry on one's wedding-day, especially if one
wishes to look memorably ravishing, as I indubitably
did. Marcus' suit and purple waistcoat were just a bit
too flash, so I smiled a sweet and bridal smile at him,
whispered a quick word, and thrust the huge cat across

his pristine chest. It stayed there long enough to leave a great mat of shed hairs, brown and white, shrieking from the immaculate velvet.

'You!' he yelled, dark brows raised, face matching waistcoat. 'You are an awful woman! Ben's got himself a handful, all right!'

Poor Ben looked anguished, so I fled quickly to the window and sat down beside the ninety-five-year-old deaf Miss Christian, a Theosophist, who sat flooded in yellow sunlight, her snowy-white hair plaited and beautiful on top of her old round head. She looked up at me with watery, washed turquoise eyes and smiled, putting out a gnarled hand to touch my arm.

'My dear, you have such happy vibrations.' And she slipped a large crumpled envelope into my hand. I gulped, and kissed and thanked the old lady, who delicately touched and smelt the freesias and roses in my bouquet. And as she did, I watched, and made a note to remember how she looked – her hands knobbled and arthritic, pearls gleaming, her dress soft and flowery – and knew I must paint her one day. I peeped into the envelope, which contained twenty fivers, ancient and crumpled. Nothing could have been better.

Years ago, I remembered watching, first crouched behind banisters, then through a keyhole, when Miss Christian came to visit my unhappy, tired mother, and gently stroked her aura, passing her wrinkled, aged hands above my mother's supine body, as she talked softly to her in her strange, duck-like, deaf voice.

Miss Christian wanted some tea, so I walked through the din and hurly-burly of friends and relatives – now rather red-faced, some of them – to the large kitchen at the back of the house. Ma was in difficulties trying to make the tea – coffee was her thing (being Swedish). Crouched over her, like a vulture, was my art student friend, Pete, talking in an almost inaudible throaty whisper, fingering his new-growing wisp of a beard, looking deeply through his new black spectacles. Pete was a nice lad, intense, but good-hearted. He didn't wash a lot, I was never quite sure if this was because he found it warmer, liked the tidemark texture, or was too poor for soap. He was telling my mother about textures in painting, admiring Jackson Pollock and various multi-syllabled French artists, which made me feel insecure because I hadn't heard of most of them, and in my heart of hearts I didn't really want to. Pete's painting was going through a slap and trickle phase, which was visually interesting, but so was burnt porridge – or even cat's hair on suiting.

I rescued my mother, who spooned tea into the urn, and gave Pete some beer.

'How are you Pete?'

'Fine, thanks, ye should get married more often. Here, fellow,' he clutched my hand, 'I started to write ye a poem.'

I was startled, but watched with interest as he unfolded a grubby piece of paper from his tobacco tin.

'D'ye want tae hear it?'

'Yes. . .' I said, a little doubtfully, because usually Pete's poems were about his unrequited love for my other great friend Zoe, who was standing only a few feet away – unrequited love and impotency, among other things.

Pete cleared his throat, moved a foot to the side to allow my mother to pour out some tea, glanced a flash of sweet smile at me, and sonorously declaimed:

'Pounds of wool are used when knitting
Used in endless work and sitting
Baby has to wear a nappy

9

If you want to keep him happy
Nappies have to be washed hourly
Otherwise they smell quite sourly
So dear Kate you should not do it,
Or I swear you'll live to rue it.'

I giggled, and caught Aunt Mabel's cold blue stare. Pete folded up the paper.

'I couldnae finish it, but I've worked out that in ten years ye'll need tae wash up and cook about eleven thousand meals, and if ye have a baby ye'll need tae wash about ten thousand nappies a year, so I just wanted tae warn ye tae think about it, fellow. It might interfere wi'yer work.'

An elderly mouth gawped, accepted a cup of tea, and exited hastily, cup and saucer rattling loudly.

'You are a beast, Pete,' I said fondly. 'If I have a child I shall keep it in a warm bath until it is potty-trained. I shall not succumb to domesticity.'

There was an intake of breath. I looked up. Ben's mother was clutching the kitchen table, horrified to think this was her daughter-in-law talking.

'Where is Ben?' she asked accusingly. Obviously she thought I ought to be by his side.

'I don't know. He *was* in the sitting-room.'

'Well I've just been in the living-room, and he wasn't there.' She sounded aggrieved.

'Maybe he's writing dirty slogans on the taxi,' suggested Pete helpfully.

'My son would not do that.'

'Oh, sorry.' Pete bit his lip and glanced at me. I was trying not to laugh – I had told Pete a lot about Mrs Mandel.

'I didnae realise ye wis Ben's mother,' Pete explained lamely, and his hand dropped nervelessly from my

10

shoulder.

'May I have a glass of water, please? I need a stomach-powder,' said Ben's mother.

Pete started to ask if she had been rinking too much, but I kicked his leg – Pete was very proud of his hairy legs, which were extremely thin with knobbly knees. He had once revealed them to Ben and myself at an Art College Revel, when he had worn a sack covered with phallic symbols drawn in ashes (very textural, as he explained to Ben).

I took a clean cup from the cupboard and tried to ignore my own mother's exasperated glances, as I reluctantly washed it to Mrs Mandel's instructions, dried it, also to her instructions, filled it with water, and gave it to my new mother-in-law to drink. Then Ben appeared, put his arms round Mrs Mandel's and my shoulders, and we went out to cut the cake and have speeches.

In the main room my brother Charlie was charging the guests' glasses. As he filled the pregnant Cordelia's, he mournfully said, 'I wish I had somebody like you,' which made her sad, because she had adored Charlie for years, but he'd been too shy to pursue her. Cordelia's own husband, Tony, was at that moment selling udder balm (for cows) to a Yorkshire sheep-farmer.

The telegrams were read out. Auntie Emma by this time had been retired to bed, clutching her sixth empty glass and a polythene basin, convulsively shouting, 'I want to see the wedding presents!'

Ben gave a very moving speech, and mentioned his long-dead father, and my own father, who had so recently died, yet had given Ben his blessing before he left the house for the last time. It saddened everyone, and there was a silence momentarily as we all looked down at our glasses and remembered.

Cordelia accompanied me to my room. 'As matron-of-honour, it is my task to refurbish the bride, put on your welly-boots, and lead you to the slaughter,' she said, shutting the door.

The bride sipped some tea, put down her flowers, and gratefully took off her shoes.

'I like getting married, but my feet are bloody sore,' I groaned, and rubbed my ankle.

'Well, you won't be using your feet tonight, darling,' said Cordelia crisply, putting the shoes away in a cupboard.

I took off the wedding dress and Cordelia looked dispassionately at my rounded figure.

'All the old ladies had a damned good peer at your tum,' she said.

'Speak for yourself.'

'I'm sure somebody could make a fortune in maternity wedding dresses.'

'I'm *not*.'

'I know,' said Cordelia. 'But an awful lot of people will be disappointed that it wasn't a shotgun wedding.'

'Ah well, can't please everyone,' I muttered, struggling into my going-away dress.

'I see you've got front buttons. That'll cheer old Ben up, I can just see him. You won't see Dublin for flashing green buttons.'

My head popped through the neck of the dress, and I gave Cordelia a shove in the back. Cordelia retreated and rolled her eyes malevolently.

'Now, now, darling, no violence.' She clutched her bump. 'We can't have the bride delivering the matron-of-honour's baby on a bouquet.' We giggled.

I looked at her fondly. 'You are an idiot,' I said, 'Try not to have it till I come back.'

'With my luck,' Cordelia sighed, 'I shall be pregnant for at least eleven months.'

She combed my hair for me.

'Is there a good beach where you're going?'

'Yes, miles of sand, super for swimming.'

'Mmm, all that lovely breast stroke, darling – and, did you know that you are not allowed to take any F.Ls into Ireland?'

I paled. 'It's not true? It can't be true?'

Cordelia combed soothingly.

'Mmm, still darling, it means that Ben won't have nearly such a heavy suitcase, doesn't it?'

Seeing my stricken face in the mirror, Cordelia relented. 'Oh Kate, don't worry, I was teasing.'

I threw my wedding dress at her, buttoned up my going-away dress, and put on a wide-brimmed hat.

'Do I look O.K?'

'Of course you do fellow, you look smashing and you know it.'

There was a knock on the door and Pete, bedraggled and red-eyed, appeared.

'Get out,' ordered Cordelia.

'Here, fellie, ye look verra nice,' said Pete swaying.

'It's private,' said Cordelia. Pete ignored her.

'I just wanted tae tell ye this – did ye know that 'Wedding' rhymes with 'Bedding'. 'Bride' rhymes with. . .'

We took him by the elbows and firmly led him to the bed, where first he sat then slowly became more and more recumbent until he lay flat out. There was another bed, he said, with an old auntie in it, talking about wedding presents.

'I offered her a fine upstanding present. . .' He tried to get up. 'I'm awfully sorry, fellie,' he muttered, 'It's been a lovely wedding. Ye must get married more often.' Then his eyes shut and he was asleep. We left him.

13

I found Ben's mother having a quiet moment in the small back bedroom filled with wedding presents.

'Well,' said Mrs Mandel, holding her white bag with gloved hands across it, 'Don't you look lovely?'

I wished she didn't sound so accusing. I tried not to look too pleased with myself, and blushed, 'I've come to say goodbye,' I said, 'And thanks, and. . .' I struggled for a moment for the right word and looked at Mrs Mandel, 'I will do my best to be a good wife to Ben. Thank you for him.' We hugged uneasily.

'My dear, I wish you every happiness.'

I left my mother-in-law to her conflicting thoughts and Jewish sorrow, and heard Ben call, 'Taxi is here! are you ready?'

We passed the piano, where Aunt Emma had risen up and was singing old Gaelic songs, off-key, accompanied by the serious young composer on a tin-whistle, watched by a glazed beetroot Uncle Lionel.

I nipped into my bedroom for a last-moment check, and fetched my handbag. Pete was now lying on the floor, snoring a little, with heavy cat asleep across his chest.

From my fading discarded bouquet I sprinkled some rose-petals across the pubic area of his old corduroy trousers, put my fingers to my lips and tiptoed out to the farewell melée in the hall, and my waiting husband.

Everybody was crammed into the hall, waiting to see us off; I noticed Cordelia struggling with Zoe to open a packet of confetti.

The bridal pair ran a gauntlet of hands, arms, hugs, kisses and good wishes. There were shouts of 'Jolly good!' 'Good luck!' and 'Jolly good!'

I muttered 'bye-bye, thanks, lovely, yes, thank you' and 'smashing', and smiled a little tensely as I tried to hold onto my hat.

14

A storm of confetti: guffaws and screeches. Cordelia loomed up and hissed, 'Don't do anything I haven't done, darling, and don't overstrain yourselves.'

Just as I was emerging from my childhood home, Ben whispered, 'Psst, watch out,' and I saw the skinny and puritanical Hazel Ochiltree coming at me, with a fixed and chilly grin and a huge packet of confetti which she viciously emptied down the front of my beautiful green dress. Then, to round off the gesture royally, she forced the crunkled packet down the neck of the dress, so that the bride had one large white hat, very askew, three breasts and a humpy back.

'Bitch.' I thought murderously, and tried to smile like a newly-wed.

Hazel Ochiltree glowed with satisfaction, and, clasping my arm with red-tipped claws, hissed, 'If you are anything like as happy as we have been, you will be incredibly lucky.' I looked at my bruised limb and gulped, glancing across to where Hazel's poor little husband sat, shrunken and white, drinking tomato juice, and managed to stammer, 'Oh thanks, Hazel, I'm sure we'll try, and thanks awfully for the egg-cup.'

Chapter 2

Like the registry office, the hotel in Dublin was Victorian and dark, muffled with carpets, and filled with flitting black-and-white-dressed servants. We had checked each other for any last signs of confetti, and I hoped my shiny wedding ring didn't look as obvious as it felt. 'We are an old married couple,' I kept muttering to myself, but from the heavily suggestive look the fifty-year-old page boy gave us we didn't look either old or married. The page boy even shut the bedroom door suggestively – over-solicitously, slow and silent – and then we were alone. I took off my hat and shoes, and Ben took stock of the room, which had a big double bed, and a smaller one, a red-patterned carpet, heavy burgundy velvet curtains, a carafe of water, a Bible and a huge wardrobe.

'Um, which bed do you fancy?' he asked.

'The one you're in.'

Ben embraced me. I was uneasy that I didn't want to consumate the marriage immediately.

'I think I'm hungry,' I confessed, and caught his look of relief. We hadn't eaten since the wedding breakfast. We raced each other to the door.

The hotel restaurant was Irish traditional – great fat sausages, chops, saucer-like plump mushrooms, and lots of floury potatoes. We gorged and talked non-stop. Across from us, at another table, was a middle-aged man and his wife. They sat in silence, each with a newspaper, which they occasionally shifted fractionally in order to impale a piece of food.

I was shocked.

'Do you think we'll ever be like that?' I asked in a small voice.

'Might.' said Ben buttering a roll. Then he saw my worried face, and put his hand on mine.

'Darling, I promise you that we will always speak, if only to argue, when we go out to eat.'

We drank coffee, and ate cheese, and my husband looked at his watch.

'Well, um. What shall we do now? he asked loudly.

'Well,um. What do you suggest?'

'We could go through to the lounge, and read the *Irish Gazette* or the *Donegal Horse and Hounds*.'

'Yes, let's!'

We got up, and Ben took a handkerchief from his breast-pocket, creating, as he did, a small blizzard of turquoise, pink and yellow confetti. The paper blew all over the table, the wine glasses, into the cream-jug. The middle-aged couple looked round and I glimpsed the waiter hiding a smile.

'Ah well,' said Ben philosophically, wiping his mouth and putting his hankie back, 'Come on Mrs' and we went up to our room.

I bathed quickly, and covered myself with talc and a nightie. Ben had gone for a shower, leaving his clothes on a stool. I looked at myself in the wardrobe mirror. 'You're like something off a Christmas tree, Mrs Mandel,' I told my reflection, but I lied, for I really thought that I looked stunning. Then I climbed into bed and waited for a while, feeling strangely nervous.

I was not a virgin. Ben had deflowered me, petal by petal, deliciously and divinely, the year before, and we had been lovers since, but somehow this was different, all legal and forever. I felt suddenly lost and tired, so to cheer myself up, and to relieve the tension of waiting for my bridegroom, I clambered out of bed, removed my nightie, and tried on his string vest. I had never seen such a garment until a couple of days ago, when we had bought it for the honeymoon – assured by the salesman that string vests were warm in winter, and cool in summer, because of their thermocellular something.

The vest was like a sack dress (popular that year), and looked odd with breasts and hips peering through the white mesh. Clown-like, I decided, as I removed it. Not romantic. Ben was still singing and water gushing, so I thought I'd try on his dove-grey waistcoat. It didn't look too bad. Next came his grey suit jacket, which I put on, and was engulfed by. Not the ideal outfit in which to greet one's new husband, I decided, and slipped the clothes off, and turned, naked to reach for my nightie, only to be surprised by a damp, rumple-haired Ben, wearing nothing but a red towel and a most alluring and beautifully textured hairy chest. He gazed at me in wonder and I gulped as he removed the towel, but after that he kissed me gently and led me to the bed, and it was all quite simple. I lay back after we had made love, and exhaustion from the weeks of preparation washed over me like a sorrow. In the night I was aware of Ben, exultant, caressing my almost somnolent body. At dawn I felt him riding on my anaesthetised limbs and thought sleepily, 'So this is marriage.'

I dozed, but woke up again to wonder worriedly, 'But is it Art?'

Then I slept like a child.

Chapter 3

We had chosen the Irish village from the map, liking its name and the lie of the sea around it. It nestled at the bottom of encircling green hills, and looked towards the west, to wide, long, lonely beaches, the Atlantic, and, ultimately, America.

A rusty red bus took us from the train to the hotel, booked blindly from an address book and chosen for its cheapness. The building was greyly gaunt, set in the middle of sand dunes.

'Lovely wild country,' I said hopefully.

'Real country cooking, I bet,' said Ben.

The proprietress was Mrs Murphy, and the large tortoiseshell comb which secured her mountain of iron curls, gave her a vaguely Spanish look. Her black satin dress was gripped at the neck by a massive green plastic shamrock, and covered two large quivering breasts. To complete the picture she had girded her ample middle with a leprechaun- and kelpie-spattered apron.

'Good afternoon,' said Ben, holding out his hand, 'I am Mr Mandel; we have a booking with you.'

'Oh yes,' Mrs Murphy sniffed dubiously and appraised his fingers as though counting sausages. She took one disapproving look at me, and I became immediately aware of my very low-necked dress, borrowed from Cordelia. ('Take it for God's sake,' Cordelia had said, 'it's no good to me in this elephantine state.')

Unwillingly Mrs Murphy admitted us; her chill glance caused me to pause as I signed the register, which pause made Mrs Murphy even icier. Our bedroom was hundreds of yards along a cemented corridor, and the room was like a solitary confinement cell, but we swallowed feebly and said, 'Oh yes, very nice,' and I sat disconsolately on the iron bed. Its mattress wheezed asthmatically under my weight.

There was, however, a view of the sea, and the bedlinen was clean, and when our clothes were unpacked and I had put some wild flowers from outside the window in the tooth-mug on the dressing-table, it seemed quite civilised. We rocked experimentally on the bed, exploring all its noises. Then explored each other and the gong sounded.

The dining-room had a few people in it; one young couple who looked animated and billed and cooed as they read the menu, an older couple with two small boys, and what looked like a spinster schoolteacher of about fifty-five.

A very young green-eyed maid came in with a huge tureen of soup. She wore black and had a small hat like a paper boat on her dark hair. She served the soup at each table, and my eagle eye – always alert to quantities in food – noticed that everyone was given two ladlefuls and that the other young couple were given nearly three each. When the waitress came to our table, the tureen was still half-full, but Ben and I were given only one ladleful each. I pointed out the discrepency to Ben in a whisper.

'It's not very good anyway,' he said spooning it down quickly.

'Of course it's good, It's food. We need all the nourishment we can get.'

The other couple were gazing, spoons hovering, into each other's eyes. Ben leaned across the table. 'D'you think they're on honeymoon too?' he asked.

'Yes, I do; she keeps looking at her ring and holding her fingers oddly, to show it off.'

'That's exactly what you keep doing,' said Ben.

'No I don't.'

'You do, you know, I've been meaning to tell you to stop gazing at your hand with such horrified fascination. It is very obvious – like Lady Macbeth.

I coloured. It did feel strange, having a ring forever, and being married forever. I put my hand under the table, and he held it for a moment.

The little waitress came out with the second course, and this time Ben watched too. When the other guests were given four sausages, we were given two. ('One-and-a-half almost,' I hissed bitterly, jabbing a cherry-sized potato with a fork.)

Pudding was the same. A tiny slice of apple-tart, half the size of anybody else's and no cream at all. Ben called the little girl over.

'You've forgotten the cream.'

Unwillingly she went to get it.

Later that evening at the pub Ben said reasonably: 'Perhaps they had forgotten that we were coming, and didn't have enough.'

'You don't suppose,' said Ben, his intricate playwright's mind eager to explore all possibilities, 'that they saw the F.L.s in the suitcase. This is Ireland, remember.'

For a panic-stricken moment I wondered if he was right. We gulped down our Guinness and had three packets of crisps each.

21

Chapter 4

In the morning after a scanty breakfast we walked to the beach. Not an aeroplane flew over; hardly a vehicle drove past. There was a priest's bicycle, the rusty bus, and a couple of donkeys, and that was all. On the beach we saw a couple of local curraghs which lay like giant slugs. These curraghs were still made as they had been made for thousands of years, from bent branches, tied with twine or reeds, covered with cowhide – or canvas – and tarred on top, so they were light to carry, black in colour, and curved like a vast basket in shape. A man carrying a curragh across the sand at dusk was a strange Heironymus Bosch sort of creature.

We swam, and slept together, and lay in the sun, read Dickens (myself) and *The Golden Bough* (Ben) and found shells and stones and a big dead drowned dog tied in a sack, washed up with his face frozen in frenzy, teeth in a death-gnash. We made whistles from grass, and wrote love-messages on the sand. Ben dozed among bluebells and thistles, whilst I put buttercups in his ears, and he dreamed of his newest play. We had two wonderful days, but we grew hungrier and hungrier.

On the second morning we were given an egg-cupful

of porridge, to everyone else's handsome helping. We were always last served, so there was no more even if we asked. We were given one rasher of bacon and a lone small egg, to everybody else's two. We noticed that same morning that the young couple seemed silent and stiff-faced. The man looked grim and pale.

'Something's obviously happened to them.'

'Maybe it didn't and that's what's wrong.'

'Oh, how awful.' My heart lurched towards the unknown couple, and I wished we could encourage them.

'Honeymoons are often ghastly for people.'

'Hard to imagine,' smugly I buttered a minute triangle of toast, and noisily scraped the gnomic marmalade-jar.

'We'll go to Dingle,' said Ben decisively, 'and have a decent meal, and find another hotel, if that's how Mrs Murphy thinks of us.'

Mrs Murphy was monosyllabic when we asked her the way to Dingle. We were hurt, and even more so when we heard her gush over the other couple of honeymooners.

Ben did look a trifle scruffy, because of his new-growing beard. Could it be his Jewish look? I wondered uneasily.

'What did you do in Dingle, darling? What did you do in Dingle?' crooned Ben as we walked through Dingle's country streets.

'I saw a dog's dugs dangling, darling, Pinkly all a-tingle,' I crooned back, pointing meaningfully at an obscene bitch bull-terrier with a bad go of mastitis.

There wasn't a lot to do in Dingle, but we had a good meal, and booked into a hotel for the following day. Then, on making our way to the bus-stop, there was suddenly a great deal to do. It was the day of Dingle races.

The Irish bookies talked even faster and louder than Scottish bookies. The horses were tired hacks, and the jockeys a motley, ill-dressed lot.

23

Shouts from the far side of the big grass field attracted us, and we saw a large crowd shouting and watching something. The object of their attentions was an old tramp, deeply wrinkled and grey-haired, wearing laceless boots and an old raincoat, inevitably tied together with string.

He had a big sack of wooden bricks – saw-mill off-cuts – and for sixpence the young and some older lads of Dingle could buy themselves the joy of chucking a brick at him, as he stood beside a piece of tarpaulin on a wooden frame behind which he ducked when the missiles were thrown. The lads were mostly drunk, as was the old tramp, and a lot of sixpences passed hands. One great lout bought himself a veritable pyramid of wood. The tramp then walked unsteadily over to his tarpaulin hide – which barely reached his waist, and urged his clients to take aim.

It was quite horrible. A mediaeval nightmare sight. The rain suddenly came on, sky and grass grew dark, and there was thud upon thud as the wooden blocks hit sometimes the man, sometimes the ground, and occasionally the tarpaulin. Ben held me back from running out to shout at the men, then there was a more sickening thud than before, and the old man fell sideways, gnarled face sheeted with blood. Cheers from the louts, and a further volley of bricks, then they stopped and were silent, and walked in a muttering group, uneasily fingering their last pieces of wood, to see how damaged the lying-down man was.

Ben hurried me away as stretcher-bearers arrived. We didn't bet on either of the chronic winners of every race; on the way to the bus we saw all the lads walking towards the pub, the old tramp with them, with a bloody rag round his head.

'What a way to earn a living,' said Ben, 'Almost as

24

bad as playwriting.' I glanced at his serious face and shivered, stifling my fear. He hadn't had a lot of success so far, for all the plays he'd written, and he was thirty-five. Not a youngster.

Back at the hotel to collect our cases, we were greeted by the vivaciously friendly little maid who asked us in detail about our day, discussed her love-life and told us that there was roast pork and roast potatoes for supper. Then Mrs Murphy emerged from her little office and gave us a huge saccharine smile.

'Mr and Mrs Mandel, how nice to see you, have you had a good day, you must be hungry, would you like some tea and scones?' she asked in a blarneyed gush.

I was nonplussed and heard Ben gasp audibly, before he stuttered, 'Why, yes Mrs Murphy, that would be wonderful.'

Drooling and delighted, we followed her to the conservatory, overlooking the sea, where we ate big dollops of home-made jam on sticky scones, and balls of fresh butter winked at us from a flowered dish. I poured Ben tea from a pretty and generously large teapot, silent with disbelief at our changed Luck.

Mrs Murphy came through to see us, still beaming; 'Some letters came for you,' she said, 'And a telegram.'

Ben took them eagerly, and Mrs Murphy smiled maternally towards us yet again, and shut the door tactfully as she left us alone.

We were excited to have letters from home, it was good to see our names written as the single statement of Mr and Mrs B. J. Mandel. As he was slitting the telegram with his teaspoon, Ben suddenly stopped, his mouth open.

'What's wrong?'

'I've just realised. Why are Mrs Murphy and co. so generous all of a sudden? Look. It's here!' He thrust the envelope towards me. 'Mr and Mrs. She now knows that we are really married.'

'But we were.'

'What – you with your tits hanging out, and me all unshaven and gipsy-like!'

And, as he called for more scones, we decided to cancel the Dingle hotel booking and stay on at Mrs Murphy's.

'Lechaim,' said Ben, 'To life,' as we clinked rose-spattered teacups.

The telegram was from Cordelia's mother: 'CORDELIA HAD DAUGHTER 7 a.m. WEDNESDAY – FLUE-BRUSH HAIR – 7lbs. 10ozs. – CATHERINE JANE'

We were silent.

'Gosh,' said Ben at last, 'Imagine Cordelia with a baby. I hope she holds it the right way up; Tony will probably anoint it with udder balm.'

I felt strangely removed from the fact of my best friend's motherhood. When I had finally said yes to Ben, I knew that he was longing for children, and, being older than me, he wanted them soon. I certainly did want his children, but my yearning was amorphous. When we were asked how many children we wanted, I'd say, 'We'll start with one.' But I still had two years to do at Art College, and we had agreed that I must at least finish my course.

'When is Graduation Day?' asked Ben.

'A year next June,' I said, and I realised with a thud that he was counting backwards, calculating that we could start trying in just over a year, in September, which seemed inordinately soon to me; but he looked so happy at the thought, and of course I wanted him to be happy. All unknowingly, I was beginning to breathe in from the anaesthetic mask which was to provide me with the sweet oblivion of family life.

Chapter 5

One sun-drenched morning we went up into the nearby hills. There was a small donkey-track leading through the fields, with their maze of little grey walls, some of the fields were as small as a house. We supposed they had originally been enormous and had been divided over the centuries among the dozens of children of the Irish farmers. Soon we were on a heathery flower-fragrant slope of hill above the little village, and we lay and listened.

There was bee-song, and bird-song. A clatter of milk-churns from the village, a barking dog, and the sighing of the wind on the hills. Occasionally a laugh or a shout, music from a distant transistor in one of the houses. We were sure that we could hear the sea's incoming, and Ben swore that the few sheep on the hill were bleating 'Bog, bog, bog' as they squelched through the Irish marshland. Then a little black-and-white dog suddenly appeared, and the sheep scattered as it bounded up to us. One of his pointed ears was erect, but the other one folded in the middle and was in need of an armature; his stump of a tail wagged hysterically when he looked at us and he pulled himself abasingly but enchantingly towards us on his plump puppy tummy, with its wispy evidence of maleness.

'Shoo,' said Ben.

'Why? He's lovely.'

'He's filthy.' said Ben. We lay down. The dog tried to lick Ben's face passionately. Ben grimaced and shoved him away. He threw a pebble and the dog bounded after it. I winced, but remained silent, and later when my husband was asleep, head among the buttercups, exhausted from the night before, the dog crept back and rapturously devoured a chicken sandwich. I gently placed him across Ben's chest, opened my sketch-book, and did my first married drawing.

But the first real fight when it came was frightening. We had never, ever, had a real fight. We both tended to argue loudly, but usually with humour, and would finally agree to disagree, or shout in a loud but amiable way until one of us conceded a point.

For several days after the dog episode (and it hadn't been a very good drawing; Ben had simply grunted when he saw it) it was grey and cold. The sea was white-flecked and murky, the sky sulphur-yellow or lead-heavy, with cold sea-mist or freezing rain. We read and dozed, made love, drew and wrote and ate, and stayed blissfully in bed.

It was good to see the sun again, and we set out for a ruined Celtic tower near the sea, a mile or two away. When we reached it, it was steaming hot, and it seemed like the whole of Ireland was ours. Apart from the ruin, there was no sign of man; not a detergent bottle or flash of broken glass disturbed the great stretches of fine, pale sand. There were flowers and insects everywhere. No movement but the odd bird, and the gently shifting sea. I lay back and let the warmth bathe me. I looked at my dozing man, and tickled him with a thin, long grass. Ben brushed away the tickle, sniffed noisily, and rolled away from me onto his side, and dozed more deeply.

Restless, I wandered along the beach, finding tiny sea-urchin shells, with wonderful pin-pricked spirals of pattern. I watched a hermit crab crawling along with his borrowed shell and tried to find a blue shell like I had found on the first day.

'This is our honeymoon,' I thought, 'but I'm bored.' I thought round it, and realised that I was almost ready to go home and get back to work and our little flat. I came back and looked again at Ben. His beard was good and thick now, and he was incredibly handsome; I wanted him to make love to me here and now on this marvellous beach. We had never made love outside, except once, before we were married, in a grassy lane, all ragged robin and clover, with two cows and a horse watching. I slowly took off my dress, then my bra and pants, and came and lay quietly beside him for a while. He grunted again, then blearily opened an eye and looked at me.

'Hey, darling,' he suddenly sat up. 'What are you doing. You can't do that here!'

I lay curled up, irresistably desirable.

'Mmmm?'

'No, darling, no.' Firmly he handed me a towel.

'It's illegal to walk around naked. Anyone could come without warning.'

'Oh, darling,' I pouted (deliciously, I was certain). 'I only want to seduce you.' Then in a gravelly imitation of crazy Aunt Emma, I growled, 'You are mai dream lover. I wish you to take me by force. Now, immediately. I shall melt into your waiting arms. . .' and I kiss-kissed towards him.

Ben was startled. 'Darling,' he said, 'Not here.'

'Why?'

'No,' he said 'I refuse.'

'Darling,' I reached out.

'I am not in the mood,' said Ben.

'The mood?' I purred, rolling on top of him, and nuzzling his nose with my breast.

'I do not like sand!' he pushed me off, got up and stood above me, frowning.

I didn't believe him.

He picked up the picnic bag and swimming things, and looked down at me. It dawned on me that he meant what he said.

'Come on love,' he said quietly, 'Get your clothes on.'

Eventually he went back, and I stayed (dressed) and stared at the sea, with tears falling endlessly down my cheeks. The marriage was in ashes.

'He scorned me!' I thought, stunned. 'How could he?'

Briefly, I considered walking into the sea, but common sense pointed out that it was dark and cold and the sea was wet.

'Also,' I reasoned, 'it's nearly supper time. I'll go back. I need the nourishment.'

Ben was waiting for me in the hall. I couldn't bear to look at him, I felt so raw and hurt. I washed my puffy tear-splodged face and combed my hair, and went into the dining-room. He was agonised and tried to reach my hand, but I was stiff like wood.

'Darling, I love you,' he whispered. 'I had no idea it was so important.'

'I won't speak to him,' I told myself.

Ben tried to smile. He was ashen. I felt my mouth do a humourless grimace at him and saw how it stabbed him, then flooded with love, and tears fell into the soup.

The other couple across the room were playing a game of pocket chess, and couldn't stop giggling.

By the time the ice-cream was served, we had

touched little fingers. We left the ice-cream uneaten, and the little waitress stared after our abrupt departure. We ran along the corridor to our room, and only after making love did we take our clothes off.

Afterwards we lay together, and I gently held him. 'It must have been agony when you had that bit off.'

'How do you know about that bit?' asked Ben.

'I've got two brothers. Was it sore?'

'I don't remember,' said Ben 'I was only eight days old. D'you fancy drawing it?'

'Mmm.'

Early on in our courtship Ben had told me about himself, as he ate spaghetti in a cheap but characterful Italian restaurant, his face animated by candlelight from a grease-covered Chianti bottle. He had told me how, when he was thirteen, he had sung his Barmitzvah song in the Synagogue, wearing his prayer shawl, and little yarmulka on the back of his head (Sometimes now, I caught him humming the Blessing, 'Baruch atah adenoi. . .'), and he said wasn't it mean of the audience not to applaud him? I smiled as I imagined the intense young boy at the ceremony, full of the joy of performance.

Love of performance was something that we both had in common. Ben had always acted and directed plays as well as write them. I was twelve when I had first glimpsed my husband-to-be on a charity concert platform. He was dressed as a tartan crone, singing a song (written and composed by himself) about a spinning-wheel, and had a waterfall – with real water – playing on the stage behind him. I had rushed home to tell my family that I had just seen an incredibly funny man, with an enormous rubbery mouth (I was a connoisseur of funny-face-making) and that I wanted to go and see him again the following day. I did too, then lost

31

sight of him until I saw him a few years later serving my school dinners, wearing an outrageous yellow waistcoat, but still with the same hilarious mouth.

He had been writing plays in the interval and had taken up teaching science in order to pay the rent.

Before the wedding Ben had just completed his thirteenth full-length stage play, which I know had taken him a year of late, lonely nights. When we got home he would start teaching on the Monday, and his fourteenth play would begin soon after that.

I had read this thirteenth play – and the one previous to it – as each act was completed. I was convinced that they were marvellous, but then wives thought that sort of thing, didn't they? The day before the wedding, Ben had sent off his immaculately-typed play, bound in blue, to his agent. It was very funny, and sometimes heartbreaking. Mandelian, I thought, as I wondered what the agent would say. I got out of bed to pull the eiderdown up off the floor.

'Maybe the film rights will be lying on the doorstep,' I said.

Ben put his arms behind his head and gazed dreamily at the faded hotel curtains.

'I'd settle for two or three stars, and a year's run in the West End.'

'I'm dying to see the cat. He is going to live with us, isn't he?'

'What?' asked Ben, alarmed.

'The cat. Pussy. You know. He is mine, he has always been. He is going to live with us?' I climbed into bed.

'Well. . .' said Ben.

'Sure now,' I purred, in deepest Irish, 'a wife, a cat, and a London run, what more could a man want?'

'Not much,' sighed Ben wistfully, and switched off

the bed-light, and held me round the middle. And as we drifted into sleep, I thought, 'Sand. That's why they circumcised them in the first place. Desert sand. So why didn't he?'

Chapter 6

The honeymoon was over, and we reached our own front door. My mother had halved her house to provide a tiny flat for us to rent. Ben unlocked the door.

'Aren't you going to carry me over the threshold?' I smiled hopefully at my husband and breathed in to look thinner, but he was looking at a depressing, all too familiar quarto envelope lying on the inside on the doormat. I wished he'd stop and turn to me and carry me, but he bent down and I watched hopefully as he opened the letter, then sagged as I watched his face. His agent had returned the play, saying it was the worst play Ben had ever written, and that she couldn't handle it. It was unbelievable.

He didn't speak much that evening. The news was too stunning. Silently we busied ourselves with making the house ready. The builders had made a tiny new bathroom with a window looking on to a grey tenement wall. One end of a fair-sized room had been used to make space for the bathroom, so next door to it we had a small, square bedroom. It was a ground-floor flat, there was grass and even a tree outside, in the shared tenement garden, and beyond that a wall, and then more tenements. Our sitting-room was next door to the bedroom, and this was scarcely big enough for our large old mahogany table with drop-sides. The kitchen was small but practical, with blue floor, shiny white cooker, and a white porcelain sink and draining-board – the cheapest arrangement we could find. Ben's study was a windowless box-room at the end of a corridor, just inside the front door.

The big striped cat was the first to welcome us, and rubbed his great sides against our legs. Ma came down from her house above us, with gifts of cooked chicken, strawberries and cream. We ate together, then she left us; she was going to lecture on living positively to a small but select group of self-improvers. Ben busied himself with hammering and the fixing of hooks for cooking knives, colanders and whisks. He sawed and sandpapered a gigantic wooden towel-rail he was making from an unwanted Victorian curtain-rod. I shopped and carried, and unpacked my paper bags of food and cleaning things, and filled my new cupboards. I took a little time over choosing my washing-powder, torn between the different bright packets, trying to envisage which one would look best with the blue floor.

I prepared our new bed, with wedding presents of blankets, and a blue chintz quilt from Ben's mother. I patted the swelling down-filled pillows – donated by Ben's fellow teachers – and looked at the bed's welcoming perfection with joy. Then I eyed the telephone and dialled Cordelia, expecting hoots of joy and shrieks of welcome and hilarious tales of the new baby. But Cordelia sounded like a different person; she was dull and listless, miserable. Yes, the baby was lovely; yes she felt O.K.; yes, it was nice to hear me. No, Tony was away again, so she'd be at her parents' house for a few days. I felt chilled; she sounded like a stranger.

I tried to tell her how disappointed we felt about

Ben's rejection. 'Yes, it's a pity,' she intoned. Then there was a resounding silence. From Cordelia! My friend! I was nonplussed. I tried again:

'Shall I come over? I must see your baby? She's three weeks old already, isn't she?'

'Yes. Come if you like.'

'Hey! Cordelia! It's me! What's happened? I'm sorry I wasn't here when you had her.'

Again a pause. And I knew she was crying.

'I'm sorry, Kate. It's just I don't get much sleep. . . she yells a lot. It hurts to feed her. . . Come over tomorrow.'

She was still crying. I promised to come.

Filled with his own problems, Ben, in the kitchen, swept up his sawdust carefully, and tidied away the tools, nails and screws. He put the gleaming silver kettle on, then went to brush his teeth. When he returned, the price-tag was fluttering in the steam.

We were both tired, and drank the tea he had made, gratefully. Once in bed, we at last spoke about the morning's letter. Ben was so shattered that he was ready to abandon the play, and put it away in a cupboard until he was less bruised. But I was indignant and furious. I jumped out of bed, scaring the cat, and went to fetch *The Writers' and Artists' Year Book*. I suggested two repertory theatres and another agent.

'O.K.' said Ben, 'I'll try again.'

I slid into bed beside him and he snapped off the light. Silently we savoured the feel of our very own bed in our very own house. 'That agent,' I said, snuggling down against my naked husband, 'is just a tasteless idiot.' Ben fondled me, the old cat twitched at our feet, until Ben lifted him out and put him in the sitting-room, and climbed back into bed. We turned, hungrily-loving, to each other, fondling, touching,

36

stroking, kissing, and murmuring. And those gentle-
nesses swelled into the rapturous oblivion of a . . .
'What?' I asked afterwards. 'A celebration-consolation
consummation,' said Ben.

Chapter 7

Cordelia's name was an unusual one, considering the environment from which she sprang – far out in the nether suburbs of Edinburgh. She had been thus named in a poetic moment by her mother, Mary, whose great release from her world of paper-doileyed housework and an unrewarding marriage was a deep involvement with amateur dramatics. When Cordelia was conceived, Mary was the wardrobe mistress of the East Ravelston Ladies' production of *King Lear*, and the Shakespearean name she chose for her first child was a secret yelp for better things, an expression of her longing for a deeper and grander shape to her life-pattern.

There were roses blooming, and a rustic plastic wishing-well by the circular goldfish-pond in Cordelia's parents' garden, when I walked up the crazy-paving path; I felt strangely shy when I rang the doorbell. Cordelia, lonely because husband Tony was away selling sheep linament to horse-dealers, had come with the new baby to her parents' lush bungalow, a few miles from the city centre. Cordelia's father, Bill, was a successful grocer – a large-built man, with an upside-down crescent of a moustache. Like many alcoholics he had a sweet and gentle manner, but got himself imbecilically drunk several nights a week, and unfortunately tonight was one of them.

Cordelia and I had disliked each other intensely when we first met, aged five, in kindergarten. Later, when we were nine, Cordelia claimed to have been terrified of me, whom she still vividly remembered wearing green shorts and beating up the boys. I, for my part, before my tomboy stage, had been falsely accused of stuffing shoes and jerseys down the school lavatory, and had only learned after her marriage that in fact Cordelia had been responsible, but was too scared to own up. Our enmity had lasted well into adolescence, until one day, coinciding on the road home from school, we had mutually confessed to having fathers with drink problems, and this had rendered us inseparable.

I found Cordelia in a large beige-and-pink tapestried Italian armchair, wincing as she breast-fed her black-haired baby. I looked at my godchild-to-be, and wondered at my sense of disconnection from this small human. A gulf had suddenly appeared between myself and Cordelia in the weeks containing my marriage and her giving birth. Now her glance slid secretively sideways, away from me, as she uncommunicatively answered my questions about the event and the newcomer. My beloved friend and maniac had disappeared with the arrival of the child; I could barely recognise her as she listlessly held the baby like a stuffed doll, and gazed into space with brooding, heavy eyes.

'It was hellish sore, fellow. It was awful,' she said dully.

Cordelia's mother, Mary, bustled about, hair perfect, make-up immaculate, dress crisp. She tidied away papers and magazines as they dropped, took away the baby's soiled nappy, spoke to the family's fat red labrador, Tassock, who sniffed everybody's genitals lovingly. Mary made tea, toasted cheese, poached eggs,

39

and fed us. It was cozy to be back in this house, with its conflicting patterns of brocade, flock wallpaper, tartan carpet, elephantine sofa with fringed bobble-trims and white lace antimacassers and arm-rests. There were photos of Cordelia and her kid sister from babyhood; it was all familiar and comfortable to me who had often eaten and slept here in the last few years.

I had always adored the warmth, softness and physical comfort I was given by Cordelia's mother. There was forever a hot-bottle in the bed, snacks on trays, cups of coffee or cocoa. A choice for breakfast – three courses if one wished (and I usually did) and magazines to read – in my home there had never been money or time for such fripperies. But today I realised that all this would never be again. Cordelia didn't live here any more. She wasn't the same Cordelia anyhow, and I myself was now meant to be grown-up. Panic swept me. We were on the other side. I looked at the baby and the nappies and Cordelia's wounded boredom, and wasn't entirely sure just how grown-up I felt.

Tassock came to me again, tail thumping tartan carpet, nostrils wide and hopeful. As I snapped my legs shut, Bill leaned lugubriously towards me, and I thought how similar he and the big mute beast were in their gestures of appeal. His eyes were heavy-drunk, and stupid, and his mouth echoed the down-curve of the moustache. I longed to paint the sorrow of him. Bill held out a photograph album, pointing to a yellowing picture. 'How could anyone love a thing like that?'

The photo showed a much younger Bill and Mary, arm in arm, by a gate. Mary hadn't changed much, and was still bright and cheerful. Bill looked thinner and more sensitive, but as unhappy as he looked today. He repeated himself now.

'How could anybody love a thing like that?'

40

I was nonplussed. I couldn't say 'Yes, yes, I agree, nobody in their right minds could ever have'. Instead I smiled feebly and said:

'Oh, Billy, my love, you were a lovely boy. If I was thirty years older, what a time we'd have.'

Bill was pleased, and chuckled. 'Ye're an awfy girl, Kate, I think I'll away out.'

The women of his family exchanged glances. Mary said sharply 'Don't forget your key.'

And Bill lumbered out, and banged the door to the street. I went home soon. I had given my present of a frilly smock to the little girl, and now there seemed little more to say.

'Bye, Kate,' said Cordelia in a dead voice. 'Come and see me soon. Come before the christening.'

Animals were happier with their young than this; she seemed to have no maternal instinct. It was joyless and alarming.

Back home the house was dark, but for the light under Ben's study door. I was lonely and longed to talk to him, so I made two mugs of coffee and a delicious sandwich for him and slid into his box-room, shutting the door with my bottom.

'Hi, darling; I'm back,' I said brightly, laying the irresistible food and drink by his elbow, and kissing his available neck. Ben's elbows were both on the table, and his outstretched fingers held his concentrated brow. He ignored me, his bride, completely.

'I made you some coffee, darling.'

There was still no reply. I paused, then started to speak again, when Ben banged his fists on the table – spilling some coffee – and, still looking downwards, shouted very loudly, 'No!'

I retreated as though burnt. I went through to the bedroom and sat quite numb, breathing very slowly,

41

staring in front of me, my eyes moving now to the left, now to the right, zombie-like and seeing nothing. Quite like Cordelia.

I lay in bed chilled and immobile, in a tight embryonic ball. I was dozing when my tired husband joined me two hours later. He crept in beside me as gently as he could, put his arm round my middle, and snuggled in as usual so that I could feel the treachorously comforting fur of his chest and the secret softness of his parts (as Pete called them).

Ben thought I was asleep until he heard my sniffles. He put the light on at once.

'What is it, darling, aren't you well?'

He was oblivious, child-like in his innocence of having hurt me. Gradually he made me tell him, and was amazed to have had such an effect.

'I was just in the middle of a scene,' he said reasonably. 'I had a page of dialogue in my head and couldn't possibly stop, or I'd have lost it.'

I wondered how he had treated his mother when she brought him gefilte fish and cheesecake at midnight. 'Did you used to shout at her?' I asked.

'Since I was fifteen,' he assured me smugly.

I felt a deep and uneasy surge of rage within me, but somehow I remained dumb, unable to express it. Ben seemed too reasonable to fight; too authoritative, and he was bigger than me. I couldn't win.

Chapter 8

Still jangling from the difficult emotions of the day before, I set off for College. Most mornings I used to be late for class; there were register books which were supposed to be signed on arrival, but usually the staff were as inefficient as the students for the first hour or so. Thus it was possible to arrive last, but in fact head the day's list of names with one's flourishing signature by writing in the space above the other names. Even if you had missed a particular class for two or three weeks it was generally still possible to find virgin space under the correct date.

On this, my first day as a married student, I greeted my angular friend Zoe in the corridor. We watched our fellow students shuffling in, greyly unkempt and unmade-up.

'See all those hollow eyes, and acres of stubble,' muttered Zoe, 'Back from parole, that's what it's like. A few bars across the windows and you wouldn't know the place from Barlinnie.'

I sighed. I wished I could feel more enthusiasm about being back at College. I had hated the Diploma exhibitions at the end of last term; somehow the students' work seemed to get greyer and deader as they proceeded with their painting course, and I could feel it happening to me.

We went into the Life-class, and I smoked and stared dully at the model on the throne, whilst trying vainly to remember some excitement I had once felt for the subject, until I was at last reprieved by the shrill din of the coffee-bell. Pete lumbered up.

'Are ye coming?'

The coffee-break was an oasis in the wilderness of early morning. The Life-studio emptied, leaving the usual three students who didn't take coffee. Two of them were known as the 'Little Knitters'. These frugal daughters of Calvin always sat in a corner, ceaselessly knitting porridge- or haggis-coloured garments for shapeless relatives. They always wore coat-overalls, one in a hideous pea-green – not the most flattering colour for its wearer – and the other a dingy grey. Beneath these they wore grey pleated skirts, lisle stockings, and home-knitted jerseys of appalling colour, and huge clumpy, tongued, thonged, tasselled and laced, brown leather brogues.

I used inwardly to curse the birdcage brains of the Little Knitters as they chattered and chirped and clicked their needles to each other. And I hated them for tittering when I dropped my drawing-board or made my easel collapse with a sleep-shattering clatter. Generally, I did knock over a board or two, or a stool, first thing in the morning. It had never been my best time of day.

The other non-coffee-drinker was a slender Welsh girl called Myfanwy – pretty girl with dark curly hair, a serious student of yoga, who often practised her Asanas in a quiet corner of the studio, standing on her head or shoulders, or jack-knifed in a silent head-hanging pose for a whole lunch- or coffee-break. Myfanwy was a good painter; she did interesting large compositions of miners, white-eyed, beneath emphatic pyramids of purple slag and silhouetted wheels of mine machinery.

At the very first coffee-break of the term Zoe, Pete and I sat at the cup-littered canteen table. We ate a packet of crisps each and resolved to work hard.

'Evening classes four nights a week. Sketch-books always at the ready. All lectures to be attended. In fact, no skiving,' said Zoe, grim and determined.

'Aye,' said Pete drawing a Union Jack on the formica table-top, 'We'll need tae bloody work. If we don't we'll get chucked out.'

He took a glass salt-cellar, and drew a skull-and-cross-bones with the flow of salt. We drank our coffee and stared gloomily at the white salt image.

Those first months of marriage passed in a haze of work for Ben and myself. We breakfasted together and met momentarily for a snatched supper, which we ate off our knees beside our old black fuel-stove (seven pounds from the Surplus Stores). Then, when we had eaten, I fled, in order to reach my evening Life-classes in time, and Ben went to the small box-room, with a bare table and a wooden chair. Here he wrote his play which grew very slowly, line by tortuous line, written in his tiny writing, criss-crossed in green, red, blue and black biro, each colour being a new version, written small, so that he could put several drafts on one page.

I tried to act normal on the mornings when I was first to collect the post from the front door, before breakfast. I knew from Ben's anxious eyes how he filled with hope as the post came through the letter-box, then drooped as he scanned the envelopes – none of which ever seemed to be about the play.

On Sundays, one of our mothers usually fed us, and we looked forward to these parental feasts and the comforts of television and big soft armchairs. The first Sunday Ben's mother cooked one of her marvellous Jewish meals. Her chickens were always done in the same time-honoured way, as were her gefilte fish, or soups with their feathery matzo dumplings. She cooked in her mother's, and her mother's mother's way, seldom improvising or changing a recipe. In Lithuania, or a Siberian cave, they had cooked this way and cheered their families. We ate rye-bread – large brown slices, bitter-sweet with unsalted butter, gherkins and gehackte herring. Chopped liver, with lovingly added dices of hard-boiled egg across its surface – and sweet tzimmes of carrots and potatoes, cooked in gravy and kissed with sugar. It was wonderful food, but we always overate to near stupefaction; our plates were filled to overflowing, and we ate and admired, and were stuffed and stuffed again.

'Is it all right?' she asked over and over, till I thought she'd drive me stupid; she knew from decades of experience and thousands of previous cookings that it was perfect. 'Have another piece. Eat more. Take a slice of cake. Here, I can't eat all of mine.' And she would spoon great unwanted portions of lamb or meltingly delicious chicken onto our already brimming plates.

Again and again she incanted to me, as I chewed and nodded, nodded and chewed, how one must add sugar, boil for four hours gently, choose one's vegetables, leave to cool, or chop into tiny pieces. So I in turn bought marrow bones from my butcher, and our small kitchen smelt of herbs and onions and bubbling meat-stock. And I added potatoes, leeks, onions, carrots, whichever was cheapest. At great speed before breakfast, or between afternoon and evening classes, I washed and scraped, cut and chopped.

Ben sometimes found me bemused by the pattern of

a pair of leeks sprawled on the table, or the starry centre of a cut carrot.

'Look at it, look at it.' I would say, eyes shining. 'And at the colour of that cabbage and all those curves.'

'Lovely, darling, lovely,' he would answer, and kiss me.

Chapter 9

After three or four weeks our house seemed good to us, and ready for family inspection. Ben had made shelves, I had made curtains and cushions, and we had painted the sitting-room. Our friends had been generous with wedding presents, and we had been given no hideosities, duplicate toast-racks, or things we could never use – except for a set of ghastly fish cutlery, which I sold in order to buy a Mexican Christmas tree.

For her wedding Cordelia had been given five trolleys, eleven teapots and almost two dozen ghastly crystal fruitbowls.

We did a check tour of the sitting-room, which had lots of cushions in different colours, with the cat on top of the heap. We had painted the walls lightest grey, almost white, and the front of the old stove looked to me like a primitive mask. It had two doors, with diamond-shaped mica-ed windows which glowed and winked like flaming eyes when the fire was burning well. The round iron door-handles were like nostrils, and the rows of vents underneath were, unmistakeably, grinning teeth.

On the scraped wood sideboard was a bronze Byzantine bowl which had been my father's – which we used

with unconcern as an ashtray – and there was an enormous chemical bottle of smokey blue glass, which I had
bought one morning in an apparatus shop from a bald
man who painted his naked skull with dark brown
boot-polish, and kept the blinds drawn across his shop-
windows in the futile hope that his customers would
think him young and generously thatched.

The bedroom was bare of all decorations except for a
Japanese print, and some old curtains – whose possible
replacements frequently distracted me as I drew knees
and plastercasts at college.

We were having our first dinner-party. We spent the
day hoovering and adjusting our cushions and few pos-
sessions by a millimetre; I cooked with great concentration in the steamy kitchen, my hair dangling untidily,
dirty dishes cluttering every surface as I studied my
cookbook. Ben, who was very tidy, shuddered at the
mess and begged me to clear up as I went, as he always
did from his laboratory training.

'I know, I know,' I said distractedly, and threw the
cat a piece of gristle.

Both mothers were coming. I had made a goulash of
venison – which cost even less than whalemeat, according to Pete. ('I'll assure Mum it's kosher,' said Ben,
'but don't use any butter or milk in the sauce, or it
won't be.') For starters there were anchovy eggs resting
on red cabbage, so it was all perfectly straightforward.
All that remained to do was to boil the rice and toss the
salad after the guests had arrived.

I tidied up the kitchen, and was ready to go and
change, when I happened to look at my hard-boiled
eggs lying on their bed of cabbage. The whites had turned a most lethal-looking blue-green. Exactly the colour of verdigris. I shrieked for my resident scientist,
and he sniffed and shook his head, and looked for

49

clues, chemical training to the fore. He peered suspiciously at a copper-bottomed wedding present, but I assured him that I hadn't used it.

'You'll have to throw it all out,' he said, 'and make sure the cat doesn't eat it either.'

Ben rushed out for more eggs and anchovies, regardless of cost.

'Potato soup all next week,' I sighed resignedly.

It didn't take long to make up again; then we changed clothes, lit some candles and waited for our guests.

My mother earned her living as an active and devoted therapist in a fringe movement for expanding the ego. She had a missionary zeal and believed that she was saving the world. She was good at her work, the frail and unhappy came to her for help and usually they left happier and stronger and more fit to face life positively. It was, however, a problem to us that Ma believed that both Ben and Mrs Mandel could be much improved by her techniques, for which she had studied lengthily, and used a sort of electrical lie-detector device. Ben had no desire to change and perhaps thereby interfere with his creativity, and Mrs Mandel was adamant that at her age she and her *mishegaasen* (daftnesses) were indissoluble. Myself my mother considered to be perfect, a fact which I reluctantly acknowledged to be untrue, but from time to time her admiration was a comfort. Undeniably it is pleasant to be adored.

The mothers arrived with contesting bunches of flowers, and Ben poured sherry into virgin glasses.

My mother made to sit on the sofa.

'Sit,' ordered Mrs Mandel pointing. 'Sit on the sofa.'

Perversely, my mother changed in mid-action, and plonked herself gymnastically on a cushion on the floor.

Mrs Mandel was aghast. 'No! No! you can't be comfortable on the floor! Sit here. By me.' she patted the

50

sofa autocratically. She meant, in fact, that to sit on the floor was unseemly in a woman of almost sixty.

'I like the floor,' declared my mother and downed her sherry and accepted a refill, to Ben's mother's single sip.

Mrs Mandel watched her disapprovingly.

'In Sweden,' my mother continued,' we always sat on the floor.'

I winced as I glimpsed my mother's knickers, and saw her grin as she downed more sherry. She was triumphant to have displayed her beloved positivity by contrasting her own agility, practicality, and simplicity with her rival mother-in-law's conventionality. I left them to it and went to the kitchen. Everything was under control, I thought; I only needed to put a dressing on my ready-made coleslaw; it was going to be a lovely meal.

Then to my horror, as I reached up to a shelf for my cooking-oil, there was a light swooshing noise as I knocked an entire packet of blue washing powder into the salad bowl, where it lay all over the slices of cabbage and apple, like Mickey Mouse cake decoration.

'Oh God!' I gasped, then wanted to cry. The shops were shut, and I had no other vegetables in the house. So I did what I must. I spooned the detergent back into its box (detergent cost money) and whizzed the entire salad into a colander, and washed it fanatically, slice by slice, chunk by chunk. A piece of red cabbage fell onto a hard-boiled egg, and I noticed with rage that it immediately turned green. Obviously it wasn't poison, but just an odd chemical reaction. Guffaws came from the other room, and Ben came through to ask if all was well. He found me like an embattled Amazon firing a sling, whirling a tea-towel, filled with something heavy and wet, round and round my head, in the tight space of the kitchen.

He ducked to avoid being splashed. Water splattered the walls, window and ceiling.

51

'What are you doing?'

'I'm just drying the salad, darling,' I gasped, handing him an empty glass.

Ben's mother was glad to see that I could in fact cook, even if I did disappear for a long time before the meal. She had enjoyed the salad, but declared to my mother that Ben looked like a beatnik with his new beard and all that hair. Mrs Mandel sighed. (And that, Ben told me later, meant that she was thinking of her stubborn son, and his writing, and wishing for the thousandth time that he'd got a decent science job with his qualifications.) My own mother, being an expert, pronounced that we seemed happy, but I knew that she constantly worried about her only daughter with this husband who locked himself away every night writing plays which might never be performed. I knew that she longed to tell Ben that some of her fringe techniques would do him a world of good and eliminate his writing compulsions, and hoped that one day she could persuade her son-in-law to have a session or two.

The mothers rose to go at a tactfully early hour. As I looked at our newly-decorated room, Mrs Mandel said 'Don't you worry, Kate, it'll be very nice when it's finished. It just needs a good coat of paint.'

'I don't find your mother very easy.' I confessed to Ben as we washed up.

'Don't you talk to me about mothers. If your mother once again says to me "In Sweden we used to. . ." I'll explode. She always knows a better way to do things. At least we don't have to live with them any more.'

There was a silence as we wiped the dishes, and I felt worried.

'Living with Ben's mother would be bloody murder,' I thought, 'And my one wouldn't be much better. She'd try to convert him to Positive Therapy.'

'I wonder what will happen when they're old. They're both widows.'

'God knows,' said Ben. 'No good worrying about it now. They're not there yet.'

Chapter 10

I enjoyed very little of the work at College. I felt that
the place was a sort of bureaucratic sausage-machine
for art teachers, who would in turn become part of a
self-replicating line of Scottish art teachers stretching
out to infinity; there were several good painters on the
staff, but they were all very 'painterly', sensual paint
handlers, who had joy from pigment and texture. My
own gift was a graphic one, and my interest, artistic and
actual, was in people and their environment. Landscape could move me and make me weep at its colour
and beauty, but if I ever painted or drew a landscape it
would only be as a setting for a figure, and I would only
use it if it was relevant to what I wanted to say about
the figure I was painting.

Still-life I found quite interesting, but the subject I
really loathed and despised was called Antique Head.
Every Monday the class was made to encircle a plaster-
cast of some Greek or Roman sculpture – the Venus de
Milo, a Hercules, or the Victory of Samothrace – and
for the whole day we were made to do just one long
sustained drawing.

I liked real Greek sculptures, and adored museums,
but these dead chipped and be-pencilled putty-

coloured plastercasts made my heart sink. One day I put an orange wig on the Venus, and, for me it immediately assumed a theatricality and interest; but Mr Angelo, the instructor, was not amused. He was a very small man, with tiny brown eyes, like currants in a bun, on either side of a long thin nose, and he wore a small black imperial. He almost endeared himself to the students one year by exhibiting a large painting in the Royal Scottish Academy, which had huge dried squelches of paint, with several plastic water-pistols embedded thereon. This artefact contrasted so strongly with the class for which he was responsible, that we thought he might have hidden depths, but for me they remained well-hidden.

I was a bad attender at Mr Angelo's classes. In fact it was war, and we openly hated each other. Part of my private battle with him and his ilk was to pretend, when bored, with Zoe, that we were gorillas, and we'd while away the tedium by grunting to each other as we drew, jutting out our jaws or thumping with two clenched fists on our chests. And the best tactic of all in this childish but entertaining game, was to do it to the other person when Mr Angelo was giving her a critique and was oblivious to the gorilla performance. His critiques were not a joy.

'Well, Mrs Mandel,' he would say nastily, transfixing me or my drawing with his hot little eyes, 'What is the problem today?' and he would thrust his tiny little body between me and the drawing, and, with outstretched arms, pencil held at eighty-five degrees to the paper, would commit outrage on my drawing, and depress me utterly, and all the while I'd be trying desperately not to catch Zoe's eye as she bared her fangs in gorilla grimace and scratched under her arms. If I looked at her it would make me giggle helplessly, and I'd have to pretend to have a coughing attack.

The real trouble was the awful repetitive boredom of the Antique classes. I could see no point whatsoever in drawing these sculptures; they seemed miles away from any artistic aims I had. To ease the tedium I would further entertain myself by imagining my gorilla wrench the plaster heads or limbs off the classical sculptures, and hurl them through the gaunt north-facing windows, which looked across grimy tenements to where Edinburgh Castle stood towering above the College on its great buttress of rock. It was an entertaining ploy, and one day I became so carried away with the image, that I impulsively transformed my dull pale drawing of a plaster Aphrodite into a strong dark one of a female gorilla, complete with bosoms and a pink ribbon on her head. It was a vital and exciting drawing, the best thing I'd done for ages but unfortunately Mr Angelo suddenly appeared at my side and saw it, and his tiny eyes almost popped off the top of his nose.

'And what, pray, Mrs Mandel, is this?'

'Oh! I yelped, my mind a startling blank, 'Its. . . It's. . .It's a gorilla.'

Mr Angelo looked interrogatively at me, but remained silent.

'This gorilla. . . it's for a play for my husband. A play that he's writing. He. . .he. . .er. . . needed me to design a costume. . .'

And then with an adrenalised gush of invention, 'This gorilla. . . it's – I mean she – She is called Queen Kong.'

Mr Angelo eyed me up and down uneasily.

'It sounds like a very strange play surely.'

'Yes. It is. It is.' I assured him, wide-eyed.

'Humph,' said Mr Angelo, 'Well kindly keep your theatrical designing to an appropriate place and time in future.'

56

Fortunately he didn't notice that Zoe was poised right behind him gesticulating murderously, her eyes mean, her mandible protracted.

After lunch Zoe and I decided that we'd had enough of the Antique class for one day, so we went junk-hunting. Much later we staggered back, Zoe with an enormous wickerwork chair on her head, myself with a filthy Persian rug. Near the College we bumped into Mr Angelo. Class must just have finished. I froze with terror and tried to hide the roll of carpet behind my back as I grimaced a feeble greeting, but he must have been day-dreaming, because he offered to help the breathless Zoe to carry the chair. Zoe thanked him, but shrilly refused. Afterwards, as we made our way to my house to recover, Zoe said, 'Poor wee gnome. He'd have been lost in it, like a shrunken tortoise in a wickerwork shell – with those totty wee feet and that horrible wrinkled neck sticking out.'

I picked up the mail from the doormat. Zoe looked at me.

'What's the matter; you've turned pale.'

'Nothing,' I said hurriedly, 'It's for Ben.'

In fact it was a rejected script, and the accompanying letter said the play was too documentary and undramatic, and didn't have enough male characters. (Next morning the second script came back with a letter which said that there was a man too many, and that the play was over-dramatic and unconvincing. The third script we never heard of again.)

I tried to cheer Ben up by telling him about my gorilla drawing, but he didn't really listen.

'I'm stuck,' he said, and melancholy filled me. I felt cut off and outcast from him, and through him from life. Marriage, I was discovering could, strangely, mean loneliness, and sex was not as frequent or available as I had expected. Often Ben didn't come to bed till after one o'clock, he worked so hard at his two professions, so it wasn't much fun when he did, with him exhausted, and me unconscious.

'How's the new play going?' I asked. I had surreptitiously looked at his re-writing of one scene; it was written over and over, and one could hardly see the paper for writing. I was afraid. It looked so neurotic, tight and obsessive, that writing.

In the morning, I looked from his white face to the rejected manuscript; obviously the two were connected.

'Darling, you must get yourself a new agent. Until the first play has some acceptance, how can you possibly write another?'

He scarcely reacted. I went to fetch *The Writers' and Artists' Year Book*, and plonked it on the breakfast table, between the marmalade and toast.

'How can I choose? It's a lottery.'

'Just pick anybody.'

He shrugged. 'O.K. Got a pin?'

I fetched one, and he shut his eyes and twirled it round and jabbed the book. It hit a blank space.

'Once more.' He almost smiled. This time he hit a name.

He peered at it. 'Barfield Scripts Limited. Never heard of him. It's a W1 address though. O.K. Why not? It'll be as good as any. I'll have a go.' He went off to work a little late, but quite bright. At tea time he typed another letter and re-packed the script.

It had been snowing when we took it out to the post, and was freezing cold. Ben bought stamps, and I watched as he licked and stuck them on.

'Don't you worry,' I intoned in Aunt Emma's voice. 'The Lord will provide.'

'Aye,' said Ben grimly, handing over the parcel. 'He'll provide a bloody wall for me to batter my head against.'

Outside the Post Office as we crunched through the snow I didn't dare ask if he was going to write tonight. I thought he might explode again. It was growing dusk, yellow and orange lights showed from the surrounding houses, and the sky was a marvellous gas-flame blue; I missed him when he always locked himself away. He turned to me suddenly, grinning.

'Let's buy some steak and some wine. We've got a free night ahead of us. What would you like to do?'

And we did. Athletically.

Later, as we lay listening to each others' breathing, arms and legs marvellously entwined, Ben asked tentatively, 'Is there any of that cheese left?'

'Ooh, you really are a genius.' I got out of bed again, and padded through to the kitchen, wearing his old orange vee-necked jersey (which I knew fetchingly revealed my cleavage and pink buttocks). I came back with two mugs of cocoa, and thick gherkin, pickle and cheese sandwiches. We ate them with grunts of pleasure.

'We're bloody lucky, you know,' said Ben.

'Yes, and rather a good fit,' I said smugly.

We sighed, set the alarm for eight for school tomorrow, and slept.

Chapter 11

Ben usually refused to come out on weekdays, but after our happy night off I was sure he would be amenable and come to a College party to celebrate the end of term. I was longing to have him meet my friends for once. But he wouldn't. 'I'm sorry. I'm in the middle of a scene. I can't.' I went into the bedroom and sat on the bed in rage and misery. Ben came through.

'Listen, darling. You go to the party. I'll work till eleven, then I'll come and join you.'

I reluctantly agreed and set out alone when the time came. An old windowless spiral tenement stairway, with worn steps led up to the dilapidated third-floor flat where the party was being held. Everybody had brought a bottle, and there was candlelight. It was odd being on my own; the other married student in the year, teeny Mary, was mutely standing in the corner with her equally teeny husband. They looked like tow-haired Babes in the Wood. I was relieved to see Pete standing looking lonesome and holding a large bottle. He brightened when he saw me, and poured me half a jam-jar of white wine.

'Hi, fellie,' he said, 'Where have ye lost yer man?'

I drank some wine. At College we talked only about

work, which obsessed us both. Now, with the alcohol inside me I expounded on the problems of marriage. Defensively at first, on Ben's side, then, as the wine glowed, my doubts flooded through. Pete put his arms round me.

'You need a lover, fellie.'

I pulled away abruptly.

'I don't,' I said. 'I love him. Without him I feel like an egg without a shell.'

Pete pondered the image, puzzled, and stared down at my cleavage.

'D'you mean a raw egg, or a boiled one?'

'Hard-boiled.'

Pete did etchings with bits of string and smudges, which were pleasant objects. You could make out the odd breast here and there, or the occasional flailing 'part'. We had one of Pete's works on our bathroom wall – his wedding present to us. But to gain full enjoyment from his work, you needed Pete to explain its meaning properly.

'Eggs,' he said, 'are very symbolic.' He was working on a painting of John the Baptist – an amazing piece with nudes and satyrs. Salome had a key in her back to make her dance, and John the Baptist's head was very decorative on the plate.

'Will ye pose for me?' he asked.

'No.'

'Ye don't want me,' said Pete sadly.

'Yes,' I assured him. 'As a friend.'

'Do ye no fancy me?' he asked.

'I'm spoken for.' I drained my jar and sighed.

Pete was watching me closely, when he suddenly grasped my right hand, and peered at my index finger.

'Here, what happened to your finger? It's shorter than your left one. Did ye bite your nails and your teeth slipped?'

61

Not many people had ever noticed, but it was true; my finger was indeed shorter. And scarred; but I rarely thought about it now, it was so long ago.

'I was bitten by an ape.' I told him.

He guffawed. 'You're kidding.'

'No,' I assured him, 'it's true. In the Ape House at the Zoo. Years ago. I was only eight.'

Pete grinned delightedly. 'I always knew there was something wild about you.'

I remembered vividly what it was like. Copying my older brother, I'd innocently offered the caged and furry beast a sweetie-paper, and it had reached its paw through the bars, grasped my finger firmly and gently, like a banana, a bitten off the top. There were screams, and horrified adults, and great drips of blood on my navy-blue school coat. I was rushed to the main gates of the Zoo, where the uniformed official said, 'Another monkey-girl, eh? I'll call ye a taxi. We've had I don't know how many bites this month.'

By taxi to the hospital, where I remembered the sinister nurse, starched, and smelling fearfully of antiseptic, coming to inject me.

'Why must you?' I asked, weeping, as she held the enormous syringe up to the light.

'Don't you worry, dear,' She loomed, and clasped me, and plunged the needle fiercely into my bottom, and I yelped. 'We're just trying to stop the monkey from getting inside you. We don't want that, do we now?'

I imagined a hairy creature, uncontrollable, and slightly bigger than me, imprisoned within my skin; and I was afraid, and gazed in horror at my newly-bandaged finger.

Pete was obviously impressed by the story. He put his arm round my shoulder and re-filled my container.

'It's probably affected ye deeply, fellie. Mebbe ye're the Missing Link. Here, drink up, It'll make your fur shine.'

We gulped, and both yelled a greeting as Zoe entered the room, voluptuous in red and black stripes. Pete was immediately lost to me and my memories.

'Oooh. . .' he breathed, 'Have a – a chair. . .or a drink, or a kiss, or something. You look utterly fantastic.'

Rebuffed, I left them to it; I was quickly picked up by a medical student called Grigor. He didn't seem to want to leave me, and his hand crept round my backside.

'That is a most excellent *gluteus maximus* there,' he said, gazing intensely at me over his glasses.

'I'm married; I'm waiting for my husband,' I said sternly. This fact did not, however, deter him in the slightest. He now clutched at my hips, a hand on each.

'Married, begod, and built for childbearing. A splendid pelvis you have.'

I wished I could bare my fangs at him, to make him go. Instead, Kate the polite, I asked brightly:

'Tell me about being a medic. Do you get very involved if someone dies? I've never seen anybody dead.'

Grigor brightened, withdrew, and we sat on a bread-strewn table, as he eagerly described the deaths he'd seen.

The vegetarian Myfanwy came rolling towards us. She was not wearing her black leotard today, but had on a sort of Eastern kimono, which showed off her slender shape, and her black curls were tied in a large, fat pigtail.

'Hello, there, friend,' said Grigor.

'Hi Kate, who's thish?' asked Myfanwy, squinting

63

towards Grigor. (Her vegetarian diet permitted alcohol.)

'This is Grigor.'

'Ah,' she swayed and surveyed him approvingly.

'Hash he got a girlfriend?'

'No.'

'Good,' she said. Then 'Hi Grigor,' with a giggle, and they were gone.

I felt deserted. Pete and Zoe were passionately entwined under a table. Everybody seemed to be paired off and was either necking or dancing to the thumping music from a piano and saxophone playing in the next room.

I took another gulp of my wine and determined, almost savagely, to go and fetch Ben. I felt quite sober when I left the racket of the party. It was quiet outside, muffled, because it had snowed earlier in the day, and the icy night cut like a knife.

To get home, I had to walk through one of the oldest parts of the city. The Grassmarket was like the bottom of a basin, the sides of the basin being steep streets of ancient tenements. There were several lodging houses for tramps and meths drinkers in the Grassmarket and in the daytime it was always filled with filthy kids, over-flowing gigantic communal dustbins, and old women with bundles of washing and falling-apart prams.

Thinking only of reaching Ben, I was unafraid till I had walked some way. An old hag loomed up to me from a dark alley and breathed croakily, putting a mittened, chapped hand on my goose-fleshed arm.

'Dinna go through the Grassmarket by yerself, lassie. Take a bus! Take a bus! It's dangerous here by night!'

Panicked, I started running past the black close-mouths and empty streets. A drunk man fell suddenly at my feet making a hideous clunk as he landed on the snowy pavement. I thought I saw two police-men, and ran towards them, but they turned invisible as quickly as they had appeared. It was like a wierd haunted play or ballet sequence; I now felt very strange, and was elatedly certain that I could fly from lampost to lampost.

At last I reached our own street, which seemed miles long. I realised that I was drunk and had better sober up before meeting Ben.

'I'm sober, I'm sober, I'm perfectly sober,' I chanted to myself in time to my zig-zagging steps.

I was rather giggly when I reached the house.

'It's a marvellous party!' I sang through the study door. Ben stopped work, put on his coat, and we went back to the party. The Grassmarket didn't seem at all frightening this time, rather romantic, in fact, but he wasn't pleased that I was drunk.

Grigor and Myfanwy had left, so had Pete and Zoe. Most other people were being sick or tangling on the floor, which seemed to be a heaving mass of beards, limbs and empty bottles. I tried to make a conversation or two get off the ground, but without success. Ben had a little wine, but grimaced, because it was Spanish, sweet and foul.

A fuzzy-haired boy, with an Italianate girlfriend who did pottery, neither of whom I knew very well, lurched towards us.

'Oh, poor Methusalah, does he not like his drinkie?' the boy asked. Ben didn't react.

I felt an animal urge to do the couple an injury and had a subliminal image of a paw with a bandaged index-finger, clutched on a bottle, poised to strike. Then I whimpered, and felt very upset. My worlds didn't mix, and I was lonely in both of them, and wanted to go home.

65

Chapter 12

A week after the party, I came home from Christmas shopping to find Ben sitting bemusedly eating a Mars Bar and pouring himself a drink of Martini – a thing he rarely did except when we had guests. 'Are you all right?' I asked dubiously, as I laid down my parcels.

'I think so.'

'What's happened?'

'I've got an agent. Quite an important agent,' (he reeled off several famous clients on the agent's list) 'and this agent thinks I'm very sensitive and unusual and talented,' Ben quaffed his glass and grinned even wider.

My knees de-boned all of a sudden, but I grabbed a glass as I simultaneously sank onto a stool. He filled it and re-filled his own, and we laughed and shrieked and the cat leapt off the mantelpiece and fled with a flash of yellow horror in its eyes. My mother heard the noise from upstairs and, greatly alarmed, rushed down to knock on our door.

'What's wrong? Is anybody hurt?'

We shrieked afresh, and gave her some Martini and told her what had happened.

'That's wonderful,' she said, 'Well done, Ben.'

I phoned Cordelia, and Ben phoned Marcus Thomson.

And day followed day and there was no further word. Then it was Christmas.

For Christmas I gave Ben a woollen shirt in an unusual and beautiful mustard colour, which had cost a lot, but I loved to see him in it. (And he needed it.)

He gave me a weighing machine, which depressed me. Its face, with the accusing little black numbers spoke truths as hard to bear as Mr Angelo's.

Ben's mother, always brilliant at choosing presents, gave Ben a showbiz autobiography and me she gave a continental cookbook, rich with coloured photographs of exotic cream-cakes and luscious paellas. We spent Boxing Day with myself incommunicado, glued to the autobiography while Ben was in the kitchen where he weighed flour, sugar and almonds like an alchemist, and chopped apples and raisins, as he laboured to make a strudel like his grandmother used to make. He succeeded too. It looked a little like a threadbare boaconstrictor, which had eaten too much plum pudding, but it tasted excellent.

I looked up from the book and admired him in his new shirt. Gradually I was weaning him away from his white shirts and pressed handkerchiefs. Not that he had many of them left now. It wasn't that I meant to dye them pink and blue. It just seemed to keep happening, when I boiled them or left them to soak. His new string vests all looked eccentric by now – rather like tie-dyed floorcloths. Anyway, this new shirt was a step in the right direction as it looked more aesthetic (although I knew Ben's mother shuddered with horror at the colour of his Christmas – or, as she called it, Channukah-shirt) and didn't show the dirt, or pink or blue dye in the same way as a white shirt. And as for handkerchiefs. All that beastly ritual of boiling cotton handkies, vests and pants seemed an awful waste of time –

and I was sure that paper hankies were more hygenic, and there were so many more important things to do.

By now Ben had a drawerful of holey socks. He used to go to the drawer in the morning, and woefully pick up sock after sock, finding a hole in every one. I kept suggesting that he wore nylon socks, but Ben liked wool. On New Year's Day I decided to consult Cordelia, who had cheered up enormously since her baby slept longer at nights.

'Oh, socks! said Cordelia lightly. 'That's simple. You just shove your fist through the hole and make it so huge that he can't possibly wear it – except perhaps as a Balaclava, or cock-warmer – then you show him that the holes are too big to mend, and he realises that he needs to buy new ones.' I envied her realistic approach, but Ben and I were on different terms. 'Well then,' said Cordelia, 'I once darned them with stringy oiled wool – like barbed wire – and made sort of horny callouses of darn. Tony found them so agonising to wear that he went out and bought ten pairs of M & S nylon socks, and now he's mad on them. 'S easy fellow. You'll manage.' She was right, I did.

Apart from boiling his nether-garments purple, which he found exasperating, but forgiveable, I had certain habits which Ben loathed. It was the awful mess I left behind whatever I was doing that drove him really mad.

Soon after Christmas Ben finished writing Act One. Early one evening he came to make himself a cup of coffee, and took it into the sitting-room where I was painting quietly. He sat down, opened the evening paper, and sipped his drink.

'A-a-a-r-gh,' he spat out a mouthful of coffee, which fizzed on the stove.

'What is it?'

'Bloody turpentine! You've been putting it in the mugs again!'

'Oh,' guilty, I bit my lip. 'I couldn't find my dipper. I thought I'd cleaned it.'

Ben washed his mouth in the kitchen, then gave an even louder yell.

'And you've put paint on the tap! Jesus! I've got a great blob of it on my jacket!'

I put down my paint-brush on my palette. 'I'm awfully sorry darling, here, I'll help. I've got turps.'

He was very angry, in shirtsleeves.

'You're not awfully sorry,' he said coldly, 'Or you wouldn't keep doing it. Here, give me the turps.'

Furiously he rubbed at the white splodge on his suit. Ben's lab training as a physicist had made him almost obsessively tidy. If he mended a fuse, the wires and pincers were immediately hung back on the correct hooks ready for next time. If he made coffee, he wiped up any spillage and put away sugar, coffee and milk. After any meal, however rushed we were, he insisted that we clear up – and I really was glad of this when I came back tired from a late class, much as I might moan at the time.

'Clear up as you go.' was his constant dictum. It drove me mad, partly because I knew it made sense. In fact I also hated untidiness, and had nightmares about my cupboard under the stairs, where I put everything not of immediate use, until the cupboard itself became unusable. But Ben kept chanting, 'Mess grows on mess,' and my messes grew into bigger messes all the time. I had somehow never learned this basic discipline of life. As a child, I had not been nagged and reminded daily to tidy my room or clothes. I had been obsessionally tidy till I was about six – or so my mother used to reminisce wistfully – then I had grown progressively

69

more and more untidy. My mother was always very busy, and worked late, and she had found that the simplest thing was to have what she called a 'Blitz' every few weeks on my room which was always strewn with books, stones, biscuits, drawings, models, orange-peel, coins, sweet-papers and apple-cores, pets and dressing-up clothes.

'Come on little monkey,' she'd say fondly, 'I'll help you.' I remembered the awful bewilderment I used to feel in the untidy room, and how I longed for it to become miraculously clear, and I still, at twenty, suffered this feeling of helplessness when I saw my own mess – which seemed to me to have come unbidden.

'That's it off now,' said Ben, looking at his jacket. Shamefaced, I had washed the mug with Vim, and made another cup of coffee. 'I don't want it,' said Ben. Deflated, I drank it myself.

Later, when we undressed for bed, I noticed that Ben now threw down his socks, jersey, and shirt in pools as he undressed. How long had he been doing this? He used to lay them in neat obsessional piles; I pointed to his untidy clothes. 'What about you?' I asked aggrieved. Ben smiled blandly. 'You're influencing me, darling,' he said. 'Like I said, mess begets mess.'

I fumed, and sulked on the sofa, comforted only by the cat, and stayed there miserably. Ben came through to fetch me at midnight.

Chapter 13

The day of Cordelia's baby's christening was doubly memorable for us. It was a grey Scottish day with a freezing wind that chilled the bones. We had breakfasted and were getting ready for the christening; I was cutting my beloved's hair: Ben knelt on a newspaper on the kitchen floor, naked to the waist, like a man due for execution. I wielded the scissors and chopped off dark hunks of hair, whilst he stroked my legs, and I caressingly brushed fallen hairs off his back and deliciously tactile chest. Then we heard the letter-box click, and the thud of mail. It was from the new agent that he'd picked with a pin, and the agent wrote that he loved the play and had sent it to a Scottish repertory company who were willing to give the play a try-out at Easter, which was really very soon. Ben was euphoric. He hummed and sang and kissed the cat as we got dressed, and I looked at his new-trimmed beard and thought how I would boast of my brilliant husband to Pete and Zoe, and even Mr Angelo. Ben wore his wedding suit, and some forgotten pieces of confetti floated from the lapels as he put on the jacket.

You're not taking your sketch-book to the christening, darling? You are the godmother, after all.' said

Ben, exasperated. I agreed reluctantly then hid it in his coat, just in case.

At the church I was glad to note, for Cordelia's sake, that Bill Brown was subdued but sober. Mary was snappily smart, all black-and-white dots, shiny fur coat, and patent leather. I was also relieved to see that Cordelia's will-o-the wisp husband was in fact there for once. Tony was a wiry, startlingly white-toothed young ex-public school man of twenty-eight, with crisp blond hair, and lots of charm. Ben and I enjoyed him as a picnic or dinner-party companion. Tony always had excellent stories to tell and he had the salesman's charm and gift for connecting apparently random pieces of information and personalities, which made conversation with him lively and often amusing.

Outside the church, Cordelia was holding the baby who, rosy and fetching, lay in layers of white lace and frills. Cordelia wore pink and white, and I hoped that I would be able to recapture the confection of colours, which were given a totemic strength by Cordelia's dark and dubious eyes brooding above them.

The women all kissed each other, and the men shook hands. 'Hi fellow,' said Cordelia, then she added jokily but with a razor's edge, 'Where's all your christening gifts then? I expected you to bring at least a silver-plated potty, or a diamond-crusted rattle.'

I replied with acid, rolled in honey, 'Darling, as soon as you give me my promised pearls, for being your lovely bridesmaid, I'll pawn it and buy endless silver trophies for my godchild.'

We smiled, and Tony came, hearty as ever, to herd us into the church, saying:

'Come on girls, let's drop wee Cathy in the font. The sooner that's done, the sooner we can get down to the serious business of celebrating' – with a slap to his father-in-law's vast pin-striped shoulder.

None of us had been near a church since Cordelia and Tony's marriage which took place·a year before ours. That had been a stark Presbyterian affair; I had a vivid memory of that occasion when the minister, a sensible, tight-faced little Scot of fifty-odd, had spoken for most of the guests present, when he gave his toast at the cutting of the cake.

'Well,' he had said sternly, 'Tony here is a charming fellow, and Cordelia is a delightful young girl. But if Cordelia had been my daughter, I would have said no. However all I can now wish for them, is that at the best they will wrastle through. So I give them my deepest hopes and good wishes.'

There had been a stunned silence as the fingers of the bankers, shopkeepers, and chartered accountants of the Scottish Lowlands tightened on champagne and whisky glasses. Then with a rustle of finery and embarrassed clearing of throats, the bridal toast was drunk. Tony, in his brief and hearty wedding speech, was oblivious of the breath of ice which had blown across his feast. All he said was:

'It's wonderful of you all to have given us both such a tremendous send-off, but honestly, all I really want to know just now, is if anyone here can tell me the winner of the Derby?'

I hoped that today's event did not coincide with the Grand National of the Oxford and Cambridge Boat Race. I went with the others into the warm darkness of the church. It was an English church; Tony's mother, who stood now, emaciated and elegant, near the font, resplendent in brown fox cape, dramatic hat and too much make-up, had begged the couple to christen her grandchild here because of family tradition. I smelt incense and saw gleams of gold and purple.

The priest was a plump genial young man in a robe, who

73

chatted and shook hands with members of the small congregation as he guided them to gather near the plain stone font. Cordelia handed her child to me, and I was deeply moved as I felt the weight and warmth of the tiny girl and saw her milky-blue eyelids, tight closed. I was aware of Ben at my side, and saw him gazing at the baby with an expression of great longing.

It was a painlessly speedy service. At one point the priest handed Tony a burning white candle, which he held helplessly whilst the congregation chanted the Lord's Prayer and the Affirmation of Belief. The baby slept, remarkably, through all of it. I shuddered for her small round head, when it was doused in chilly water, and mopped dry with a soft towel – leaving her long dark hair sticking out in all directions like a flue-brush – as she was given her names, Catherine Jane.

At the end everybody cooed and smiled and re-enacted the brief happenings and I saw poor Tony, standing now very embarrassed, with the candle still burning in his hand.

'What do you think I'm supposed to do with this thing?' he muttered anguishedly to Ben, who agreed that it would be disturbing symbolism to put it out.

Ben spoke tactfully to the priest, who was apologetic and said of course Tony might blow it out and take it home for safe-keeping, so that it could be used at the christening of any other children they might have. Tony blanched and smiled mirthlessly, and put the extinguished candle in his breast-pocket, like a large white cigar. Then we went back to their small yellow-painted flat to celebrate.

Ben stopped at an off-licence to buy a bottle of whisky to drink to the christening and the imminent performance of the play, and when he tried to put it in his overcoat pocket, he encountered my small smuggled sketch-book. The party was brief but noisy, and everyone drank too much too soon, and apologised and left. Cordelia, holding her now crying baby, agonised in the doorway, and said, 'I wish you didn't need to go.' And again I wanted to paint that beautiful but uncomfortable motherhood.

Chapter 14

Ben went to Glasgow to talk to the director, and I involved myself with a series of paintings of children and old ladies. The christening had supplied me with both. I had painted my first old lady a couple of years earlier, and since then had been constantly haunted by images of old ladies with hats, beads, earrings, flamboyant make-up or flowers. I often wondered why I was obsessed with old ladies. One of my friends' mothers had seen a drawing I had done from memory of old Miss Christian at the wedding and she said 'Oh, Kate, you are cruel,' which hurt me deeply. I painted old ladies because I was almost moved to tears when I saw them.

Since I was a child I had been hypnotised by the sadness, helplessness, loneliness and bravery of the old. I adored the almost clown-like quality of many of the indefatigable old warhorses whom I passed in the street; I found them moving, and beautiful, with their great hats, jewels, complicated shoes and burdens of flowers, handbags and umbrellas. I was haunted by them as they struggled across zebra-crossings, with honking cars pawing the ground, while lights flashed and Belisha beacons twinkled. The drama of these fragile people in cities clutched at me, and I was compelled to express what I felt about them – and the children I saw in the same surroundings, sucking lollies and reading comics obliviously.

At College I found it hard to learn the technique I needed. I had come there filled with originality and talent, like so many of my fellow students, but now, half-way through my third year, I felt I was being stamped flat.

In the Still-Life class I had been thrilled with the glint and flash of fish, and used to go to the sea-smelling, white-marbled fish shop near the College, where I bought herrings and kippers, which I painted all day and fed to the cat at night. I would go to sleep dreaming of the sparkle of a kipper's back, and longing to show the world the wonder of a herring. But College undermined me with its contradictions.

'Keep your whites down. Use more neutrals,' was all they ever seemed to say. Ben put up several ink and water-colour old ladies in his study, but I know that I still had to come to terms with my oil-painting.

Walking home on the sunny afternoon of the start of the Easter break, I saw a heap of mackerel shouting their beauty at me from their white slab, with water rippling over it. Bemused, I bought two, and walked out of the shop watched by a puzzled fishmonger, as I pulled open the newspaper they were wrapped in. They gleamed and winked in the sun like diamonds. Blue and silver zig-zagged with black. I walked home, oblivious of all but the fish, just missed being run over by a bicycle, and almost bumped into Ben's mother, who was alarmed to see me in that state. 'Are you all right?' asked Mrs Mandel anxiously. 'Yes,' I nodded vacantly.

'How's married life?'

'Lovely.'

'What news of the play?'

'Rehearsals start tomorrow.'

'Isn't it all a bit hectic?'

'No, not really.'

Defeated, my mother-in-law eyed the open newspaper of mackerel.

'You're still going on with College?'

'Of course,' I said firmly, 'I was just admiring these fish. Aren't they extraordinary?'

Ben's mother agreed dubiously, and instructed me how to cook mackerel with gooseberries.

Ben, elated by his trips to see rehearsals, would come back thrumming with excitement. The lead parts were shaping up well; the young beatnik girl was smashing – he was so enthusiastic about her that I felt a twinge of jealousy. The man playing the lover was a bit weak, said Ben, but he would improve. The most pressing problem was that the director needed a violin every day. At one point in the play the enraged husband smashed a violin on his wife's head. Brilliant theatre, Mandelian, I thought, putting my canvas away and giving one of the mackerel to the cat.

Wednesday night before the opening Ben came home in a panic. 'They're going to cut the violin scene,' he said, 'they can't get any violins.'

'But it would be like Princes Street without the Scott Monument. What will they do instead?'

'I think he'll just slap her.'

It was too weak. We must find violins. We'd go to the junk-shops.

The play took over my life too, and the violin-hunting became an obsession. The play was to run for three weeks, so we needed twenty-four violins which could be sawn through then sellotaped together before being smashed on stage. I tried all the shops in the Grassmarket but found only one violin that was either battered enough or cheap enough. I went to see my antique-dealer friend Jamie Coutts, who squeaked like a delighted guinea-pig when I told him of the violin hunt. 'My God,' he said, 'You Arty-Crafties get dafter and dafter. Ye'd think ye'd have some sense now ye're married.' But he gave me one for a few shillings and an old bowler hat for nothing, which pleased me mightily. I left the shop wearing the bowler hat, clutching the two battle-scarred violins to my bosom, hearing Jamie's cackle following me down the street.

Jamie's shop was across the road from Mrs Mandel's kosher butcher, and I liked peering in this window because he had a most extraordinary cat. Like our own cat, it was very large and square. The butcher's cat was red, but its most interesting feature was its lower jaw, which jutted out for almost an inch beyond its upper jaw, giving the beast an air of extreme agression. The thing that fascinated me more was that the butcher had exactly the same sort of mouth, and his lower teeth jutted far beyond his upper set, so he and the cat were a surreal matching set. A notice on the door of the butcher's read 'Best Worst', and I mimicked the cat's face as I peered through the glass, and saw him pad majestically across the sawdust and come to rest by the counter.

I was shocked from my reverie by hearing my mother-in-law say, 'Is that you Kate? What on earth are you doing with those violins and that hat?'

I shrieked with surprise and dropped one of the instruments with a great clutter which brought the butcher to the door, whilst I grovelled to pick it up, and hurriedly retracted my jaw.

'Ah, Mrs Mandel,' said the butcher to Ben's mother, a little surprised to see her with this strange girl, 'How are you? I have your lamb all ready for you.'

Mrs Mandel was obviously transfixed by indecision, but she quickly realised that she must admit to her relationship with me, so she reluctantly took my arm, almost making me drop the other violin. 'This,' she said with one of her sighs, 'is my new daughter-in-law. Ben's wife.' The introduction sounded like an apology. I struggled to remove my bowler, as I suspected that keeping it on didn't add to my image, but nor did the gesture of removal at the moment of introduction. The butcher wiped his huge hands on his striped apron, and smiled with his prognathic jaw, a little dubiously, and extended a hand into my tangle of black wooden violin scrolls and pegs and bowler hat. I succeeded in freeing a finger for him.

Mrs Mandel went into the butcher's shop, collected her lamb and bought a wurst sausage for me to take home. I was grateful, but by now desperate to get home and unload myself, so somehow I fitted the sausage into the hat, said goodbye to my bemused mother-in-law, and made for the nearest bus-stop, knowing within my bones that the old lady was watching me unhappily, and shaking her head as I went.

At home Ben hadn't done too well. He had only found one violin.

The theatre had phoned twice to ask if we had succeeded, as they had only found one as well. We still needed twenty more. Frantically we phoned round the music shops, the College of Music, and the Library; but we went to bed baffled. At one a.m. we were startled awake by the phone. It was Marcus Thomson, Ben's BBC colleague. For a moment I wondered if he was belatedly punishing us for my thrusting the cat onto his velvet waistcoat at our wedding.

'Ben,' he said. 'Good news, I hope! I've just edited an interview with a violin-maker!'

Next morning we went together to see the violin-maker; it was entrancing to think that there actually was such a man, still alive and working. It sounded like a Grimm's Fairy Tale trade, like the charcoal burner or toymaker. Mr Luft lived in a decaying street of tenements which were due for demolition. The brass bell-pulls had no handles, just wire guts hanging out, and the name plates were either non-existent, or, occasionally, smoothed to gleaming illegibility by generations of pride and polish. We asked some kids with yellow ice-lollies, black teeth and green snot if they knew of the violin-maker. 'Naw.' They shuffled and giggled, then they ran away and shouted 'Beardie! Feardie! Does it keep ye warm?' Ben, intent only on violins, ignored them, but I wanted to linger. It was a sunny day, and the children had marked out squares on the pavements, making patterns against the cobbles and graffiti. There were groups of kids playing marbles, and some older girls skipping and singing to the rhythm of the song:

'Catch a Perry Como
Wash him in some Omo
Hang him up to dry
Drip dry.'

You could always tell that spring had properly arrived in the city when the children on the streets brought out marbles and peevers (Scots for hopscotch). I stopped for a few minutes to quickly draw the playing children, while Ben walked the length of the street and back. The street number he'd been given didn't seem to exist, and he wondered if the interview had been a hoax.

A very fat woman came wheezing along, an old grey

coat buttoned tight round her swelling shapes. Ben approached her and asked if she knew Mr Luft.

'Oh, aye, ah ken him. He's a foreigner, is he no? He lives up the top there, number thirteen.'

'Come on,' said Ben, 'We're short of time.'

Mr Luft lived right at the top of a dirty, worn stair, which wound round and round, in almost pitch dark. Panting, we reached the top, and knocked on a door, which was answered after a longish pause by a short, grey-haired little man, wearing ancient slippers, a striped suit, and stained brown trilby. He had bright, dark eyes, gold-rimmed glasses, and a strong Germano-Scottish accent.

He took us into a room which was scruffy and white, and looked out across the city's roofs and spires and barely-green trees to the sea, and beyond, to the blue hills of Fife. The room itself was filled with violins. They lay on the floor, and almost covered a large long table. There were woodshavings everywhere and chisels and pots of varnish with ancient brushes in them. I noticed a long rope all hung with violins like washing on a line – handles at the top. It was fascinating and odd and Mr Luft bobbed excitedly about showing us now this violin, and now that. He had come over before the war, he told us. His trade had always been violin-making, as it had been his father's. 'It's just like cooking,' he said. 'Some people can make food taste extra good, and it's the same with violins, some people can give them a special good tone,' and he plucked and twanged a violin to show us how well he cooked.

'You're good,' said Ben approvingly.

He was a great help, and promised us all the rubbishy violins we needed, so we took as many as we could carry, and Ben went triumphantly to catch a train to the theatre, clutching a great posy of violins – so beautiful he looked; I kissed his empty shirt when he had gone.

Chapter 15

Ben's new agent came up to see the play being performed. We travelled to the seaside town where the play
was due to have its première, to meet him. There was
blossom everywhere and it was a sunny evening, full of
promise. The agent, Nigel Barfield, was about forty-
five, dark and elegant, well-dressed in tasteful golden
browns. I liked him, and approved of how he took Ben
under his wing, fed us both and cossetted Ben throughout the stressful evening.

We looked in on the actors and wished them luck.
The husband was played by a blue-eyed man called
Mike. He had an upturned nose, and a face which
looked alternatively harrowed and aristocratic or
humorous and proletarian. I noticed that he had very
hairy arms and broad shoulders, like a circus per-
former.

'How are you guv?' asked Mike, clapping Ben on the
shoulder 'Are you going to be out front with the
critics?'

'I don't know yet.'

Nigel took us to the circle bar, and gave us a brandy
each. We drank it nervously and watched the audience
coming in. Ben was pale, and distraught.

'I'm not coming to sit inside,' he said and felt in his wallet. 'Here are your tickets. I'll be at the back.'

I was sad, but kissed his cheek. 'Good luck!' I whispered.

And I sat near the front of the circle and counted the rows of heads. The theatre was almost full.

There was a hush, and the curtain went up. The sets were a sitting-room, an architect's office and a bedroom, all on the stage at once, each area belonging to one of these places. There was no back-cloth. The designer had decided to use the texture of the bricks at the back of the theatre, which gave a drab sense of space. The audience looked at the sets, and then slowly from left to right an old man wearing a boiler-suit walked across the whole width of the set, carrying a cup of tea.

'Here's yer tea, Jimmy,' he called to the wings.

'Who the hell was that? hissed Nigel.

I was horror-struck. There was no such character in the play. Nigel glanced at me, puzzled, and I shook my head at him. The audience was completely quiet, still looking towards where the old man had disappeared. At last Mike made his entrance, called for his wife, and the play got under way. I admired Nigel for the convincing guffaws of laughter he let loose at every joke. There were quite a lot of laughs. In the interval we found Ben, ashen, with another glass of brandy.

'It's very good. It plays beautifully, Ben,' said Nigel with professional enthusiasm. 'I shall get all the managements up from London to see it. But who, tell me, was that old man who made his début?'

'Oh God,' sighed Ben. It was the bloody theatre fireman. Nobody had bothered to tell him that there was no back-cloth.'

During the second act a woman got up and walked

out when the wife reminisced about being discovered making love in the bath. There was warm clapping at the end of that act, and we assured Ben that it was going very well.

In the last act Mike had to talk for a time about death. At one point he asked his wife, 'When do you think we'll die Jean?' and this caused several hysterical titters. I was furious, but Nigel whispered that it was very Scottish to laugh at death. At last it was over. The management gave us drinks and some limp sandwiches. Mike and the rest of the cast were very animated and there were all sorts of local newspapermen. Ben answered endless questions about his age, his hopes for the play, and I gave a rather indiscreet interview in which I mentioned the aunt and uncle Ben had used as models. 'They even sent Ben a telegram and the play's about them. Wasn't it sweet?' It didn't matter in the end because the reporter was from the *Ayrshire Farming Times,* and they'd never see it.

The Scottish papers had some very flattering notices during the next few days. Even the mothers quite liked the play. Nigel went back to London and kept phoning to say that Michael Codron or Binkie Beaumont or some impresario from the States was coming up to see it and Ben, manic with hope, would travel over to meet them. But nobody came. Promises yes, managements no. There were three weeks of excitement and notoriety. Newspapers and radio interviewed Ben, then nothing. It was all over, and the play of all our hopes sank into oblivion.

I cut out the notices and put them in an envelope. Ben sat in a chair staring unseeing and chewing his beard.

I wept inside myself for his — and my — disappointment. He was so hard to talk to when he was sad like this. He was like an ancient Ruritanian stranger with no English. Nigel had written to say that he was terribly sorry that none of the managements had come, but he hoped they would read the play and the good notices. I sighed, and went to put the envelope away beside my tangle of paints and papers in the cupboard under the stairs. I opened the door, and from among the brushes and bottles, sewing and overdue books, a dead and smelly mackerel stared at me.

Chapter 16

It was hard for us both to settle down to the dullness of work and poverty again after our glimpse of a golden future. Ben swallowed his disappointment. At least he had had a professional production and a lot of people had liked it.

He went back to writing the play he had tucked away in a dark drawer in the autumn. And I went to work in a panic, because there were only a few weeks of term before all the year's drawings had to be gathered together, mounted, and shown to the staff. A lot of people were to be weeded out, before the hard work of the Diploma year, and I had nightmare visions of toppling Antique sculptures with Mr Angelo peering through their legs like a garden gnome.

At the second Antique class of the term, Mr Angelo told the students that they must all bring their entire year's work for him to see next week. Panic registered on at least half of the faces in the room. The Little Knitters stood looking very smug, arms outstretched, pencils poised between thumb and forefinger, and drew in military unison. 'My God', said Pete, to the trembling Zoe and myself, 'What are we gonna do?'

On my way home that evening, I was clutching a

huge piece of white-painted hardboard that I wanted
to work on at home. Zoe and Pete and I had decided
to work through lunch-hours on Antique heads, to use
some drawings from last year's portfolios, and Zoe
had had the brilliant idea of borrowing some old
Antique drawings from the fourth-year girls who
shared her flat. It was a sunny spring night, but windy,
and I felt like a ship in full sail, because the board
caught every puff or gust and threatened to whirl me
across the street.

Across the street was a junk-shop I rarely visited,
because it sold mostly reproduction horse-brasses and
little china cups from Stockton or Darlington. As a gust
of wind took me round the corner to our flat, pressed
against the hardboard like a painting on a kite, a subliminal image remained with me.

I struggled into the house, and dumped the board
against a wall. Ben wasn't due home for a good
half-hour, so I grabbed an apple, and ran back out, I
was soon staring through the filthy window of the
junk-shop, with open mouth and half-eaten apple in
hand, feeling like Eve after the first bite. There, in the
middle of the window, was a mask. It was about twenty
inches high, and was basically a carved wooden face,
with boat-shaped holes for eyes and a strange large
shape – separate from the face – which I realised later
was the tongue, which started wide from the mouth and
swooped up like a flat blade into a point above the forehead. It was painted all over in angular lines with tiny
squares of red-ochre, black and white. It was filthy with
dust and pieces of old twine and sacking hung about it,
but its presence was Christ-like, magnificent and regal,
yet full of suffering. I had no idea what it was, or where
it came from. For a while I wondered if it was a Swiss
mountain mask, because the mood was gothic. I didn't

care what it was, or whence it came, I only knew that I must possess it. My blood was pumping with excitement, and I went to the shop door and rattled the handle. There was nobody there. All I could find was a notice which said 'Back in ten minutes', but it had cobwebs on it. I asked in the sweetie shop next door if they knew when the shop would be open.

'Oh aye,' he's been away on his holidays. He'll be back at the end of the week.'

Today was only Monday. I couldn't bear it. I went home, with nothing but the mask in my head. The white board remained in the hall till Ben fell over it and cursed. I couldn't tell Ben about the mask because he was understandably jumpy about money. It had been expensive travelling so often to see to the play, so it had in fact cost money. Thoughts of a summer holiday had now receded; I knew he would veto any purchase of an antique – even if it was only a pound or two – and I knew well it must cost much more than that.

It was a fraught week. I hoped that Mr Angelo cricked his neck with surprise as he walked past and saw me working in the gaunt corridor where sculptures loomed from grubby plinths and cupboard tops. After my snatched lunch-hour drawing, I would dash across the nearby daffodil-starred park, and arrive panting at the junk-shop, where I would gaze at what I considered to be my mask, and hoplelessly rattle the round brass door-handle. I went every day, either at the end of the lunch hour, or just before the evening lectures. The History of Architecture lecturer was thin and bald and had a very large moustache ('He knew he needed some texture somewhere,' muttered Pete), and we had a weekly ritual when I creaked guiltily in, several minutes late, of his peering over his glasses at me and saying: 'Whenever you are ready, Miss Lawrence,' and

I would blush and feel tearfully guilty, but be late again the next week.

The junk-shop man didn't come home on the Friday. Nor was he there on the Saturday. I became very tense.

'Are you premenstrual?' asked Ben.

'No,' I snapped, 'I'm overdue.'

'What!' Ben's eyes popped, half with hope, half with horror.

'I am actually. I'm two days late. And I couldn't drink my coffee this morning.'

'Oh darling.' Ben came and cradled me. We neither of us wanted a baby at this particular point, yet we were both beginning to long for a child. Spring, daffodils and cherry blossom and little birds all were having their effect, and my goddaughter was fast growing more delicious and amenable.

I was still overdue on Sunday. I woke up at six on Sunday morning feeling the stew of the night before swilling blearily about my stomach and burst into tears.

'I don't want a baby right now. I want to get my Dip. I must learn more about painting first. I'm not ready.' I dashed out of bed to the bathroom, where I was sick.

Ben was very comforting. 'Don't worry. We'll handle it somehow. You could even have it in the Christmas holidays and keep on going to College.'

I wept again, and then wept louder as I realised that I wasn't well enough to go to check on whether or not the mask was still there.

I was sick several times on the Sunday, but felt better next day, and went to College, still slightly wobbly. I finished my still-life of fish and a mincing machine and gathered up my basket of pencils, blades, fish, drawing-books and purse, and counted my money. I had exactly four pounds for the week's housekeeping. I went to the cloakroom for one of my hourly checks, but my pants were spotless: I was still pregnant. Then I went out of College.

The shop was open. I could hardly believe my luck. The owner was dark, plump and mayby forty. He had a khaki-brown overall on and a checked cap. I put down my basket and examined a white china dish from Whitby.

'They're verra popular, these wee pots,' said the man.

'Mmm, they're lovely,' I cooed.

I flitted from object to object, weighed a brass candle-stick, and admired a teapot in the shape of a cottage. Then I said, 'How much is the funny head in the window?'

'Seven pounds. It came in wi' a lot of missionary junk. Calabashes of lime, stuff like that.' He showed me a few uninteresting broken gourds and a dusty model of a native hut. I dismissed them and went to look at the mask. 'You must be kidding,' I said, all wide eyes and naïveté. 'Seven pounds for that! It's just a joke.'

'Oh, I dunno,' said the man, scratching his head. 'It's quite old, and it is a real native thing, whatever it may be.'

I cocked my head to one side. 'It's quite creepy,' I said as chattily and ignorantly as I could. 'It would look really funny above my mantelpiece.'

The man chuckled. 'Aye, he might give ye a fright in the night, dear.'

By now I had conjured up for myself a job, a pink-painted room, and a father with a small garden filled with dahlias. 'I think it would make my Dad laugh,' I told him confidingly, 'if I came home with that. He was in Burma in the war and is always going on about those sort of funny things.'

'Oh aye,' The man wasn't very interested.

91

'Listen,' I said, 'I've got thirty bob. I'll give you that for it.'

The man snorted like a horse. 'That's very handsome of you dear. But ye'd need tae give me six pounds. I paid a lot for all that stuff.'

My heart sank. 'I just can't,' I said. 'I'm only a student nurse, and I'm over from Crieff for the day. Please, would you take two pounds?'

'Nah,' said the man.

I didn't know what to do. I rarely ever spent more than a pound on my finds, and two pounds seemed an awful lot. I couldn't use up all the house-keeping.

'Listen,' I said. 'I really just fancy that thing. I think I could manage three pounds. But my father would go for me with the lawnmower if he knew.'

'Honest, dear, I'd like ye tae have it, but I've a living tae make. I can't go under five pounds.'

My adrenalin was pumping. 'What a shame,' I said. 'I'd really have liked to take it back to Crieff. I collect wee glass animals and this would have been a change.' I wandered over to a dark corner of the shop where there was a hideously carved modern tourist-trade African lady. 'This might do,' I said. 'How much is it?'

'Four pounds.'

'Oh, what a shame. Dad would have liked that too.'

Then, as though the thought had just struck, I said, 'Would you take three pounds then for the funny mask?'

The man shook his head, and locked the back door of the shop.

I was desperate. I've got to run for my train home in a minute,' I said. 'And I won't be back for ages. Please, would you take three pounds ten?'

'I'm sorry dear. I can't.'

I gulped. 'Three pounds fifteen?'

The man shook his head again. 'Come on dear, I need tae lock up now, it's after five.' He jangled his keys.

I took out my purse and emptied three notes and a lot of silver and copper onto a brass salver. 'Look,' I said, 'That's my lot. Four pounds exactly, and I don't know how I'll get from the station to the house. Please can I have it?'

The man shook his head dubiously and counted the coins, and examined the notes.

'I made them myself,' I assured him. 'They're all right.' The man shook his head at me and pocketed the money.

'O.K. you win,' he said. 'I'll get ye some paper to put it in.'

I felt as though all the birds of the world had burst into song. I tried not to look too excited. The man came out with a bundle of what looked like firewood – about ten sticks, maybe fifteen inchcs long.

'They belong to the top of it,' he said. 'They're like Red Indian carved feathers.'

I gawped at them. It was true. The flat, slightly curved pieces of wood were also painted and carved, and I saw round the top of the mask the broken bits where I would fit them on. It was the broken pieces round the mask's head that had lent it the Christ-like crown of thorns look.

I carried my precious burden home to the upstairs flat and hid it under the bed in my mother's spare room. I knew Ben would be home downstairs and I didn't dare take it into our own home. As to how to confess to spending four pounds, I simply didn't know.

I made macaroni cheese for supper which we ate quietly. I became worried and alarmed again when I found no sign of a period, and had bad dreams that night. Next morning I lay staring into space, very worried, full of fears and doubts. Ben brought our toast and tea into the bedroom and we ate, again silently.

I went to wash and dress; and came back to Ben swollen-eyed. He reached for my limp hand, and soothed me. Tears fell down my cheeks.

'I'm not preggers,' I said dismally. 'My period, it's come.'

'I don't get it,' said Ben, as he hugged me.

'I didn't want to be preggers,' I wept 'And now I'm not, I wish I was.'

Ben had to laugh. He held me. We both felt a sense of loss, but it was better this way. He wiped my eyes and kissed me. 'I love you,' he murmured.

'I love you,' I sobbed. 'And Teeny Mary's pregnant, and I feel jealous.'

I ran up to my mother's house. The door was answered by Ma, surprised and pyjama'd. I fetched the mask out from under the bed and was relieved to see it was still beautiful. With a rush of confidence I took it down to the flat. My mother followed. Both Ben and Ma saw the rarity of the thing at once. They held the wooden feathers against the silent, powerful face, and planned how to glue them on.

'My God, we're late,' Ben realised. As he pulled on his coat he said 'What did this thing cost?'

'Three pounds seventeen-and-six,' I said very quickly. I couldn't confess to four whole pounds.

'Was that the housekeeping?'

'Oh no!' I shrieked.

He reached into his wallet; there was a fiver in it.

'Here,' he said, 'I'll see you for supper.'

Chapter 17

All through the Antique class I thought about my marvellous mask and how beautiful it would be, mended and hung above the old black stove. Zoe, Pete and I had succeeded in making impressive fat folders of Antique drawings. The Little Knitters were bewildered by our cheerful and confident smiles, and Mr Angelo spent most of the day crouched over the folders, breathing heavily, and grunting in despair before he handed them sourly back. I was quite pleased with myself, because I had actually worked on the same drawing all day (it was of a dreary headless torso), and I hadn't drawn any gorillas or crossed swords with Mr Angelo. There were only fifteen minutes of the class to go, but I was glazing over as I drew, for at least the third time, the same highlight on a plaster toenail. I did after all need glue for the mask's feathers, and it had to be the right kind of glue. Also, I needed to buy paint, because it was essential to change the colour of the end wall where the mask would hang. Convinced by my own persuasion, I glanced across to where Mr Angelo stood, correcting the newly-pregnant Teeny Mary's weeny drawing and, satisfied that he wasn't looking, I crept quietly out of the class.

I intended to go back in an hour's time, after the tea-break, to collect my drawing-board and the folio of drawings.

When I got home with the glue and paint, Ben had finished the first typeable draft of his new play and was relaxed and happy. I cooked supper, and after we had eaten, we drank coffee, and admired the mask, which lay in pieces of newspaper on the floor. It took us a long time to fit the wooden feathers on. It wasn't an easy job, and we couldn't do them all at one go, because they needed screw-clamps, twine and rubber-bands to hold them in place. We managed the front four. The very front one was a tall barbed extension of the carved tongue, and the mask looked wonderful, more wonderful than before, now that it was mended.

I raked through my History of Design books. 'I think it's Melanesian,' I ventured. Later I was sure. 'It's from New Ireland.'

After we had done all that we could in the way of repair, I mixed my paint – a warm ochre – and painted the end wall of the sitting-room, ready to receive the mask. The wall was a perfect colour, and enhanced the room hugely, but the glue on the mask wasn't dry.

We went to bed, and Ben promised to buy clamps the next day for the last four feathers. As he put out the light I suddenly remembered and yelped, 'My God! My Antique drawings, I forgot to go and get them. I hope to God they're still there!'

For once I was early as I walked across the park to College the next day. I watched the seagulls shriek and soar above the lines of bright green trees, with blackened town trunks. It was Life-drawing today, and I would need my drawing-board which I trusted would still be standing on yesterday's easel.

It was silly, I decided, to worry about my portfolio

which would still be by my easel. I fixed my mind on the models, and hoped it wouldn't be either Hairy Mary or Saggy Jim. Hairy Mary was a black-haired female model, scraggy and worn, with generous amounts of pubic and underarm hair, which accounted for her name. She had quite an interesting body to draw, with tendons and bones showing through all over, but she drooped as the day went by and lost the line of pose with which we started the day, which made drawing her very difficult, because her whole centre of gravity would change from one leg to the other in a matter of an hour, and this exasperated the students. Saggy Jim was a large, puce-coloured man, with popping eyes and a loose-lipped mouth, which hung open as he posed. His pendulous stomach and flabby chest made him look pregnant and his feet were odd and ill-fitting, like side-ways snow-shoes.

The female models posed quite naked and the men wore G-strings. Saggy Jim's G-string looked like a crepe bandage round his vast stomach, and held his genitals in a tired, heavy bag. He was disgusting to look at and often scratched his bottom unawarely, but he looked characterful – especially if the drawing teacher posed him in a hat. But I was tired of both these models and hoped we would have Alberto Rotondo instead. He was a marvellous model. He had told me that one of the Pre-Raphaelite painters had discovered his grand-father as a young shepherd sitting on a Tuscan hill; the painter had brought the boy to London where he had founded a whole stable of Italian models – men, women, children, babies and grandparents. Alberto Rotondo had a barrel-shaped top, and was aged almost seventy. He had a fine head, not much hair, a Roman nose, round red cheeks and intelligent eyes. Most of all, he knew how to keep a pose. He felt his way into a pose, testing the ground, moving his feet, and feeling his body weight distribute itself correctly. He knew exactly what an artist needed, and how important it was to take up the same position after a break. He was a real professional, reliable and dignified. We all adored him. Often, after easing his way back into a position, he would ask me, 'Is that all right, Miss?'

At the last Life class, I had been given a particularly vicious criticism of one of my drawings; the instructor, a large untidy man, Hamish Mackenzie, had drawn all over my simple linear drawing with large rough lines and said:

'You mustn't be afraid to make a mess, Miss Lawrence,' and he then urged me to make a sort of bird's nest of pencil lines from which the figure woollily emerged. I felt hopeless and miserable. Furious that I wasn't technically good enough at the simple linear drawing I longed to do, to prevent such assaults on my work. Alberto came to me during the break, with a maroon dressing-gown round his shoulders. He gave me a mint imperial. 'You really care about this lark, don't you, Miss?' I nodded miserably.

'Well, don't you let them get you down, Miss. You've a lifetime ahead of you, and that's more than they've got. Just keep going.'

I passed some pigeons eating crumbs on the cobbled road by the park. So soft and perfect those colours were. Would I ever catch their subtletly and splendour? Maybe I could paint that old lady in the red coat and hat, feeding them, or might that be too sentimental?

In College I went straight to the Antique studio, and found my drawing-board with the headless torso drawing on it, but my Antique folio was nowhere. I had left it beside the easel. I looked on the radiators, and climbed up to the high windowsills with their grim north-facing windows. I looked beside and under the sink, where there were large pieces of paper pinned up to collect the multi-coloured scrapings from a thousand palette-knives. Panicking, I asked everybody in the room if they had seen it. I looked behind the Venus, and the Apollo and the anatomy skeleton, and under chairs and tables and in the painting rack. I pulled out dozens of dreary paintings and graffitied drawing-boards in my desperate hunt. I saw Pete who assured me that he'd seen the folio where I had left it. I searched out Zoe, desperately hoping that she might have saved it for me, but Zoe shook her head. 'Mr Angelo will murder you, Kate,' she said comfortingly, and Pete fondled his beard and dolefully said, 'Well you'll be chucked out now for sure.'

The starting-bell shrilled, and we went to Life-drawing. I saw with relief that Alberto Rotondo was on the model's rostrum. He winked at me as he positioned himself comfortably and interestingly, leaning on a long wooden pole. I forgot about the folio, and made a good start to my drawing. I was using a cheap Japanese brush with black ink, which was a medium I always enjoyed. The brush had about a dozen delicate and complicated Japanese characters incised on its side. I looked at it, and wondered what the poem on this particular one said. 'Folio lost, student dismissed.'

'Well, Miss Lawrence?' (I had given up telling him that I was now Mrs Mandel.) 'How are we doing today?' asked Hamish Mackenzie.

'I don't know,' I said, 'It seems not too bad to me.'

Mr Mackenzie pulled at his lower lip and gazed from drawing to model. 'Well,' he said heavily, 'I suppose it will do, but make sure you explain properly what happens in the dorsal region there. And I'm not keen on these brushes. It's awfully easy to be over-flashy with them.

I made a sick gorilla face behind his back, and saw Zoe

scratch under her arms. I snorted, then grovelled in my cluttered basket for an ink-stained hankie. 'Excuse be,' I said to Hamish Mackenzie, sniffing into the hankie, 'I have ad awful code.'

After the class as I fruitlessly searched along the corridors for my lost drawings. I noticed a toffee-paper stuck in the navel of one of the Venuses. I looked at the letter-rack, where there was never a letter for me, and read and re-read everybody's postcards. On the noticeboard most of the notices were half-obliterated with lewd pencilled comment. I asked the Cockney janitor, Fred, if he had seen my drawings.

'Lost your etchings 'ave you, dear? Why don't you come in and see some of mine?'

I had enjoyed some highly suggestive conversations with Fred, but today I was much too preoccupied, I turned, and found myself face-to-face with Mr Angelo. I nodded hysterically to him and hurried past.

'Oh, Mrs Mandel,' he said. I stopped. If I'd been pregnant, I said later to Pete, I'd have had a miscarriage.

'Mrs Mandel,' repeated Mr Angelo. 'I would like to see your Antique folio.'

I was faint. 'I . . . I . . . I don't know where it is, Mr Angelo. I did have it. You saw it when we handed them all in.'

'I would like to see it again, Mrs Mandel.'

I became tearful. 'I don't know where it is, Mr Angelo. I've looked everywhere, even in the College dustbins. It has utterly disappeared.'

Mr Angelo was silent as an Antique head.

'I noticed,' he spoke after a minute, 'that you left the class extremely early last night. Could you kindly explain your reasons for doing that?'

I blinked, and looked at my awful little enemy, and

100

for a strange moment it was as though thick fur had grown on my body. My breathing became a deep grunt, and my pale hands became leathery; the moment passed, and I was myself again, but I saw looming in front of me, alive and bulging, complete with pink ribbon on her head, the very gorilla I had drawn weeks before. Her nostrils dilated as she gazed at the oblivious Mr Angelo; then she roared and beat her leathery bosom with her huge fist.

'I am Queen Kong!' she shouted, and I watched, entranced, as she leapt a wondrous leap to a far-off cupboard-top from which she swung by means of the light-fittings from easel to easel, roaring her rage. 'You, little man, are a bird-brained idiot, a waster of Life, Time and Talent!'

My heart beat in triumph at her words, and Mr Angelo seemed smaller than ever. I drew breath, and looked straight into his squinting little eyes and sighed.

'I'm terribly sorry, I know I shouldn't have left early, but my drawing was finished, and I needed to do some shopping.'

Mr Angelo stared into space, then he said, 'Come with me, please,' and walked into a private room at the end of the studio. My knees were shaking as I followed him. He took a key out of his pocket, unlocked the door, and went over to a dark cupboard. He reached inside it, and slowly withdrew my lost folder. I looked at it, hardly believing my eyes.

'Is this what you were looking for, Mrs Mandel?'

I held my breath in rage as my dear gorilla lifted the tiny trembling Mr Angelo up in her huge paw and said, 'You know it's what she was looking for, you bloody midget sadist.'

And I, frightened student Kate, simpered my relief, grovelled, thanked him even, and promised not to

101

leave the class early in future. Queen Kong went home munching his head between her fangs, and squeezing his little suited body in her gigantic muscley fingers. I walked beside her, a little light-headed from the strength of her image.

Ben was home early for once. He'd had a phone call from Nigel at school in the morning, saying that an impresario called Abe Bramstein had read the play and liked it. Ben had taken the afternoon off to come home and rake out all his other copies and send them off express post. I had heard of Abe Bramstein, because he was a television personality. Ben was on his way to the post. 'I'll be about half-an-hour,' he told me.

'Why so long?' The Post Office was across the road.

He smiled his pussy-cat smile. 'I'm going to call at the travel agent. We need more honeymoon.'

I hardly dared believe it. 'Is the Bramstein thing definite?'

'No,' he admitted, 'But let's chance it.'

This was a new Ben, a Ben with the scent of success. I liked him even more this way. I felt wonderful; an optimistic husband, and a secret gorilla, what more could a girl want?

Chapter 18

The good weather brought outbreaks of romance to all the students, the staff, and even some of the models.

Saggy Jim was one morning reported to be wearing a new sports-jacket instead of his ubiquitous dirty rain-coat. Pete and I rushed to look over the balcony surrounding the sculpture court, and there indeed he was, lumbering by, his great bulk encased in violent green, white and red checks.

'It's for the Venus de Milo,' said Pete, 'He's fancied her for years.'

And Zoe fell in love with the dashing and highly successful painter who taught Still-Life, Michael Phoenix. I went with Zoe to his enormous annual exhibition, and we were deeply impressed by the number of large romantic canvasses he had painted in a year. In the Still-Life room he dashed past us.

'Oh, how I envy him that neat little bum,' said Zoe longingly, and I knew that she was in love.

I found Michael Phoenix stimulating as a teacher. The things I wanted to express seemed to me remote from his art, but his own enthusiasm and delight in sheer paint-handling and colour was excitingly infectious.

When I was bogged down by my inability to make a still-life 'sing', Phoenix would appear at my side like a parachutist landing in a field, and enthuse me with a few brief words. He always asked permission to paint on a student's board or canvas, which was a good habit. This morning I watched, bewitched, as he transformed my unpoetic rendering of a black-and-white alarm clock into a marvel of insinuation and pleasure.

Then I noticed Zoe's look of intense jealousy.

'Look girl, I'm not interested in him,' I told her.

'I know,' said Zoe, 'but I can't help myself.'

'He's unattainable, is that why you fancy him?'

'Certainly not!' snapped Zoe, and she turned and smiled alluringly towards Pete.

And Myfanwy and Hector fell in love. Myfanwy, the yoga expert, wore very short straight skirts and infuriated Zoe and me by boasting that at three in the morning, during the College Revel, Michael Phoenix had remarked on the perfection of her knees. An academic remark, Pete assured us, because he'd made it from beneath a large and active sculptress. Big Hector, from Dingwall, was an enormous bearded teddy-bear of a lad, who always wore the kilt and a multi-striped jersey. We overheard them chatting, and Myfanwy taught him to say the long Welsh place-name which requires six-inch railway tickets, and he fell visibly in love with her as he repeated the strange Welsh syllables after her soft voice, and gazed into her black eyes.

I put a blob of titanium white on a fish's scale, and wondered if Myfanwy would now teach Big Hector yoga, and if he would then stand on his head like Myfanwy. And, if he did so, I wondered, would he then also abandon the wearing of the kilt. For, as Hector often said, there is nothing worn under the kilt; it is all in good working order.

104

The following afternoon, on my way home from College, I saw Big Hector striding along towards Myfanwy's flat, through pushchairs, old ladies, and traffic, as though through wild heather. His face was filled with beatific Celtic ardour, and his arms were filled with what must have been a couple of hundred daffodils.

He was a splendid image, but Myfanwy milked it, and described it hourly, along with her perfect knees, until Queen Kong threatened to string her by her leotard from a light-fitting. Even the Little Knitters went courting now, I saw them sitting outside the College on a bench – still knitting, as they chattered to each other across their companions who looked like a bespectacled Harris tweed clone.

Pete responded with alacrity to Zoe's rebound from the unattainable Michael Phoenix. He would stand vulture-like, and watch her as she drew. Pete, as with his John the Baptist period, was still using the Bible for subject-matter. He did an interestingly painted, and quite obscene, Susannah and the Elders – the Elders were in great states of excitement, and Susannah was soaping her breasts. His work, however, was still very abstract-expressionist, so it was just as hard to decipher which piece of anatomy was which as it had been with his Salome etchings.

During the coffee-breaks Pete sat with the slender Zoe on his knees, his skinny arms round her enviably thin middle, hand-rolling his own cigarettes on her knees. And then he smoked and talked incessantly about the thought-processes he went through for his painting, with Zoe nodding violently every time he took an in-breath on one of his thin, shaggy cigarettes.

Pete was proud to have won Zoe for himself because she was rated high by the College men. To celebrate, he wrote a neat pencilled message on every buttock and nipple of every plaster sculpture in the College. The message was 'Phuck Phoenix'.

Back home, Ben was busy with school work, as his pupils were about to sit their exams. The mask hung in splendour on our wall, and Nigel Barfield wrote to say that Bramstein was having twenty copies of the play printed and was this O.K. by Ben?

It meant that Bramstein was serious, I crowed to Pete and Zoe, who were very impressed. 'Abe Bramtein,' mused Pete. 'I've seen him on some of these telly panel-games about antiques and funny objects.'

'What does he look like?' I begged.

'He's big and fat, and has a very cruel face. Real strong.'

I went back to the antique shop where I had found the mask, half-hoping I might discover its brother. The dealer greeted me: 'Back from Crieff are ye?'

I was surprised, then remembering, yelped, 'Oh, yes, I had a day off from the hospital. I just wondered if you had any more things like that mask I got?'

'Do I hell,' said the man sourly. 'But I tell you what; I'll give you fifteen quid if you bring it back.'

I could hardly believe my ears. For a split second I was tempted, then I smiled and said, 'Er – no thanks. My father really likes it an awful lot. It looks great with the glass animals.'

Ben had booked a cheap little house in a Spanish village for a month; we asked Tony and Cordelia to share the cost by joining us half-way through. 'You must come,' I insisted on the phone, 'You need a holiday; of course your mum will keep the baby.'

And the rest of the term flashed by. There were a few written exams, which were straightforward things like a slide of the Great Pyramid shown briefly on the screen,

106

and you had to write all you knew about it. I enjoyed that. There was a costume-drawing test, for which we drew Saggy Jim, complete with spectacles and hanging mouth, dressed as a Beefeater, in tired old velvet togs which hung limply from his great appendage. And there were other drawing tests – Antique and Life – before we finally handed in our folios.

During the last week of term, I noticed Myfanwy sitting by the radiator, with weary eyes, leaning against Big Hector's protective bulk. I sat beside them, and we compared drawing-marks and how many mounts we each still needed to cut.

Myfanwy sighed bleakly. 'I don't care if I never see another piece of paper or tube of paint in my life,' she said.

'You feel like that now, because you're tired,' said Hector gently, 'But you're dying to get on with your big miner painting. It's going to be the best thing you've ever done.'

Myfanwy really seemed to have found her artistic voice recently, perhaps because of Hector, I grudgingly admired her work, although her chronic boastings of her unparalleled knees, and daffodil-laden lover continued to aggravate.

'You just need to get on and do more yoga, surely,' I said. 'You're always telling us how it revitalises you – all that standing on your head in the lotus position.'

'It's no that she needs,' said Hector, 'There's nothin' wrong wi' her that a big fat steak or hunk of meat will no' cure. She doesn't get proper nourishment wi' all that yoghurt and beans. I keep telling her. But they're stubborn, these Welshies. She wouldnae even eat ma auntie's cockie leekie soup, which is full of her national vegetable.'

Myfanwy got up quietly. 'I think I need to go home,'

she said, picking up her bag made from an embroidered coal-sack, with hundreds of buttons sewn onto it. 'I just feel too tired. Can you tell Mr Angelo that I didn't feel well.'

Hector got up, ready to take her home, but she shook her head heavily, and said, 'Please, I feel hellish unsociable. I need to go home and sleep.'

She left, and Hector shook his head. 'She's too exhausted to do anything just now. She's listless and off her food, just like an old sick collie. I think she should see the doctor and get some vitamin pills, and he might at least make her eat properly.'

I nodded. Now that Hector pointed it out, I realised that Myfanwy had been doing much less yoga lately. 'It's because she's been wrapped up in Hector,' said Zoe. I imagined Hector and Myfanwy entirely cocooned in a highland plaid, of the same dark green tartan as Hector's kilt. Anyway, I shook off the thought, probably Myfanwy was missing her beloved Welsh mining village, which she was always painting, with its slag heaps at the bottom of brilliant green valleys.

My own work was improving. I had just done a small painting of a teenage bride, inspired by Cordelia, and the blonde, bewildered lassies I saw on buses all peroxide beehives, plump knees and short skirts, holding their babies like dolls. And this one broke the College bounds and reassured me. This was Art; I might really be a painter one day.

On the last day of term came a momentous letter. Could Ben arrange to meet Abe Bramstein in London as soon as possible and sign a contract?

We sat in the bed and screamed our joy and disbelief, and I saw Queen Kong turn cartwheels on the carpet. Ben phoned his BBC friend and colleague,

Marcus, who displayed avuncular but genuine delight, and I phoned a half-asleep Cordelia, and we screeched in unison. Ben re-booked the sleepers to London en route for our Spanish village; could Abe wait till then? Then he phoned Nigel, who laughingly said the contract-signing could wait of course. I went to College like a helium baloon on a string, and the first person I met was Hector, carrying some of Myfanwy's paintings.

'Hi, Hector!' I roared cheerfully, 'Where's that Welshwoman of yours?'

'She's in hospital, Kate. They're doing all sorts of tests on her; they think she's anaemic or something. I just hope they'll give her some liver and iron and stuff; I said I'd clear out her locker for her.'

'Oh God. Poor Myfanwy. Give her my love. She's probably just been working too hard and not eating enough.'

Hector nodded, and we said goodbye till the autumn.

My one beloved teacher, William Wyllie – or Willie Winkie as everyone called him – passed me on the way out. Willie Winkie gentled his students to paint, as a gardener waters and watches his plants unfold. He joked with Zoe, Pete and me, told us about Keats and Blake and argued as to the best way to casserole tough chicken. He was a small man of about fifty-five, with thinning grey hair, and a puckish twinkling face when animated, which often looked stern and private when he was contemplating some thought of his own. Ben had met him once and been entranced by the culture, humility and width of the man's mind. Willie Winkie was never a prolific painter; older people who knew him, told me how he used to paint in a minute, badly-lit bedroom, and how his palette was crusted thick with ancient layers of dried paint, which had lucent wet craters of fresh paint, where he dipped and stirred his

109

singing brush. I adored his paintings of nudes and flowers and streets and houses. They were slightly whimsical, like Willie himself, and in them partridges pranced, stars glittered, and shambling pink-faced country boys embraced their plumpkin girls, with garlands on their suits and ties.

I loved Willie most of all because he seemed to believe in me as a artist. Once or twice, after swapping a recipe, describing a concert, or telling of junk-shops as they used to be, he would look at my painting almost in passing and say, 'You're really coming on, aren't you?' and it was the greatest praise and encouragement I could have asked, because it seemed like he meant it, and understood that I was on a journey.

'Hallo there Kate,' he said today. 'Zoe tells me your man's play is for London now. If your London management do it half as well as they did it up here, it should make your fortune. Wish him luck for me. I'm away to my neglected garden at last.' He twinkled, and made me happy and was gone.

I noticed that the janitor was cleaning one of Pete's graffiti off a female statue. The term was well and truly over. I went to clear my own cluttered locker, and day-dreamed of Spain and fame.

Chapter 19

It was the Big Time now. Riches sparkled within our grasp. We flipped from poverty to wealth in a blink of hope. We packed for a month in Spain and travelled overnight to London, where Ben's agent Nigel met us and primed us up on Abe Bramstein in a dark red and mirrored Victorian pub.

'He's a well-known and successful writer and promoter of plays,' said Nigel, 'He's delightful. He is determined to put the play on soon and wants to discuss casting and direction with you and sign the contract.'

Abe Bramstein's office was above a shop off Bond Street which specialised in African art. I was enthralled. The shop was painted a dark reddish-brown and dimly-lit, and marvellous masks, dolls and fetishes were hung in niches on the walls, all dramatically spotlit. Everything had a little printed label as in a museum, with mysterious reference numbers, but no price, and the whole place was thickly carpeted. Ben pulled me to follow Nigel through an almost invisible door at the back of the shop, just behind a sublime and terrifying mask which was blandly featureless, with gaping circle eyes, and grooves from the eyes to a silent howl of a mouth which had a few inset teeth.

111

We climbed up a generously-carpeted stairway and reached a small office with hundreds of Victorian programmes plastering the wall. There was green paintwork here and there and a busy desk with a typewriter. A dark young man met us who seemed to know Nigel, and we were ushered into a further room. I, still reeling from the African sculptures, felt myself sink into a deep white carpet, and glancing above the desk, saw a real Maillol drawing, in red chalk, of a nude woman. Beside it was a modern gouache, very simple, bright and primitive, of a theatre queue and a London bus – the name in lights on the theatre front was one of Abe Bramstein's biggests hits. I felt Ben's hand pulling me and walked into an almost circular room which overlooked a busy street. It was quiet in the room; clever lighting, a sense of bright green, archetypal black leather and steel chairs, an enormous telephone-strewn desk and a smiling, thickset man sitting behind it. I thought, yes. He had a strong underlip to his muscular mouth, a thick neck, bright brown eyes, and, I noticed with fascination, a frayed blue shirt.

'Hi,' he said extending a large hand to Ben. 'I'm Abe Bramstein. Nice to meet you.'

The young man who had brought us through from the first room was a sort of henchman-manager. He poured us enormous drinks from a dazzlingly-stocked drink-cupboard, which looked like a Portuguese ivory coffer. I sipped from my goblet brimming with Martini, and dazedly looked from object to object. The door on this side consisted of what looked to me like a complete carved and painted Persian temple door. There was a splendid Augustus John pencil drawing of an angry child, and a general feeling of lushness such as I had never experienced.

Abe was direct and amusing. He asked Ben almost at

112

once how old he was and was he a Yid. Ben told him and Bramstein declared that he was thirty-six and his people were Russian Jews. 'Are the people in the play your family?' he asked Ben with a sardonic smile. 'Yes,' Ben admitted. 'And some of hers.' He pointed at me.

'I had trouble from my own family,' said Abe, 'but you can't make a family omelette without breaking somebody's eggs.'

After several minutes of talking and drinking, I asked about the masks. 'Of course,' said Abe, 'I'm an expert, darling. I did the source-book on African Tribal Art.' I accepted my second glass and thought, 'All this, and ethnography too?' It was beyond belief; and the phone rang. The dark young man came through from the other office and said Sophia Loren was on the line. I, groggily staring at the Persian temple door, heard this, and vaguely thought, 'How funny, he's trying to impress us.'

Abe sighed, shook his head and grinned before he took the phone. 'She's the most beautiful woman in the world,' he said. 'That dame is so sexy that I get the hots just talking to her on the telephone.' He reached his paw for the red instrument and crooned into it – 'Hello my darling. Here I am.' There was lots of excited talk on the other end of the phone, and Abe nodded and muttered 'Yeah' several times. He beckoned to his henchman to prepare him a cigar and sat smoking it while he grunted to the phone. At last he said, 'O.K. darling, I'll fix it. Don't worry, we'll have them all lined up' and put down the receiver. Ben had watched this with a dazed smile and Nigel winked at me.

'Now,' said Abe, 'Where were we?'

'We were talking about the setting of the play,' said Nigel.

'Yeah, Yeah,' Abe relaxed back onto his chair. 'I love the play, but I think you need to set it up a class. Audiences long for a bit of space and glitter. A diamond or two. A stately home here, a nice painting there. We don't want to give them tat. Life is dull enough. We're here to bring a bit of the circus to our audience.'

I, quite hypnotised, and reeling from Martini and sublime aesthetics, felt like roaring 'Hooray, hooray!' but I realised in time that Abe was merely warming up to something stronger.

'Now,' continued Abe,' I think that instead of being an ordinary architect in a semi, your hero should be a real big time architect. Then we can have lovely sets and frocks and give more to the audience. If we get someone with good tits, we can have some sparkle and excitement.'

'But, but . . .' said Ben, very worried.

'Never mind,' said Abe. 'Let's go eat. I have a restaurant not far away.'

Abe led us through the marvellous masks once more. I paused by the terrifying carving on the way out. 'You like it?' muttered Abe. 'You have good taste. For four hundred pounds, my darling, it's yours. It's Ziba.'

The henchman drove us in a silent Mercedes to Abe's restaurant. (He owned it, as he also owned the African shop.) It was a very theatrical restaurant. Abe told us that the waiters made fortunes by eavesdropping on plans for shows as they were made, and then backed their fancies like horses, thus becoming angel-waiters.

It was dark and discreet. The gold cardboard menus were as big as newspapers and I felt my mind jam like typewriter keys hit simultaneously.

114

'You just order for me,' I whispered to Ben. 'There's too much to choose from.'

'What you mean is you want it all,' said the gorilla hoarsely. I was pleased to see her here.

During the meal Abe made it clear that he thought the play should be moved from its small town setting to somewhere not Scottish, but amorphous and refined like Chichester and that the incomes of all the protagonists should be upped by several thousand pounds per annum, so that they were accentless and rich.

Ben was not happy and argued firmly and coolly his reasons for leaving things as they were – mainly that the play was about real people. They shelved the matter until they had a director, then Abe suddenly said piercingly:

'You write women's parts very well, are you heterosexual?'

I, my mind swimming with excitement and wine, wasn't sure at that moment exactly what heterosexual meant – a glance at Ben told me he was in the same haze.

'I love my wife very much,' said Ben, embarrassed. I wondered if he should have said 'very often'.

They talked again about changing the setting and I became quite angry, 'You're going to fillet the play like a haddock, if you're not careful,' I declared, – flushed, 'and it will be dead, white and gutless.'

Abe looked at me with an expansive smile and touched Ben's shoulder.

'She's beautiful, this girl, but aggressive,' which two-handled compliment silenced me briefly, while Queen Kong sucked her thumb behind a palm tree.

Abe mentioned a director's name. 'I hate him,' Ben said, abruptly downing his coffee.

'Why?' said Abe.

115

'Because all his productions are full of himself strutting and crowing all over the stage saying look at me, how brilliant I am!'

'O.K.' said Abe.

'Well,' said Nigel at last. 'I think we've covered everything.'

'Except,' said Abe, 'The title. We need a new one. We can't call it *A Marriage Disarranged* when we go into Town. You think up some ideas.'

'We'll send you them from Spain,' said Ben, rising.

'*Mañana*,' shrugged Abe, and his henchman wrote down our Spanish address. Nigel walked with us to St James' Park, where we sat briefly in the sun.

'Don't worry,' said Nigel. 'Abe is renowned for his impulsiveness, and tends to gild the lily a bit. Ride along with him, and it will sort itself out. You have a good holiday and think up a new title. And above all don't worry. You are actually having a West End production, and that's wonderful.'

Ben nodded dubiously, but Queen Kong was excited; she appeared suddenly before me, a-flutter with anticipation, wearing a sparkling sequinned dress with a velvet bandeau round her forehead.

'How about this for the première?' she asked, eyes wide, and she waltzed dreamily backwards out through the park and into the street where she became lost in the milling crowds of Piccadilly.

Chapter 20

The Boulevard St Michel was as green, wide and vital as we remembered it from a weekend two years before. We drank iced Parisian beer, and walked by the Seine. We visited the Renoirs again and went to the Musée de L'Homme to see if we could find anything like our beloved mask. We found several, but liked ours best. In the museum foyer, Ben said, 'Let's send Abe a card.' We chose a picture of an Ashanti fertility doll and wrote: 'YES BEN HETEROSEXUAL. WASN'T SURE WHAT WORD MEANT. REGARDS MANDELS'

Puerto de los Pinos was just over the eastern French border. It was a small village, with few tourists and a large sandy bay. South of the village were cliffs and rocky coves, with hillsides of olives and grapevines. The landscape reminded us of Scotland oven-hot.

The courier for the house wasn't there to meet us as promised. Ben had a photo of the house, white, two-storeyed, with a balcony, and we asked a small boy in pidgin Spanish and sign language if he knew where it was. He nodded, and skipped along the dusty track in front of us, while we staggered behind dragging the ever heavier cases, sweaty and swearing. We found it at last, after endless back-streets, steps and cart-tracks.

The house was locked and deserted. We sat disconsolately on our suitcases and realised that everyone must be siesta-ing and we hadn't seen anywhere where we could get water or food. Ben found two polo mints and gave one to me and we sucked them. Then we heard a woman's voice calling:

'Mandel! Mandel!'

We looked up and saw a fat, moustached girl of maybe twenty-five, dressed in a dull grey cotton dress. 'You are Mandel?' she asked, waving a bundle of papers.

'Yes, I'm Ben Mandel,' said Ben, squinting up at her.

'Chi cham chyour chagent,' she said, prefixing every word with a gutteral 'ch' as in Scottish 'loch'. 'Chi cham sorry Chi did not meet you. Chusually the bus is very late. Today it was very chearly.' She spread her hands in endearing Latin helplessness. 'Here, I chave your key.'

She unlocked the door and took us into the welcome shade of the house, and showed us the rooms. There were tiled floors, blue-washed walls, two shady bedrooms and a ladder which led onto a flat tiled roof, hot from the baking sun. From the roof we looked across more orange-tiled roofs, to the olive-clad hills behind the village, and the large bay in front. The girl pointed to a small refrigerator in the corner, which we were glad to see. We ran the water tap in the kitchen and held our hot faces under it, drinking and enjoying the freshness. Chuachina, as the girl seemed to be called, told us she was a teacher in the school, and was studying to be an interpreter. She showed us from a window the road which lead to her house, and told us when she would be home. (Or 'chome', as she put it.) 'Your cook, Rosa, will come to you tomorrow,' she told us. (The house-rental included a maid.)

'I must go now chand meet the chother charrivals.'

She left us to the house, and we rested for a while in the shade, then wandered into the dusy street, smelling wonderful smells of charcoal cooking. A man with a face as wrinkled as dried mud, in patched faded denim shirt and white hat, was cooking small silver fish on charcoal, in the street. The local grocery and vegetable store had big tomatoes, bananas, oranges, pimentos and melons heaped in baskets. We bought some of each, and bread, sardines and wine. The wine was hilariously cheap and the olives fat and rich. The local rope-soled sandals were also cheap and sloppily comfortable. We kitted ourselves out with these and Ben bought a straw hat and looked like a Mexican gunrunner.

Back at the house, we laid the food on the table and poured rich red tumblers of wine, and ate and drank till we were full.

'Chave you thought of chany titles yet?' asked Ben. I spat out my seventeenth olive-stone and shook my head. 'How about *One, Two, Free?*' I asked, pouring another tumbler.

Ben shook his head, not amused, then:

'Twenty Years After.'

'Ha, ha,' said Ben sourly.

'Well, hell, you suggest one.'

Ben drank more wine and put his hat on and frowned, chin sunk on hands, elbows on table.

'Let's think,' he said, 'what it's about. It's about a middle-aged man having an affair with a beatnik. And we discover that it's because his wife has lost her purpose because her children have left home.'

I nodded and ate another olive.

'How about *The End of the Affair?* – That's a good title.'

119

'Graham Greene thought so too.'

'Oh.'

'It is also,' continued Ben 'about marriage.'

'What do you know about that?'

'I've had a lot of ups and downs,' said Ben modestly.

'Eleven-and-a-half months,' I said. 'Chave a cholive.'

I pushed the dish across to him.

For a blissful two weeks we slept in the sun on our roof and swam and wandered throughout the silvery olive-groves. I drew cactuses and photographed tortured rock formations. We ate, drank, and made love, and all the time, day and night there was the warm excitement of knowing that the play was under way in London.

Nigel sent word that a director had been appointed. We had heard of him – David Lee – but had seen nothing that he had done. He was meant to be an up-and- coming man, so all we could do was hope. They hadn't got any Sirs or Ladies for the cast yet.

One night, after another day of sun, wine, food and titles, there was a violent electric storm. It was straight above the village, which trembled beneath the terrifying thundering. We watched sheet-clad from a back window, entranced as the heavens roared and flashed, and the hills and roofs were momentarily lit in silver. Then the rain came and poured until the streets were streams, then rivers, gushing in torrents down steps and into doorways.

It rained for hours and we went to bed and listened to its roar. 'That will fill the wells and reservoirs,' said Ben. And we made love. It was so much easier and better together, now, than it had been a year ago in Ireland – and even then it had been good. We knew each other's rhythms as we tangled, stroked and nuzzled. And we comforted and applauded, admired and gazed in wonder at the beauty and detail of each other's bodies. And the joys of flesh on flesh were always changing, yet remaining the same. 'We've never done exactly this before,' we would say, time after time. Touch was a constant miracle of pleasure – the passing cuddle, or the way one body moved in sleep as the other shifted or turned, or a shoulder twitched in friendly response to a living dozy hand or brushed cheek. These were ever-present delights.

Titles occurred sporadically to us. We were lethargically pedaloing along in the water, a couple of hundred metres from the beach; it was much cooler where we where, and we watched the tiny figures on the sand, prostrate beneath bright umbrellas.

I, who had been dozing , came suddenly to.

'*Affairs in Order!*' I shrieked. 'That's it! It makes sense dammit! Your characters all have affairs because they are bored and have lost their purpose, and it helps them ultimately as people. It's a lovely title!'

Ben pedaloed half-heartedly, and the machine creaked tiredly; he mused, slowly lit a Spanish cigarette, mused again, then nodded.

'O.K. We'll send Abe two titles. He can best decide.'

Queen Kong, I saw, was sitting on the back of the pedalo, dressed in a tight floral bikini and straw hat, trailing her mighty feet in the water. She stretched and yawned.

'I think it's O.K.' she told me. 'And anyway, how important is this title business? After all, *Macbeth* and *Hamlet* didn't do too badly.'

Chapter 21

We had our golden fortnight by ourselves, then Tony and Cordelia arrived. Cordelia bounded in, burnt dark brown, and we immediately compared suntans. Tony looked relaxed and healthy as he usually did, and slapped Ben on his sunburnt back. 'How's it going then Ben? The heat hasn't made John Thomas wilt has it?'

'Not that I'd noticed,' said Ben, uncorking a litre of wine. Cordelia was her old self, delighted to be without her baby. 'I miss her of course, but Mary adores having her,' she said. We ate greedily, spitting out peach-stones and carving big chunks of bread, with tomatoes which must have weighed a pound apiece, and Spanish almond cakes and chocolate.

'Can I have a shower?' Cordelia asked after the meal.

'I'm afraid we've only got two poly-buckets of water,' said Ben, and explained how the water was cut off every night. Cordelia used one-and-a-half of them; 'It's me crevices, after the long drive,' she explained.

We two couples wandered arm-in-arm under the stars to look at the harbour. There were lots of small boats out, fishing by the lamplight. It was a warm night, filled with cricket-chirrups, buzzings, and laughter from the nearby houses. There was music being played on an accordian, and a man's voice wailing Catalan songs. The harbour was unruffled and calm, and the lights of the houses and boats were reflected in perfect mirror-images on the darkness of the water.

We'll never ever want to go home,' crooned Cordelia breathing in the atmosphere ecstatically.

We swam and picnicked and lazed blissfully for the next few days. Tony had a snorkel, flippers and a harpoon gun, and spent most of his time underwater. He harpooned only one small jellyfish and almost hit an octopus, but he enjoyed trying.

I tried half-heartedly to paint, as Ben had begun to write, but it was going badly, and I dragged a brush, loaded with blue paint, across the canvas beside a donkey's head.

'Oh hell,' I moaned, 'It's no bloody good. I'm bored.'

Cordelia, who was writing postcards in the same room, looked up.

'It's too hot to work, Kate. Let's go for a drive.'

'Where's Tony?'

'He's on the roof,' called Ben from the next room. 'With *Fanny Hill*.'

'I'll get him.' I put down my brush, and clattered up the ladder to the roof, and cursed as I hit my head on the crossbeam. Tony was bright red from sun, and lecherous.

'Come and read a chapter with me,' he said, rolling towards me. I dodged him, and he held my ankle. 'Come on, Kate, have a giggle. Here, have you seen this?' He moved his towel slightly.

'Oh that!' I giggled. 'Yes, it's very funny, darling. Come on downstairs. The others are waiting.'

And I retreated. It was all right to joke about sex with Tony when Ben and Cordelia were there. Alone it

123

was alarming. Tony followed after a few minutes, and the three of us got into the car. Ben stayed at home with his play.

We drove inland, and stopped at three tavernas for Martinis and olives. Then on to a dusty farmyard where Cordelia took pictures of the farmer's family and we all shook hands at least twice.

We wanted to go, but Catalan hospitality was too strong to resist. The family eddied about us, cackling and comparing. An old woman in black stockings, dress and shawl touched my blonde hair gently and asked *'Rubia verdadera?'* Cordelia became involved in showing the old woman photos of baby Catherine, and she cooed and admired her, then gesticulated towards me and asked *'Niño? Niño?'*

I smiled and shook by head. *'Mañana, mañana,'* I said, and they all clucked and screeched with laughter. The farmer's wife arrived with some bread and a length of dark sausage, about an inch thick. My heart sank as I watched her cut it, because either the knife was blunt or the sausage was hard, and I guessed it to be the latter. The farmer had disappeared but now he came back, waving two bottles of rosé wine.

'Now we're getting somewhere,' muttered Tony. The several small boys of the family stood behind the door and stared at the crazy adults. The wife succeeded in sawing through the sausage, and she clunked the pieces onto earthenware dishes and handed everybody a hunk of bread and a cotton-reel of sausage.

There was nothing for it, so I picked up my sausage and tried to snap a piece of meat off the end. It wasn't easy; I felt my jaw creak – or was it the sausage? It tasted exactly like mouldy wood. The old lady was chewing hers like a cow on the cud, and she again grinned and nodded to Cordelia who grinned and nodded back.

The Spaniards all seemed to manage the sausage easily and even took second helpings. I chewed and chewed, and ate some bread which was also hard, to push it down, and I saw Tony's chin going up and down, up and down, like a yo-yo. Across the table I saw Cordelia's alarmed eyes as the husband yelled at her to have some more. Cordelia mimed being full up and how lovely, but Señor Farmer shouted Spanish encouragements as to a matador, so she was forced to take a second piece. I was relieved when I realised it was the last of the sausage. His wife, meanwhile, had found enough glasses for everyone, and handed us each some wine.

I trembled with apprehension as I sniffed it. If it was anything like as awful as the sausage had been, I doubted my ability to drink it. The wine was, in fact, fantastic. It had a bouquet like no wine we had ever had. It tasted of summer, fruits and sun. The taste was a poem – and it was incredibly strong. We drank a series of Spanish and Scottish toasts, and then the farmer gave us a second glass. We asked his wife where the wine came from and she pointed to her old father, who winked and pointed to his chest and then his espadrilles. He moved them up and down as though trampling grapes. The wine, we understood, was only three months old and trampled with his own bare feet, at least I hoped he'd removed his espadrilles.

'It's divine,' said Cordelia, quaffing it.

'One of the best,' said Tony, 'I wouldn't mind marketing that.'

At last we were allowed to go home. It was dark and we wrote the Spaniards' names down, and Cordelia and I promised to send postcards from Escocia. They shouted goodbye, and we drove off, leaving the heavily pregnant wife holding a crying child in each arm, with

125

her beaming husband standing empty-handed beside her.

'My God, that was an incredible sausage,' said Tony, veering to avoid a lone white goat.

'An acquired taste,' I grunted.

'Sausage!' cried Cordelia, 'I've got severely bruised tits from that bloody sausage!' and she reached into the cleavage of her dress and withdrew first one, then two pieces of half-gnawed sausage.

'You could use them as souvenir Spanish paper-weights,' suggested Tony.

We reached the village and decided to stop off and have a drink at the hotel bar. The old man's wine and then more Martini on almost empty stomachs affected us quite suddenly. I looked at Cordelia.

'You're very flushed.'

'Speak for yourself, dearie, you look just like the harvest moon.'

This made us giggle till we ached.

'I must go for a pee,' gasped Cordelia.

'Me too,'

We swayed on our feet, and beamed at Tony who was talking to a couple of English tourists at the bar. Inside the hotel we searched for a bathroom. We surprised a man wearing nothing but a vest.

'Wow,' said Cordelia, 'He looked like a hairy taran-tula.'

'With goitre of the groin.'

We found a fuzzy-haired little maid struggling vainly to make a double bed. She pointed along the blue-and-white corridor at the end.

'At last,' we gasped, and wrestled with each other like nine-year-olds to be first on the throne. Cordelia won, and I reclined across the nearby bath, exhausted.

'Hey!' said Cordelia, as she made way for me. 'This

is fabulous! Let's have a bath! I'm sick to death of those spider-filled buckets of cold water every night.'

The bath filled slowly, so I again slung myself across the bath, bottom downwards. Cordelia blew bubbles in the basin and came up snorting like a whale, redder than ever.

'That's much better,' she puffed. 'I really cooled myself down. Hand me the towel, would you, I can't see a thing.'

I looked blearily around the bathroom. 'There isn't one,' I said at last.

'What!' Cordelia shrieked and opened her eyes, and started to laugh again, then I yelped and jumped up from the half-filled bath with a large wet area on my backside. 'Hell. I'm soaked. I didn't realise it was getting so full.'

'Well you are quite low-slung, darling.'

I glared at her. 'What are we going to do?' I asked, 'I've got a dripping wet bum, and you look like a Piper's Lament.'

I pulled the plug out of the bath and it gurgled like an old man being tickled. 'We'll just have to stay here until we dry out a little.' We wiped ourselves as best we could on a cardigan, then, exhausted, I lay on the floor, wet side up, and Cordelia had hysterics on the basin.

I suddenly took off my wedding-ring and squinted at the inscription on the inside.

'Hey, what's the date?' I asked.

'The nineteenth,' said Cordelia.

'Tomorrow's our wedding anniversary!'

We reminisced about our weddings. 'You know,' said Cordelia, sounding quite sober now, 'I really didn't love Tony much at all when we got married. It seemed like an escape from earning a living, and Dad's boozing.'

127

I nodded. 'We knew that. We did try to warn you.'

'I know, but nothing would have stopped me. But the funny thing is, Kate, I really do love him now. He's an idiot, and unreliable, but I love him.'

I was silent, remembering Tony on the roof.

'How about the baby?' I asked.

Cordelia sighed, and stared into space for a while, then she said:

'Well, I've got her haven't I? All I can say is I'll make jolly sure *she* doesn't get married at eighteen-and-a-half.' Then she looked at me.

'When will you be preggers?'

'As soon as possible. As long as I'm on my feet enough to get my Diploma next summer, that will be O.K.'

Cordelia counted her fingers, then rolled her eyes. 'Hey, fellow,' she carolled, 'That makes it any day now!'

'Well almost.' I drew on the floor with a splash of water. 'I'm worried about it really. I'm dying for kids. But how will I manage to paint?'

'Oh,' Cordelia dismissed my doubts with a regal gesture. 'You know you will. Nothing will stop you. Your kids will piddle on the floor and eat oil paint, but you'll manage.'

I was aware that the gorilla had appeared, and was listening intently. 'She's kidding,' she said.

'You're pissed Cordelia,' I said uneasily. There was a loud knocking on the door and a lot of voluble Spanish. 'Come on,' I stood unsteadily up, and wound my damp cardigan round my middle.

There was some talc on a shelf. 'Let's put some on so we don't look so flushed,' said Cordelia. This seemed clever, so we dusted our faces, rather too liberally.

'You look like the Scarlet Pimpernel, with his pow-

128

dered periwig,' said Cordelia peering at me and swaying.

'You look like a piece of unbaked pastry.'

We brushed off the surplus, and went to find Tony. He had his shirt rolled up and was demonstrating to an English couple, 'I saw this chap in Alexandria once, and he had terrible scars all down his arm, where the octopus suckers had been pulled off him.'

Cordelia pirouetted towards him and kissed his ear. 'I thought those were shark bites, darling,' she whispered. Tony gave us another glass of Martini each, and Cordelia sat down looking totally sober, and started talking to the wife of the English couple about tinned Spanish baby milk, as she sipped her drink.

I remained standing. My dress was still damp, and the patio was whirling about me.

'I'm going to fetch Ben,' I said.

'Drive her, Tony, and bring Ben back,' said Cordelia, 'I'll hang on here.'

Tony drove us to the house and we went upstairs.

'Darling!' I called, but he wasn't there. There was a note on the table: 'Have gone for a walk. Time 5.30, back at 7.00. Ben.'

'We've just missed him, I'll go and hunt for him,' I said, disappointed.

Tony came through from the kitchen with a half-bottle of wine. 'Come on, Kate,' he urged, 'We'd better drink this, or it will go sour and be full of dead flies.' I smiled vaguely. He handed me the bottle, and I took a half-hearted swig and gave it back to him, and went into my bedroom to change.

'I'll just be a minute and put on something dry,' I said.

I dizzily undid my zip and plonked down on the bed to pull my dress over my head. The bed felt like a ship and heaved from side to side.

Next thing I knew was an arm round me and a warm hand on my thighs. I yelped, and couldn't get out of my dress.

My bra was undone for me as the dress came off, and my breasts plopped into warm hands.

'You've got lovely tits,' said Tony's voice, 'I've been dying to do this.'

I shrieked 'Tony! For God's sake! What are you doing? Stop it!'

He gave me a thrusting kiss, fondled my breasts and struggled to undo his straining trouser zip.

'I thought we'd never get a chance,' he muttered.

The room was whirling dizzily.

'No' I thought distantly, 'This is wrong. I want Ben.'

Tony was kissing me again, and pushing at me. I was in the sea, swaying, swimming, sinking. His breathing was heavy.

'I'm just a big sexy Swede,' I thought faintly.

'Ben,' I said, and the waves wafted me on their surge, and his breathing was the rhythm of the water.

'Don't call me Ben, love,' said Tony, and hungrily pushed his mouth onto mine. He tasted of wine. It was strange kissing a different mouth. Interesting.

I floated and wafted, backwards and forwards. What? I realised dimly that I was physically quite helpless. I looked down on my body in the green water from far above. Then I saw that Queen Kong was on the ladder leading to the roof, glaring down at Tony and me. She was very angry. Her fur was all on end.

'No!' she shouted. 'You mustn't let him! He must not fuck you!'

'Come on Kate,' muttered Tony. 'Just a quickie.'

A handful of alien genitals swam into my inert and drunken hand. His cock, I noted detachedly, was smaller than Ben's. I thrust the handful aside, and heard my voice murmur, 'Ben, Ben, Ben.'

'Don't call me Ben,' said Tony, aggressive now. His face hot, eyes intense.

I shoved at his chest and crossed my legs.

'Ow!' he yelped.

'I don't want to Tony! Get off! Ben will kill you!'

'Only a bit of fun Kate!' he grabbed at my thigh.

'No,' I moaned.

And suddenly the gorilla came to the rescue. She leapt from the top of the steps in one bound, and together she and I made a massive effort to thrust him off the bed. He fell with a resounding thud.

'Go away!' I yelled. 'I want Ben!'

Tony groaned from the floor. There was a silence, then I heard him say 'Shit' and he crawled from the room, clutching his trousers at the waist.

I lay on the bed with the room still revolving, and heard him go to the bathroom and be sick.

At last his retchings stopped. I heard the door unlock, and dimly heard him shuffle past the door and mumble, 'I'm sorry, Kate.'

And the outer door closed, the bed was still moving like a ship, the room still sped round. Queen Kong pulled the coolly comforting sheet over my aching head.

'Ben will come soon,' she promised. And I slept.

Chapter 22

The next morning we all found the sun a trifle bright, and we girls drank coffee on the hot tiled roof, with newspapers like cloches over our heads. Ben was trying to write inside the house. Earlier, as I made coffee in the kitchen, Tony had whispered to me, 'I'm sorry. I was pissed. Thank God you stopped me.' I felt foolish but said nothing to Ben. Then Tony went out to stride the hills like a bandit, looking for a rabbit to kill. Surprisingly, the heavily-armed customs officials at the Spanish-French border had allowed him to bring his shotgun into Spain, or so Tony said, though Ben only half-believed him. About mid-morning there was a great kerfuffle of shouts and door-bangings in the street outside the house. We peered over the roof-parapet, clutching towels to our sunburnt bosoms and saw an agitated man waving an envelope at us. *'Telegramia! Telegramia!'* he shouted.

We scrambled down the ladder, heads wincing at every step. 'My baby! Maybe something's happened to her!' agonised Cordelia.

We found Ben in the street surrounded by a grinning circle of expectant Spaniards. 'It's O.K.' said Ben, 'It's from Abe.'

We went into the house and he showed us the telegram which read: 'TITLES USELESS- STOP – SUGGEST TO HAVE AND TO HOLD – STOP – CONFIRM SOONEST –
BRAMSTEIN'

Ben swore quietly. 'I will not allow my play to have that title. Come on you two, make some more coffee. We need a new title immediately.'

We drank coffee and had blank minds. Queen Kong snorted and cursed in silent resentment. 'Bloody play. Bloody titles. This is supposed to be a holiday. Can't he ever forget about work?'

Cordelia kept saying, 'But I liked the title you had in Scotland *A Marriage Disarranged* is a super title,' till Queen Kong's hot little eyes threatened injury to her.

Ben looked at the telegram again. 'My God!' he said, 'This was sent on Monday, and today is Thursday! It's taken seventy-two hours to reach us! They'll be printing the posters in a minute.'

I could think of nothing except titles I had already suggested – and I had been rather proud of some of them. Maybe one day I could write an anthology of unused titles, I mused, my mind miles away from the terracotta-and-blue kitchen. An hour ticked by. Ben at last spoke.

'*Personal Story*,' he said, 'How about that?' We savoured it, and said it in Serbo-Croat, Edinburgh, Glasgow, Spanish and Irish accents.

'I like it, I like it,' I declared, determined that I did. Anything to stop this boring game.

'Me too,' said Cordelia. 'It's simple and I'd want to go and see a play called *Personal Story*.'

'Right,' said Ben. 'Let's send a telegram.'

Ben composed the telegram as follows: 'TITLE NO GOOD – STOP – INSIST ON QUOTE PERSONAL STORY UNQUOTE – REGARDS MANDEL'

133

The woman in the characterful and colourfully domestic shed which was also the telegraph office, read it, checked the address with Ben, then looked up a heavy directory which lay beneath a dish of bananas and aubergines. She ran her finger quickly down the page and told Ben how many pesetas he owed her.

'What is Spanish for quick?' he hissed to Tony as he paid the woman.

'*Pronto,*' replied the lady crisply, sitting down to her headphones. Then, wired up, she shooed away a hen and proceeded to tap her keys and send the message. A cat jumped onto her knee; she winked at us and said '*Adios,*' and was lost to her bleeps and knob-pulling.

Ben produced a bottle of champagne for our anniversary, and popped the cork over the balcony, surprising a sleepy donkey in the road. And we had a seafood feast cooked by Cordelia, with lettuce and orange salad. Then she appeared with a great dish of flambéed bananas, rolled in brown sugar and brandy, which burned now with its ghostly blue flame. It was marvellous, and Ben and I felt very sentimental. We looked over the balcony, and the sleepy donkey had a three-foot erection. We were impressed.

Later, when we tumbled into our respective beds, we were rather noisy, and I shouted through the wall, and Tony shouted back and reported good progress.

'Hey, what are you doing?' asked Ben.

'Just being friendly, darling,' I replied, and kissed his navel.

Chapter 23

Our month was up, and it was time to go home. We were reluctant to leave, but excited that the London production was now properly under way.

In London, we checked into an inexpensive but gloomy hotel in Bloomsbury, that Nigel had booked for us, overlooking a square of threadbare grass, where bulging pigeons waddled and picked up pieces of bread and orange-peel. It was about half-a-mile from the hall where David Lee was to hold the first read-through of the play, so the next morning, after an enormous hotel breakfast – neither of us felt able to refuse anything on the menu, as we were paying for it anyway – we wandered through the crowds, advertisements and traffic of Shaftesbury Avenue, until we came to the hall, which was in a small side-street.

David Lee, the director, was a close-cropped, black-haired, little man of maybe thirty-five. He bounced dynamically over to us, with twinkling feet and bright eyes, exuding charm, and introduced us to the actors, who were sitting around on stackable chairs, looking at their scripts.

'This sunburnt couple,' he said in a ringmaster's voice, 'is the author and his wife: Ben Mandel and Mrs Mandel; straight back from wildest Spain they are.'

We shook hands and he introduced us to the actors. Ben asked David if he would mind if I watched some rehearsals, but he threw out his arms in welcome and cried, 'No, my dear, it's wonderful to have you with us. You sit over there and watch to your heart's content.' Then, fondling his incipient bald patch with one hand, and his incipient middle-age-spread with the other, he said to the actors, 'Now, my loves, I want no performances. Let's just have the text unadorned.' Then he plopped into a chair facing the actors and snapped open his script, saying crisply, 'Right then, boys and girls. Let's go. Curtain up. Act One, Scene One.'

The next hour was magic. The actors read their parts in neutral voices, making sense of the text, but in no way dramatising or emphasising what was there. I was moved. It was a smashing play, of that I had no doubt. I laughed and Ben cackled at several of the jokes, and one or two people were in tears towards the end, when the wife walked out on her bewildered husband of twenty years' standing.

I watched the actors with great interest. Theo Stanley, whose sublime Sir Andrew Aguecheek I remembered now, was about forty-five. He was a tall man, sandy-blond, going grey at the edges, and he had a long Irish face, with deep creases down his cheeks and ridiculously blue eyes. There was a suffering hilarity about his mouth, and he wore a carelessly-knotted blue scarf at the open neck of his beautiful brown silk shirt. I knew I would like him. Clarice Bowen, who was to play a divorced psychiatrist, had been a witch in a gloomy film I had once seen. She had pale blue, heavily-hooded eyes, and was maybe forty-five. She had almost no eyebrows, a high forehead, and her strange long face was like a marble mask. She looked cold, and I was surprised to hear later from Ben that she had ever been considered a great beauty. She didn't seem to have much chin and her mouth was nastily mocking. When she smiled, her eyes were reptilian and unblinking, and only her lips moved.

Hazel Norton, who played the wife, looked sensible and approachable. She was perhaps forty, with short hair, and an expressive face with enormous eyes, surrounded by lots of make-up and false lashes. She was obviously theatrical, as though her very clown face had led her to the theatre.

After the actors had read Act One, David Lee ordered coffee and everyone relaxed and put out tentative social feelers. Ben and David had a long talk and I listened. The clown-faced Hazel Norton was already using a Scots accent in her reading, and for both Ben and myself, this gave authenticity to the play.

'Well, let's do it Scots. I'm willing,' said David. 'Abe isn't keen at all, but let's do it the author's way until we've felt ourselves into it more thoroughly. O.K. darling?' He clasped Hazel's shoulders, and she nodded. 'I think it must be Scots,' she said, only makes sense if it is.'

'How about you, darling?' David put his ubiquitous arm round Clarice Bowen's (quite thick) waist.

'I am in your hands, dear David,' she drawled, and withdrew to speak to young Larry Marker, a twenty-year-old East End boy, straight out of drama college, who was making faces at his own outstretched legs and baseball boots.

'See him,' grunted the gorilla.

He was, I realised with a shock, outstandingly good-looking. He had haunting, dark almost purple eyes, wide cheekbones, a sculpted sensitive mouth, and beautiful strong hands and wrists. Abe had picked him from hundreds of likely boys at an audition. 'That boy,' he was to say several times, 'has got star quality. He will make the big time.'

There was a commotion at the double doors of the hall and Abe entered, with at least three henchmen clutching clipboards and cigars.

Abe still wore the same spotless but tattered blue shirt, and kissed or shook hands with everybody. 'How are you, my darling, I like your suntan,' he said, gazing appreciatively at my bosom. I was glad to see him again.

He gave a welcoming pep-talk, and told everybody they were wonderful, and it was a fantastic play. Simultaneously with Ben's play, he said, he was going to present another play, this one being by the Irish child-prodigy, Mary O'Donovan. This was interesting, because this girl had made a big splash during the last couple of years with a play she had dashed off after seeing a boring touring production of one of London's longest-running dramas. That play was now being filmed and had been performed all over Britain and Europe.

'I've just been to the first read-through of the O'Donovan play, and it looks great,' said Abe. 'Now, you're all costing me a lot of money, my darlings, so let's make it fly.'

He told us that the tour theatres had been booked. The play would go to Scotland, Manchester and Oxford before it came to Town. Negotiations were still going on for a London venue. In Manchester, he added, the O'Donovan play would be on at the same time. He'd taken both big theatres. 'So it's Bramstein week in Manchester, and we won't let them forget it,' he said with a sardonic grin.

'He likes this game,' I thought.

The read-through continued, and was just as striking as the first act had been. My pre-marital belief in Ben's talent was strongly re-affirmed.

We sat at a table in a sort of stall, with David, Theo and Clarice Bowen. By the end of the meal I disliked Clarice Bowen as much as I adored the other two. The actress seemed to remain purposely aloof from everything about her. She read the menu like a cat disdaining fish-scraps, and asked for two extra-menu poached eggs on toast and a glass of water. (I was too young and heedlessly plump myself to realise she was battling with her bulge.) Everyone else ordered baked potatoes, butter, pork chops or roast beef and glasses of beer. David Lee and Theo outvied each other with funny stories and reminiscences and made everyone but Clarice guffaw. She simply watched with her mocking mirthless smile, as she slowly lapped her meal. Queen Kong longed to push the poached eggs into her frozen face. If she yowled as the yolks dripped from those pale blue eyes, it would at least be a reaction.

David claimed to have been expelled from a well-known choir school for being discovered in a laundry-basket with a redhead.

'He was such a lovely boy,' he said sadly. 'All freckles and orange curls, he nearly broke my heart. We used to sing hymns together in a beech tree when I was supposed to be playing cricket. I always managed to be bowled out in one.'

After being thrown out David had tried to learn his father's business, which appeared to be property-stealing. But he'd tried to sell a man his own house, and was consequently given the sack. Then he joined the Navy, where he was asked to entertain the boys on a troopship to Cairo. 'And here I am,' he said. 'I've been trying to entertain them ever since.'

As he told his stories, David became, in turn, the freckled schoolboy, his nearly senile housemaster who couldn't pronounce his 'L's, or his Naval Commander,

139

who was so bemused by the Navy that even his ordinary conversation sounded like hiccuped commands to his sailors.

In the afternoon, back at rehearsals, David removed his jacket and rolled up his purple shirtsleeves. One of Abe's henchmen had brought a model of the set which made Ben freeze, and my heart sink, because it was far too flamboyant and over-scaled. But it was already being built. A *fait accompli*. It was £6,000 worth, said the henchman. There was no glimmer of a hope of changing it. David proceeded with chalk and measuring tape, to plot the spaces, steps and furniture. Then they set out to do a blocking-out rehearsal, and David instructed the actors where the enter, stand, sit or cross the stage. He was brisk and efficient. The camp clown from the lunch-table had gone completely and a ruthless, hard-driving craftsman appeared. He took great trouble to listen to suggestions, and dealt with them efficiently as they arose. Theo or Hazel or Larry would question, and David would deftly re-plot a move. Ben watched, approvingly, loving everything that happened, and forgot about the set. He was an involved professional. A Man of the Theatre.

After rehearsals, we wandered through the London streets. It was getting dark and the dusk was a rich all-pervading blue. Thousands of starlings buzzed, chattered and swooped from a theatre at the end of Shaftesbury Avenue. The city thrummed with incident and colour; it was strange after the peace of our Spanish village. We stood on a corner of Piccadilly Circus and watched lights flash and the relentless crowds go past as tickertape letters two feet high spelled out their adverts and film villains stared down at us with gleaming flood-lit eyes. Great red buses roared past, and taxi meters flashed and ticked. We watched an old woman, wrinkled as a walnut and older than the Prime Minister (the one who never had it so good), singing with a sweet, plaintive, girl's voice to the cinema queues. She wore flapping blue-and-white gymshoes, and her old man collected money for her in his cap, after he had stood by, quiet and bald, until her song was over. When her repertoire was finished, she yelled raucously to him and they shuffled off to the nearest pub.

'What do you think of David Lee?' I asked as we ate a hot-dog on the street.

'I'm impressed,' said Ben. 'He's a real tough professional. He's obviously queer, but I think he understands the pressures of marriage in the play.'

'The pressures of marriage?' I muttered, looking at my frankfurter. 'Long may one's marriage pressure, as they say in Auchiltibuie.'

We spent a couple of nights in the navy-blue gloom of our hotel room. At the daily rehearsals we watched layers being peeled off the actors, and I was shocked at the raw nakedness and vulnerability being exposed.

'Darling,' said Abe quietly, 'I think you should stay away for a while.'

Ben gave me a tenner from his advance. I did the museums and art-galleries, and shopped for a dress for the London First Night.

Clarice Bowen was half-heartedly trying to do a Scots accent, Ben told me, but she sounded awful. I met Ben, Theo and David for lunch again and Theo practised his Scots on them until he became almost perfect. 'Tomorrow and tomorrow and tomorrow,' he intoned like Auntie Emma 'creeps on this petty pace from day to day.'

David warned Ben that there might be trouble from Clarice. The rehearsals had reached the minutiae stage, so Ben decided to go home and leave them to it. There wasn't a lot he could do.

At home we unpacked our pottery and wine and went upstairs to give my mother her presents from Spain.

'Where's Pussy?' I asked.

Ma looked up 'He's probably in the garden. He's not very well.'

I went to the window. The old cat sat in a puddle of water staring madly at unseen things.

We went to Mrs Mandel's for supper. Ben answered his mother's questions with uncommunicative brevity whilst I burbled on with my embroidered tales of foreign travel and the theatrical world. And Mrs Mandel said, 'Don't you worry, you'll see. It'll be all right.' When we got home Ben saddened me by saying his mother and he had been on a different wavelength since he could think for himself.

Next day the cat was worse. 'We'll have to take him to the vet.' said Ben.

Hopefully, I found a square shopping-basket, and tied on a cardboard lid, and laid the old cat in it, on top of an old jersey. He didn't like the basket, and yowled weakly as I thrust him down. I carried him to the bus, aware of his weight like a baby in my arms. He'd been a warmth and comfort since childhood, when I'd shared my blocks of Highland toffee with him, alternate licks, for blissful hours, ensconced on cushions with the hiss of the gas fire and the cat's purr.

He fell over on the vet's table and lay limply.

'Aye,' said the vet,' he's an old man now. We'll need to help him away. Will you want his remains?'

I shook my head, and tenderly stroked the cat's great striped body for the last time and left him on the cold table, surrounded by bottles and medical smells.

I travelled back on the bus, clutching the basket on my knee, light now.

142

'Aw, what have ye got in there? A wee pussy?' The conductress peered at the basket.

I held it to me. 'It's empty,' I said, and wished that I didn't want to cry.

Ben was understanding and hugged me. 'I know, darling, you'd had him since you were five. For most of your life. Of course you're sad.' He kissed me. 'Tell you what, though.'

I sniffed. 'What"

'As soon as we can I'll give you a replacement.'

I'd always wanted a Burmese cat. Maybe . . .

He stroked my cheek with his nose.

'A lóvely soft replacement. Soft and cuddly.'

I looked hopefully at him through my tears.

'Soft and cuddly;' he smiled. 'And hairless. And pink.'

He gazed dreamily at me, and Queen Kong frowned and bit her lip.

Ben and Marcus made a tape of Scottish talk and sent it down to David for Clarice and Theo to practise with. David acknowledged it with a short note of thanks in broad Scots.

I tried to settle down to some serious painting. I was quite pleased with my few Spanish water-colours, and cut mounts for them; I even put one of them up in the bathroom. I did some drawings of the old woman in gymshoes singing to the cinema queue. They weren't bad, and I eagerly planned to do a lithograph of one of them, when college started again in a couple of weeks. I tried to paint the hurdy-gurdy, but abandoned it again, confused by that awful gap between intention and reality. I was frustrated and depressed by my inability to transfer what I saw in my mind onto canvas.

Ben had to buy some text-books for school and did several days of swotting, to prepare for the new exam

143

syllabus. It was hard to settle, we kept meeting in the kitchen, jumping guiltily as one discovered the other making an unnecessary, but comforting, cup of coffee. The phone rang a lot with newspapermen enquiring about rehearsals, and Cordelia, Marcus or Zoe kept looking in or telephoning just as I was trying to get the right colour for the old woman's gymshoes, or when Ben was working out a complicated equation.

Abe sent a telegram saying: 'CLARICE BOWEN THREATENS WALK-OUT IF SHOW IS SCOTS'

Ben had anguished phone calls with Nigel, Abe and David Lee in turn. I wished Clarice Bowen would walk out, but David felt that rehearsals had gone too far for a change of cast. Abe declared sardonically that she was a queen bitch, but they needed her for star-billing. Ben argued and agonised. Hazel Norton and Theo and the rest of the cast had developed almost perfect accents. Rehearsals were held up for a day whilst this was discussed then there was another urgent telegram for Abe: 'PERSONAL STORY TITLE NO USE – SEND NEW ONE SOONEST'

'My God,' Ben pulled his fingers wildly through his hair. 'Think of a title, quick.'

I dropped my brushes and sat frowning amid my topless oozing paint tubes.

Then the phone rang again. It was David, with a long, complicated problem. He was frankly worried, he said, because he didn't think smashing the violin on the head was going to work. I was crouched next to Ben, eavesdropping on the phone call, and felt that this was utter disaster. A fancy, too ornate set, an amorphous English setting, and, to crown it, no violin being shattered. They wanted to castrate the play. The violin smashing was utterly integral, tragi-comic and organic. I made agonised faces at Ben, and mouthed 'No! No!'

144

at him and shook my head. He looked very sad, and kept saying heavily, 'Yes, yes.'

The doorbell rang and I thought my mind would blow a fuse. It was the laundryman and he had brought back two wrong pillowcases and one wrong sheet. Queen Kong dictated a rude letter to the manager, and I dashed it off on a page of the laundry book, handed it to the bewildered laundryman and zoomed back to save the play.

The phone tinkled as Ben rang off and I found him sitting desolate on the bed. 'I'm travelling down tonight,' he said, 'I've got to be there for a few days. You stay here and come to Manchester for the weekend before the première.'

I nodded and kept saying, 'But the violin smashing is bloody marvellous. We know it works – it worked fabulously for three weeks in Glasgow!'

Ben listlessly shook his head, chewed his beard and rocked as though he was wearing a praying-shawl.

'Yes, it did, but I've an awful feeling that this is going to be a different play. Have you thought of a title? They need it by tonight, to give to the printers, for the programmes.'

I hadn't.

'We all liked *Personal Story,* why not simply *Personal?*'

'I can't tell one title from another any more. I'm numb.'

Ben was limp. 'I'll phone Abe, then I'll book my sleeper.'

I hated being alone at home while Ben was in London, but I did a little work and longed for his nightly phone calls. He had been depressed when he left, and was even more so the first time he phoned.

'What's happening?'

145

'Well,' Ben's voice sounded remote and unfamiliar. 'It's not Scots any more, and its called *Personal*. At least that's one point of agreement.'

'What about Queen Bitch, Clarice?'

'Well, she just couldn't handle the accent. So she played up and made a fool of the part and was poised to leave. But Abe bought her two feather-and-sequin gowns for Act Two . . .'

'Feather-and-sequins!' I screeched in horror. 'But that's utterly wrong visually and out of context and character! They're mad!'

'Yes, they are a bit,' said Ben faintly.

'But darling, you must fight all this.'

'I'm afraid I can't, love. Time is short and I'm too busy doing re-writes.'

'Re-writes!' I almost pulled the phone out by its roots. 'What sort of re-writes?'

'Well, they want me to write in bits and pieces to explain all the gloriousness of the set. For instance, there's a great gold-framed portrait of a general in full regalia.'

'Whaat?' – an anguished howl from the writer's wife.

'And they wanted me to write in about Theo's plushy job and all that.'

'But surely you're not going to?'

'Some of it I am. Some of their suggestions are quite good really.'

'What about the violin?'

'Well . . . ' Ben seemed to tail off at the other end of the line.

'Well, what?'

'Well, Theo now bangs it down among the crockery, and actually that is very exciting.'

That didn't sound too bad. 'Yeah,' I said. 'Maybe that's O.K., but it's not as Mandelian as on her nut.'

The pips went for the fourth time so Ben rang off.

146

The next day he sounded happier and by the end of the week he was positively ebullient. 'It's really coming now,' he enthused. 'It's looking great. Theo and Hazel are terrific. I cried like a baby today and the American girl is utterly fantastic. She's made more out of the part than I thought was possible. I'm dying for you to see it. Have you found out your train time?'

'Yes,' I said, 'I'll be in Manchester at two o'clock tomorrow. 'How about you?'

'We arrive about one. I'll meet you at the station. I miss you terribly.'

Chapter 24

Manchester was wet and grey when Ben met me off the train and we could hardly stop hugging each other. He took me to the hotel through desolate rain-swept streets and I kept seeing down-and-outs and cripples. Abe's henchman had booked us into a vast hotel, all carpets, plush and whispers. Our room was gracious after Spain and our own simple house, and we padded on the thick carpet into the bathroom and gazed at everything. I at once climbed into the bath, shedding my clothes in a heap on the floor; Ben almost immediately made me climb out.

Dreamily, five minutes later, he mumbled, 'We must have a fitted carpet one day.'

I saw a rehearsal at the large Victorian theatre in the middle of Manchester and was deeply impressed. I had reservations about the set, but it looked solid and opulent and worked well as a space for the actors. I thought Theo and Hazel and Sue were outstandingly good, but hated Clarice Bowen's constipated manner. Larry Marker was disappointing and I said so to Abe, who was in the darkened auditorium just in front of me.

'Yeah,' said Abe, 'You wait. He'll be a star. He'll come up like magic on the First Night. The boy needs

148

an audience and Bowen is the same. She's not going to waste her energies in rehearsals, she'll keep it all for when its really happening. She looks great doesn't she?'

I mumbled something neutral and hoped that he was right.

I had always loved watching a play take shape. When you read a play for the first time you imagine it so vividly and see what each character looks like and imagine their voice. With Ben's characters I had still the original archetypes in my head, but the magic now was that each actor took that archetype and changed it. Each time a new actor plays a part, it becomes different, sometimes better, sometimes worse. This is, to me, the main fascination of the theatre.

Abe intended to stun Manchester with publicity for his two productions and for this purpose he had rented a large suite in the hotel for a double press conference. He had spent about £20,000 by now, and didn't intend to stint at this point, when he was entertaining the gentlemen of the press.

We took a long time beard-trimming, hair-spraying, washing and perfuming. I straightened Ben's lapel and picked something off it.

'There's a pubic hair on your shirt.'

There was one large mirror in the bedroom, and we thumped each other out of the way with our bottoms as we fought to practise devastating smiles for the photographers. There was always hope for me, that I would gleam from the background of one of the pictures or that the photographers would want the playwright standing beside his lovely wife.

We each felt attractive and witty and poised to give columns of publicity to the panting newshounds.

We walked nervously to the door of the press conference suite. Then we entered the smoke-filled room exuding debonair confidence, imagining the next day's headlines.

'Talented Scot takes city by storm.'

'Wife always knew he'd do it.'

'Mandel is huge success.'

I could see it all, interspersed with our photos, captioned with our wryly shy, masterfully funny comments.

There was quite a crowd of journalists, and there were all grouped round someone at the far end of the vast stretch of carpet. There were lots of flashes and clicks from cameras and eventually we discerned through the fumes a tall, dark-haired young woman in a white mackintosh, who was smoking and talking with great animation. We had forgotten that the press conference was being shared with Abe's other gamble-child – the famous young playwright Mary O'Donovan who, though Irish, had in fact been to primary school in Manchester, so was a local girl. Her play was due to open the night after Ben's première, two hundred yards up the road from his theatre.

We stood by discomfited on the carpet and watched. At last someone came towards us. He looked charmingly at me and asked:

'Can I connect your face with any of the photographs?'

'No, I'm afraid I'm just a camp follower. I belong to my husband here. He's the auth . . .'

The man's face almost fell, but he caught it, and left me hurriedly, with only a pickled onion to remember him by.

Ben and I offered each other drinks and cigarettes, and had an enthusiastic discussion about the view from the window – which was all trolley cables and cobbles. Very expressive, sort of kitchen-sink cityscape.

After what felt like hours, I suppose that the sand-wiches down the other end must have collected too many cigarette stubs, because a few people began to percolate towards us. I saw Abe surreptitiously lay a trail of bottles leading towards us, and he encircled us with gin and whisky – which was handy really. Also, one or two journalists arrived late, and by that time the smoke was so thick that you couldn't see as far as Ben's rival, so the journalists settled for Ben and myself.

The first one was a charming girl, who did woman's pages. She decided to miss out on Ben and get his wife's-eye view.

I started to be entertaining, but the girl was in a state of ecstacy over my new fur-trimmed suit and Cossack hat (bought in London, between Art galleries). I was quite pleased about this. 'Mrs Mandel wore a darkly subtle suit of stunningly sophisticated simplicity . . .' but it transpired that the Woman's Page girl was about to get married, and wanted to find a suit exactly the same. Here her personal interest stopped short. Her professional interest wasn't within hailing-distance.

Meanwhile, things were looking up for Ben. The photographers were onto him. Wanted him to pose with Mary O'Donovan.

'I'm telling them that you and Mary have a great thing going between you,' Abe hissed to Ben with a hoarse chuckle. He slapped away Ben's startled expression with a rib-rattling thump, and turned to me, stroked my cheek with his finger and gave me an intimate wink. He was really rather a lovely man.

Ben was now given a match and told to light Mary O'Donovan's half-smoked cigarette. It looked as though it would be a really good picture, with the two intense faces dramatically lit by the flame. We turned from this, flushed with success, to meet the next assailant. He was young, and belonged to the most important paper, and had specs and affectionate pink eyes like an albino rabbit. We both thought to win him by asking him just a little about himself first, before we told him all about our fascinating artistic life. Unfortunately he was an unhappy fellow, and only too eager to talk. He lived with his mother and was frustrated, felt that he had missed his vocation in some pedagogical paradise. His face matched his eyes and shone as he talked. Ben managed to escape politely to light another cigarette for the prodigy in the mackintosh.

I felt sure I was lulling the young man into a sweet mood for a discerningly enthusiastic review of the play that night. He looked much happier when he at last left me. After another reporter had told us his tedious drinking memories of Scotland we each considered that we had given good curative therapy sessions to all these unhappy journalists. We retired confidently to await the papers. The photographers had even photographed us together in the end.

Evening came. Abe had said that some of the evening paper people had rushed off early to file their copy. We tried to display our nonchalance to each other as we walked the streets to pass the time. At last our restraint broke and we inundated a surprised little man with copper coins and brought a sheaf of evening papers – a pair and a spare, and one for luck, and one for home, another for each of the mums, because the photos were sure to be good, what with our beautiful suits and quizzical smiles. The papers had a lot of pages, so we went to a café and ordered tea. Each of us searched every inch of every page of every paper.

There was nothing except for a paragraph and a couple of photos of Mary O'Donovan. Then Ben discovered a tiny hazy picture which I had by-passed twice. It showed a bearded octogenarian and his old-age pensioner wife, who had a Cossack hat exactly like mine. They were called Mr and Mrs Bin Handle, and that was all it said about them.

Neither Ben nor I spoke when we had scrutinised our respective heaps of paper twice. We were drinking tea, and I poured some into Ben's pocket, trying to show that I was not upset.

'Of course, we could hardly expect it to be in the evening papers,' said Ben, stubbing out an unlit cigarette.

'No, it's too early.'

'They've got those pictures of *her* though.'

'I bet they're old ones, she's a local girl.'

'But I'm sure they were taken in that room in the hotel.'

We sipped our tea, then in a tight-nostrilled silence we went to send Mrs Mandel flowers for Rosh-Hasonah.

The Manchester First Night of the try-out was not too harrowing. I became a little short-winded, running from auditorium to bar, where Ben was huddled feebly, waiting to hear from me if the few people in the audience were laughing or not. The theatre was enormous, and yawned above us like the Dome of Discovery. I sat perched on the edge of my seat for most of the show, desperately trying to listen to the comments of two frosty old ladies sitting in front of me or adding valiantly to the occasional weak ripple of isolated handclaps. The hard-working pink-eyed young man from the paper we most cared about, was sitting across the aisle, and I flashed my loveliest 'Hello Friend' smile at him, but he responded with a cold uncompromised state. I remembered all that I had done to inflate his crumpled little ego, and Queen Kong gnashed her teeth

153

and roared with rage, and pushed his beastly pink body into a jungle river with a hairy foot, and watched, swinging from a jungle creeper, as he drowned, eaten by piranhas.

At the expected point in the play, when Hazel was reminiscing to Theo how once they had been discovered making love in a bath, an entire family, who, as far as I could tell in the murk, were dressed in matching flannel suits, marched out in a body. 'It must have been a carefully-planned family,' pointed out Queen Kong throatily. I looked and saw that the children went down in precise six-inch levels from eye-level to seat-height. The gorilla winked.

By the interval I was quite hoarse from laughing as loud as I could at the jokes, and my forehead ached from the strain of frowning at my neighbouring non-laughers. Nigel had arrived breathless from London, just before the curtain rose, his laugh was fiendish loud, and he was very comforting between scenes.

Next morning we lay in the hotel bed, almost submerged by newsprint. The notices weren't bad, except for the pinkly bespectacled boy. He definitely did not like the play or any of the performances. Obviously he was insensitive and had no taste or discernment, which I should have realised from the start.

The pink boy (he also had dandruff, Queen Kong reminded me, and blackheads on his nose) was evidently a hard worker. He had a full two-page spread, with about a dozen very fine photographs, which were all – except for a hand holding a burning match – of the local child-prodigy playwright.

The bluff man seemed to think that Abe had written the play, and there was a photograph of Ben looking like a moron, with Abe's name mis-spelt beneath it.

The woman's page had nothing, except a slightly

154

off-beat article on Harris tweed wedding dresses for winter weddings.

Theo, Hazel and Clarice all had pleasant mentions and the set was praised to the skies. Larry Marker – who had given a powerful performance – was admired for his animal grace, and threat. Sue, playing the beatnik, was barely mentioned, but her performance had been uneven, because she was so nervous.

Abe had called a meeting for everybody in the theatre at ten a.m. to discuss the notices and plan any changes. Ben and I arrived to find David Lee slumped in a chair, worn out, puffy and bleary. He fluttered a faint 'Hello, my loves,' at us, then closed his eyes.

Abe arrived smoking a cheroot, henchmen ranged behind him. One of the henchmen, a fat untidy man called Wilby, had a bottle of whisky, half-empty, peering out of his coat-pocket. The actors trickled in and sat around on the plush seats. I noticed with surprise that Clarice Bowen was sitting next to Larry Marker, smiling and whispering. He had his arm round her neck and she stroked his cheek with the back of her purple-taloned, bejewelled hand. 'They've been going at it like crazy since the third day of rehearsal,' Abe whispered in answer to my startled look.

Abe got down to business.

'Act Two is too long,' he said. 'We need to cut it. Larry has an entrance too many in Act One, I want that fixed, and I want Theo's violin speech to have more build-up. How do you feel about that David?' He looked towards David, who suddenly jerked out of his slump, wild-eyed.

'My God!' he said. 'My pills! That's what's wrong. I haven't had my pep-pills this morning!'

He fumbled in his pocket and took out a bottle of bright blue-and-yellow capsules, and swallowed two

155

with a sip of Wilby's whisky. 'Thanks, lovey,' he said, and I noticed Wilby wince.

'Right,' said David, 'I'm with you. Let's work it all out.'

The theatre cleaners were wandering along rows of seats, emptying ashtrays. The stage manager was on the stage, clipboard in hand, calling numbers to the electrician, tucked away in his lighting-box at the top of the theatre, and the feeling was of anti-climax.

Ben was told what changes were needed. He was totally bemused by now, and had lost his bearings. His play had turned into a different creature altogether from the one he had written and seen happily performed in Scotland. He realised that he was now a cog in a huge business machine, and felt unable to make a stand anywhere – indeed there was nowhere he felt certain enough to make a stand, because so much had disappeared and reappeared, changed, in the last few weeks.

He went to the hotel room and wrote for three hours, making the changes, which were given to the actors, who had to learn them and rehearse them for that night's performance. Ben watched the rehearsal and did rediscover some of his bearings. 'The changes have got to go,' he said with certainty.

He wrote all night, while I turned in my sleep and heard the keyboard clatter. He demolished the changes and he found a copy of his original play – the one Abe had read, liked, and bought – and he restored much of the original. There was a matinée that day and he and Abe sat together.

'It's good,' said Abe. 'It's really good.'

I saw the gorilla glower regally at him. She was not amused.

At breakfast next day, under the chandeliers, with flitting white-coated waiters and a delicious smell of coffee and bacon, we saw an elderly, distinguished man and woman; she was aquiline but beautiful, and wore diamond earrings and a hat of exquisite brown fur; he was frail, military and aristocratic. Ben whispered to me that they owned one of London's nicest and oldest theatres and that he was a Sir. They had come specially to see the play, and to consider if they wanted it to play in their theatre. I almost choked on my toast and sent a fleeting dewy-bride smile across the room.

They simply shook their heads as they said goodbye to Abe after the show that Night. They didn't like it.

At the end of the week the play seemed healthy and on an even keel, and the performances were maturing well. Mary O'Donovan's play had opened the night after *Personal*. We went, but didn't enjoy it much, we felt too numbed to be objective. 'I think she'll not be heard of till she's forty.' said Ben. The play had made headlines in all the local papers because of an accident at the theatre.

'Mary O'Donovan brings house down,' we read. The roof of the theatre proscenium had fallen after the second performance, which was a matinée, so the theatre had to be closed, which meant more financial stress for Abe. We returned to Scotland.

Chapter 25

The play came to Edinburgh and on the first night Abe
sat me in a box with an aged and well-known Scottish
novelist, Sir Toby Farquarson, who had an ancient,
handsome, satyr's face, with straight backswept white
hair and an imperial goatee. Abe considered that the
renowned octogenarian would look good in the box
and help business. I was pleased to be sitting next to the
famous old man. My father had often told me how he'd
met the writer in Constantinople, in the twenties.

'I believe my father knew you in Constantinople.' I
ventured.

Sir Toby looked quizzically at me. 'What was his
name?'

I told him.

'Lawrence?' he repeated vaguely.

'Captain Henry Lawrence,' I said.

'What year?'

'About 1923, I suppose,' I said.

'Where?' he snapped.

'Constantinople.' I repeated weakly.

'Lawrence,' he said, and shook his head. 'Never
heard of him.'

As we waited for the curtain to go up, Sir Toby

leaned back, eyes half-shut, bow-tie gleaming, and held his silver-topped cane with gloved hands, and started to reminisce about his early youth. 'I performed in this theatre when I was nineteen,' he said, and then he went on and on and on, until I was driven nearly stupid. He was obviously going to talk during the play, so I firmly turned my back and pretended not to hear his monotone, until he at last stopped, long after action had commenced on stage.

The play was swinging along splendidly and I was dying to see Ben when the interval came.

'Shall we go for a drink,' I asked.

'No, I don't feel like it,' said Sir Toby rather tersely. My heart sank, the Queen Kong offered to hurl him over the balcony, and I imagined the aged writer bouncing from a caryatid and smashing onto the heads of the audience beneath.

I glared at him and wished that Abe and Ben, whom I knew were in the circle bar, would come and visit myself and Sir Toby in the box. The old man said nothing about the play, except, 'It seems to be going rather well. You and your husband must come and drink some whisky with me one day.' Then he launched off into another interminable series of reminiscences. I kept saying, 'Really, how fascinating,' and, 'Goodness that's amazing,' while I tried to spot the faces I knew in the audience. Cordelia and Tony, still sunburnt from Puerto de los Pinos, weren't far away, and Cordelia kept leering up and crossing her eyes most foully; and Zoe grimaced from the upper circle. Mrs Mandel and my mother were sitting in a large group of relatives from both families and I was sure that I could see Mr Angelo peering beadily out from behind a pillar.

'. . . don't you think?' asked Sir Toby.

'Oh, yes,' I said enthusiastically, wondering why the hell Ben or Abe hadn't come to rescue me. 'Yes, I do!'

The old man opened one eye rather wide, and popped a

monocle in it, looked fiercely at me and said 'Hur-umph' and I wondered what on earth he had been asking.

We gave a party in our flat for friends and press after the opening. Abe had suggested that this would be poli-tic. 'You need to ask all the influential people you know,' he said. We thought hard but then decided that we didn't know anybody influential, or that if we did, we didn't like them enough to ask them to a party. Sir Toby was tired from talking so he was driven home in a taxi. Old Mrs Mandel was the highlight of the evening. She had made some of her chopped liver, and dozens of tiny fried gefilte fish, orange-coloured, with a gleaming dot of pickle in their middle. Abe was delighted to find good Jewish food in darkest Scotland and ate lots of gefilte fish, with great gusto. Theo fell quite in love with Mrs Mandel and listened to her stories about how she cooked her food, and how clever her son was, and how I was always doing too many things at once. I glimpsed them both, holding each other's arms and roaring with laughter. Larry Marker seemed to have cooled off his passion for the Queen Bitch, who had declined to come to the party, and he was standing with arms folded, in a corner, wearing a navy-blue tee-shirt, nodding, and talking intensely to Zoe. Tony drifted around, and patted my bottom as he passed. A couple of gossip column reporters were there but today I was careful not be become involved with their psychiatric problems. Cousin Louise was handing round a bowl of fondue, and wearing a skirt with green stallions gallop-ing round it on a red-and-black ground.

'Never, never marry a playwright,' I hissed, dipping in a crisp and spilling a blob of fondue on her front.

Louise's eyes popped and teeth bared in a gash of a smile. 'It's hardly likely!' she neighed.

David Lee was having a long, involved argument with Ben about open-stage and proscenium productions, and Tony was lost in admiration of the American girl Sue's beads, which he was examining too closely.

Abe took me into a corner. 'I like your house and your *objet* sense,' he said. 'You've got a good eye. You could make yourself some money, if you find any good African pieces here, you can be my agent. I'll give you *carte blanche.*' I was thrilled, but not at all sure that I'd want to pass any good pieces on to anybody, even someone as pleasant as Abe.

'Where did you get the mask? asked Abe. I recounted the saga, and he grinned appreciatively. 'Listen,' he said, 'I'll give you fifty pounds here and now for it.'

I looked at it, sitting all beautiful and peaceful on the ochre wall, lit by candles, staring across the chattering guests.

'Never,' I said. 'And anyway, it's worth much more.'

Abe roared with laughter. 'I don't believe that you're a Shiksa,' he said. 'What would you say to two hundred pounds.'

I paused and slowly ate a sausage on a stick. 'I'd say I'd rather have the mask,' I said, a little surprised by myself.

Abe nodded. 'I think you're right. It's a beautiful piece, you keep it.

After the party, it was back to work. The play ran its course in Scotland, and played to large, enthusiastic audiences, and College started and we slipped back into routine, feeling odd, living our usual lives while our minds dwelt with the play and how it was faring. There were two-and-a-half weeks before *Personal* opened in London. I started a large Spanish landscape painting – done from a small gouache I had painted sitting in an olive grove one morning while Ben sang beside me and ate grapes.

Ben was bored with teaching. 'It's an awful profession,' he said at supper, after his first day back. 'You get a year older, but the kids stay the same. It's depressing. And three-quarters of the staff are indelibly stamped by their teaching. You can tell a teacher a mile off. I'll be like that soon if I don't get out.'

'Oh, darling, if the play has a good run, you could leave next year. That would be bliss.'

'If it runs, we could have several thousand pounds in a few months, and a car and a house of our own.'

'And lots of beautiful primitive sculptures,' I sighed.

'It's like having a horse drawn in a sweepstake' said Ben, 'You don't necessarily stand to win, but at least you've drawn a horse, so you have some hope.'

Chapter 26

The week of the London opening came at last. We had been understandingly given time off from school and College. We flew to London, found the theatre, and saw '*Personal* by Ben Mandel' up in lights. We stood and gazed at the glorious words in silence for a moment, then went inside to the foyer. Abe had arranged another press conference, to be held before the final dress-rehearsal.

We entered the conference-room and were greeted by Abe with David Lee spruce in a lilac-sprigged shirt. There seemed to be hundreds of sophisticated women in the room, all wearing little black, dull dresses. They had rows of white predatory teeth, shiny beads, virulent nail-varnish and lipstick, automatic charming smiles and stone-cold artefact eyes under half-a-week's wages of hairdo. Abe had invited all the women's magazines, because any West End play success depended on block-bookings from women's clubs in the provinces. They were mechanical, precision-instrumented women; elaborately-jewelled robots, with tinny voices. Automatic inanities clicked on and off and sparkled, while cold steel wheels silently gyrated in relentless mindless motion behind their glittering façades.

'How old are you? How long does it take you to write a play? How long did it take you to write this play? How long will it take you to write the next play? Is this your first play? How do you feel about it? Do you hope it will be a success?'

Queen Kong swung from chandelier to chandelier, pelting the journalists with sandwiches and pickled onions, screaming:

'No you fools! Of course we don't! We hope it will flop and be booed to its grave!' Ben was humorous and dignified with his interviews and enchanted the women. I found myself thinking, almost nostalgically, of the Manchester spectacled pink boy, and the girl-about-to-be-married. At least they had themselves to be interested in.

A bulging man in florid nine-inch checks, with a fruity mellifluous voice, spoke to me. I wondered to myself if he knitted in his office; I felt that it would suit him. Theo later told me that he in fact crocheted. The man asked me what I felt about the play. I explained evasively to him that the original concept of the play, and what remained in the sieve after being mixed up and re-created by the innumerable interdependants of any single production, are very different things. My words took flight, and I was sure that I was enlightening him about the theatre. Later, David whispered his name – renowned for forty years in showbiz literature – and I choked on my olive.

Ben was standing nearby, grinning at a ring of vampires. I then had a lovely cosy chat with a dear little fellow with a soft blond haircut in a chi-chi fringe, darling tapered trousers, sweet cuffed jacket and a silver-and-amber cigarette holder. He told me that he wrote food and wine copy for a famous glossy. He was hurt when I said there were too many adverts in his magazine, but he admired my Cossack hat, which endeared him to me. We had an excited exchange about exhibitions and shows we had both seen – furniture, fabrics and buildings. It was all lovely, darling, lovely. Only, the little man kept saying he was only here with a friend, so none of my sparkling comments would be printed. It was a miserable waste, but he kept refilling my glass, and I didn't want to hurt his feelings by going.

Again the same inanities buzzed round.

'Do you hope the play will be a success?'

'Do you expect to have a long run?'

'What do you think of your husband's impresario?' – as though one would be indiscreet enough to say if one hated him, so that they could spread it all over their rag.

People were trickling away, and the males dwindled to a few hardcore drinkers. I noticed David Lee and the little blond man exchange addresses. The little blond man was watching himself in the mirror and smoking through his holder with delicate panache.

The last reporter to leave was a haggard wretch who bitterly complained about the social drinking he was forced to do by his job. 'It's wrecking my marriage,' he said, taking a final gulp of vodka before he staggered out.

A woman started clearing glasses, tinkled a breakage into a shovel, and offered me a final piece of celery and cheese. Ben and I said goodbye to Abe and David until the evening and wandered down the red plush stair, with brass handrail, past the gilded mirrors and erotically cavorting cupids above the door, into the big empty auditorium. A couple of dim lights picked out the dust-sheets on the empty rows of seating and the set looked unreal and abandoned in the eerie light. All was muffled, silent and deserted and we stood quietly for a moment, wondering.

We took a taxi to Bayswater where Abe had lent us a

165

company flat, and slept, exhausted, till the phone rang. It was Marcus, Ben's friend and colleague from Scotland. 'Come to the dress rehearsal,' urged Ben.

We sat high up in the theatre because Ben wanted to see how the show looked from the top. The curtains were down, and Abe, the henchmen, David Lee and half-a-dozen people were dotted round the large auditorium. Everyone was excited; tension was mounting throughout the company. Abe had a constant grim smile.

'House lights out please' called David, looking up at the electrician's perch. The auditorium was darkened, and the curtain rose.

Everything seemed to have gelled. Even the set looked well. They had removed the general's portrait and put a flower-piece in its place. Clarice Bowen was striking and looked remarkable tonight. The rehearsal went smoothly with no mishaps. After the violence of the shattered violin, Theo and Hazel had a reconciliation scene. Tonight they played it very quiet and intimate, and I was disturbed, wanting to weep for the sadness of them, but filled with joy because it was such good theatre. When the house lights went up at the end, I was amazed and touched to see that the normally controlled and Scottish Marcus was weeping, tears streaming down his cheeks. He gasped and sniffed, and Ben handed him a (paper) hankie.

When he had recovered himself, he said bewilderedly, 'I have never, ever in my life been so bloody moved by a performance in the theatre. It's wonderful, Ben. I haven't greeted like that since I was a wean.'

We were all three moved, and sniffed simultaneously. Ben stood up and stretched:

'Come on,' he reached for me. 'Let's all go for an expensive life-affirming slap-up meal.'

At the plush restaurant in the lane behind the theatre I couldn't think why roast duck should taste of cod, but when, after a quarter-glass of gentle wine, I felt vastly drunk and heard waterfalls in my head, I began to wonder. I chewed the fish-flavoured duck and found that the orange sauce had the same taste. I held valiantly onto the hidden table-leg beneath a damask cloth, whilst my right foot kicked at my left in exhortation to balance better. The waterfalls swelled into fuller spate, and Ben's beard now swirled round like a Catherine-wheel. I knew that I must not be sick on the table, because it was a very famous restaurant (it's name was reverently dotted through the pages of my better cookbooks), and Ben was going to be famous tomorrow.

I tried to make intelligent conversation:

'What did you think of the second act finale darling?'

I saw Ben's beard turn and whirl round in a anti-clockwise direction and then I definitely saw the waiter lean to forty-five degrees and swing slowly back, so I said, 'I think I'm going to faint.'

And as I proceeded to do so, I wondered how a tiny glass of hock could conceivably wreak such havoc.

'Put your head between your knees.'

It was a monsoon, not a waterfall. It was only sad that my nicest dress was also my tightest, and was not improved by being yanked half-way up my thighs.

'You can't look chic, when being sick,' muttered the anxious gorilla feebly.

A man's voice came. 'Madame needs some fresh air.'

'Huh,' I thought, 'You mean you don't want a drunk-looking woman in your plushy place.'

In fact, my thought was uncharitable. He was really a nice waiter, even if he did drop his aitchcs in his cock-eyed Cockney French.

167

He sat me outside the restaurant, on the pavement, on a velvet-seated chair of spindly elegance, and fanned me with a large and spotless napkin. Then he produced a crystal bottle of smelling-salts which made me weep like onions and shudder in the cold night air. Ben's beard was back to normal, and somebody had turned the taps off, or damned the river. I stared dizzily up at Ben in the sudden silence. He looked very concerned, and handsome, and husbandly. Between the worried bits of his face lurked an expression I'd never seen before.

'Oh cripes,' I said, and realised why the duck was cod.

And Marcus was grinning 'Congratulations,' he said. 'The pair of you.'

It was opening night. I had had a battle about Ben's dinner-suit trousers which were elephantine and positively swirled and coiled around his ankles. He didn't want to taper them – his tailor being an old family friend – but I managed to filch them from him and put them into a little tailor-shop near the flat that Abe had lent us. The tailor narrowed them beautifully, cutting off what would have made scarves for several men, then I quietly popped them back in the wardrobe. When we were getting dressed, I waited nervously for indignant noises, but Ben's mind must have been miles away, because he didn't seem to notice that it took him ages to squeeze his feet into the leg-holes.

We arrived early at the theatre, and the ever-cheerful stage doorman presented Ben with a sheaf of glossy golden telegrams, which we read with great sentimentality. We went to wish the actors good luck. I half-expected to find them surrounded by noisy well-wishers, but it was quite different. We found each one of them quite alone – putting make-up onto their dark-eyed, pale faces. Clarice watched us enter, in her mirror, with her wintry blue eyes, and mocking smile. Yesterday I had said 'good morning' to her, at the stage door, and the actress had simply stared coldly in wordless reply. Tonight though there was a total nakedness of person in each of the stars. The strain of an important first night on any actor is immeasurably great and I realised that this limboid pause in the irrevocable half-hour before curtain-up must be deeply lonely and self-confronting.

Clarice was real and warm for the few moments we had with her. It was the first time either of us felt we had made any positive contact with her.

In front, the house lights were blazing and chandeliers with crystal festoons glittered above the colourful first night crowd. Mrs Mandel and my mother were there, and Marcus Thomson, keeping his promise of many years' standing to be at Ben's London première. Unexpected and half-forgotten friends and acquaintances kept rushing up to kiss us, thrust a note or gift into a pocket or hand and wish Ben good luck. There was a pulsating sense of excitement and a constant rich rattle of chatter.

The curtain rose – Ben sat on in the bar with Abe's henchmen who were remarkably affable tonight. I stood at the back of the circle feeling dramatic and wondered if I really was pregant; I wore a backless, high-fronted, long-sleeved black-and-blue brocade dress, and frequently dashed in and out to the bar to tell them all how it was going. The theatre was filled to capacity. The audience seemed to be enjoying it after a sticky start. They were clapping and laughing quite nicely, but it seemed to me that the play wasn't going nearly so well as the dress rehearsal. There was the usual lonely maniac at the back, laughing at all the wrong bits, whose ignorance I forgave because of his obvious goodwill, and guessed him to be a Scot because he laughed hysterically when Theo said, 'When do you think we'll die, Jean?'

In the intervals Ben, myself, Abe, henchmen and David and friends huddled together drinking and smoking avidly, and compared notes on critics.

'Tynan was looking very serious.'

'I don't think the *Mail's* going to like it.'

'The two big dailies always disagree.'

'Hobson was chuckling a lot.'

'They seem pretty warm.'

'A bit slow in the first act.'

Despite the doubts and fears, I was elated with the excitement of the night, and utterly happy. Ben seemed quite unruffled and not visibly tense. He sat on his bar-stool grinning like a kid at Christmas.

At last it was over, and the curtain came down and as the applause blazed, I was touched to see Queen Kong on her feet, clapping hysterically, jumping up and down, shouting 'Encore! Encore!' Everybody seemed a little blurred and there was a welter of flashing eyes and teeth as innumerable people said 'Lovely, darling, lovely' and pummelled, patted or shook everybody in any way connected with the show.

We went backstage again, expecting this time that the dressing-rooms would be filled with friends. Clarice was having a quiet talk with her mother, a tall dignified woman of perhaps seventy. We told Clarice that she had been wonderful, and her eyes mocked us again for an instant. We provincials; we innocents.

Hazel was also with her parents. Her father was a sandy-haired moustached old Scot. Ben grinned, 'So that's where you get the accent from.' Hazel winked. We went to see Theo. His dressing-room was packed with people, all talking and laughing and saying 'Wonderful' and 'Darling'. Theo, sweaty, excited and anxious, grasped Ben's arm and immediately asked if his mother had enjoyed the show. We assured him that she had adored it; then Theo held out his hand, which was wrapped in a white cloth and showed them it had been quite badly gashed. He had had trouble with the violin when he smashed it down among the crockery, but swore that he hadn't felt it at all. David Lee's Whitby blue-rinsed mum of sixty-five was there, standing proudly by her son, in musquash and blue glass diamonds.

We went back to the flat with Marcus Thomson and several old theatrical friends. The mothers had gone to their hotel. After raking the kitchen cupboards and opening what few tins we could find, three of us cooked a strange but delectable meal – it wasn't quite sausages and sardines, but something similar – which we ate and washed down with a little champagne and some beer. We all kept drinking toasts to the play until at last Ben looked at his watch and said, 'It's getting quite early you know, how about some sleep to prepare us for the notices?' We said goodnight and Marcus promised to wake us with all the newspapers; he was doing an early morning radio report on the play to Scotland. We fell into bed and slept within minutes, with high-speed visions of the day's happenings swirling through our heads. Ben's last words were, 'It'll run for six weeks.'

I heard a doorbell ringing and couldn't for a moment imagine why Marcus should be on our doorstep so early in the morning, but he flourished a handful of newspapers at me and looked grim. Some of the notices were grim too, and a couple were so rude that we laughed out loud. There were also some nice ones (obviously written by sensitive people). The nastiest notice was

171

read out by Ben, who sat bare-chested and unkempt in a pair of trousers, drinking tea.

'Personal Rubbish,' was the headline, and it continued, 'You have failed, Mr Mandel to write a play.'

'Insensitive cretin,' groaned the gorilla.

It was a strange breakfast we had that day in London. We knew that good or bad notices were important in terms of box-office, but emotionally we were too shattered to react fully to them. We both knew that the original written piece was good, and trusted its artistic integrity, but we had lived too long with the present actuality of the play to see it objectively. We had real doubts about the production, but knew that it had had its own urgency and pressures and organic growth to make it what it was. The good notices still made us feel good, but the bad ones seemed hilariously irrelevant somehow, to our own knowledge and view of the play.

Nigel met us for lunch and seemed surprisingly pleased by the press. He said that Ben had made a distinguished start, and Abe had taken an option on Ben's next, as yet unfinished, play. Then he said goodbye until the next time. We went to the theatre to see how the bookings were going. The foyer looked splendid, and was lined with huge blown-up quotes from the notices. All the charmingest bits had been cut out, photographed and enlarged to great size that morning, and were pasted by the doors and windows to entice the passing masses. It made the play sound terrific.

In fact, from the writing on the wall, nobody would have dreamed that the show was not already a huge box-office success. The bookings they were told, were above average.

We said a fond farewell to Abe; he patted my tum.

'I hear you have a bun in the oven,' he said. 'Call him after me.'

For an emotional moment I thought this was a great idea.

Chapter 27

As soon as we were home I went to see the family doctor, Dr Wilts, who was a very jolly fellow – a wearer of cavalry boots, and a passionate skier and sailor. I had been about ten when he first became our remarkably young GP, but I noticed today that his hair looked like a heel in a holey sock, and was in need of darning at the back. He told me to bring him a urine sample and assured me that he would let me know the result as soon as possible.

Unfortunately, Dr Wilts was absent-minded, so it took about a week to find out if the test was positive or not. I tape-measured my middle about three times a day and tried to talk myself into feeling sick. When I assured myself that I wasn't pregnant I felt upset, and doomed to perpetual barrenness, but when I decided that I was, both Ben and I bit our nails and wondered. Every morning at eleven I would phone the doctor from the College phone booth. He took his coffee at eleven, so he was always bright and jolly, and asked how I was, or what was my trouble. I daily reminded him about my fateful bitter-lemon bottle (it was the only bottle I could find) and he would chuckle.

'Oh Lord, yes, don't worry, I'll see about it. Phone me again tomorrow.'

He had four children, I knew, so I supposed one became blasé after a bit.

In the Life class we were painting Saggy Jim, which I found terribly distracting. I kept using him mentally as a model for the kinds of maternity dress that I thought I might wear. Pete was doing a good painting, or so he said, but the he had always liked those purplish, mottled colours.

Zoe had given up Pete, and she and I were trying to give up smoking, so we took it in turn to buy twenty a day, instead of buying ten each every day, which was quite a saving we rationalised. Zoe was fed up because Saggy Jim upset her delicate sense of the aesthetic. She made me feel all nervous again. Saggy Jim yawned repulsively on the rostrum and scratched his bottom. Zoe opened her shopping bag, and pretended to be sick into it. On the seventh day of the bitter-lemon bottle, I again went to phone the doctor. I didn't have any money for the phone, so I went to the janitor's office and asked Fred for some change.

'What are you goin' to give me for it?' he asked with a hideous leer and I had such a struggle to persuade him to give me the coins that I was late when I at last thrust three sweaty pennies into the box. I dropped the fourth, picked it up and pushed it in, then I dialled the wrong number.

I had to fetch more money, and the gorilla appeared and efficiently dialled for me this time. At last I got through and the doctor immediately told me the test was positive.

'Oh . . .' I gasped weakly, my blood pounding with strange shock. I felt a funny overwhelming happiness, then I felt utterly limp.

'Of course your last confinement was quite normal, wasn't it?'

174

'My what?' I shrieked, my enraged senses flooding back.

'Oh, ha ha, of course, yes, ha. I forgot. It's your first isn't it? Come and see me on Monday. How's the play going?'

'He could remember that!' snarled Queen Kong in outrage.

'Very well, thanks,' I mumbled.

I hung him back on the hook, and staggered out of the booth, where, although it was a drear Scottish autumn everywhere else, there were birds singing and sun streaming down. I obtained another handful of pennies which I tried to push into the shilling slot. Ben, who was at school, registered almost speechless delight, and anxiously asked if I felt all right. The gorilla, outside the phone booth, was grinning idiotically, tears making her leathery cheeks glisten.

Zoe was by now stamping up and down outside the phone box and she and I wept together. We decided very soberly not to tell anybody until it was vastly obvious, because I didn't want anybody to make allowances or otherwise for my pregnant paintings. We agreed on secrecy, nodded vigorously at each other, then went upstairs to class. Teeny Mary was busy painting. Teeny Mary was already six months pregnant, so I couldn't restrain myself from whispering that she was no longer alone. Teeny Mary beamed and hauled out her cigarettes. The three of us collapsed, suddenly weak, onto high stools, and puffed long excited puffs in unison. Then Myfanwy, who still looked ill after the hospital X-ray treatments, and was still taking lots of pills, sensed our excitement and came across. When she was told the news Myfanwy stared all dewy-eyed at me and hugged her own thin body and rocked rhythmically with delight, crooning 'Ooh, how super! You are lucky!'

175

My mind was barely focussing. All I wanted was a curry for elevenses.

We somehow did a day's work, arguing on the radiator, at break-time, about possible names. Myfanwy read out an article from the paper about a young mother who had gone mad from overstrain and had kept all her child's used nappies till she had five sackfuls, which she had set on fire before abandoning her baby. Pete came up and shook his head at me. 'I warned ye at your wedding, fellie,' he said. 'I told ye not to do it, and anyway, I hope it's no a monkey.' The girls kept putting their heads sideways to gaze at me and decide whether or not I looked any different. We borrowed a Little Knitter's Girl Guide diary, and worked out that the baby was due exactly the day after the Diploma exams finished.

At teatime I realised that I couldn't possibly attend the last class of the day, as it was imperative for me to buy some books. So I crept out of College and went to a bookshop which was full of antenatal exercise books, stuffed with pictures of bulbous women in beastly underwear, their faces blacked out like prisoners. There were also books with bulging wonder-babies on the front, with fleshy toothless smiles and spotless nappies, and these were crammed with advice on how to bring them up. I bought a green book about natural childbirth, filled with poetic passages on the joys of parenthood, and another one with a reasonably unrepulsive baby on the cover. I read them on the bus home with my head half-hidden in my basket in case somebody thought I was pregnant.

Ben was waiting anxiously at home for me. He had cooked supper and even hoovered the sofa for me to recline on. It was a lovely supper, but I kept craving curry.

We sprawled on the floor and read the books and I almost ruptured myself doing the exercises with too much gusto.

The child-rearing book had some awful things in it. There was one picture of splodges of porridgy food, through which two presumably baby eyes peered malevolently. This was ominously labelled 'Mixed Feeding'. And there was another photograph beside it of a little darling in a nappy, with a negative paragraph beneath it which advised the reader to use a nylon scrubber on the worst-soiled of the twenty-odd nappies one would have to clean each day. There were pages which looked like advanced chemical text books with lurid diagrams of bottles and shchedule charts, and the whole book was punctuated with pictures of clocks. There was feeding-time, potting-time, sleeping-time (I looked forward to that one), burping-time, relaxing-time and weaning-time.

It all seemed too complicated and daunting and a subdued hour-and-a-half later, I wondered if, had I known all these things, I might not have reconsidered the matter. When did one paint in this twenty-four hour schedule?

'Three months colic. Many babies cry for four hours every night for the first three months . . .'

We stared at each other appalled.

'I don't like this game,' snorted the gorilla. She rocked by my side, gnawing her lip.

'How to keep baby warm. Projectile vomiting. Hernia from crying. Loose stools. Teething,' and, most chilling of all; is baby breathing?'

We looked at each other, speechless with fore-boding, and turned, trembling, to the next page, which was the first of several which listed the basic necessities for the average baby.

'Cottonwool swabs. Disinfectant. Nappy-soakers. Gripe-water. Milk of Magnesia. Probes for ears and nose. Soothing ointment and feeders – for baby is often a little sick . . .'

There was also an article on breast feeding; how painful it could be and how awkward it was to have dripping breasts, which soaked one's clothes, and how one was tied down by feedings times – but yet how satisfying and delightful it was to feed one's child oneself.

The book assured me, with unconvincing schmaltz, that one must not worry (had Mrs Mandel written it?) because one would bloom like a ripening rose and glow with the joy of one's little secret.

This was more than enough for me. 'I need a cigarette,' I said. Ben pulled one out and lit it for me. I took a long rich pull at it, and my head immediately whirled about sickly. Our unborn barley-grain-sized child was already taking over my life, and dictating what I might or might not do.

'I'll have to stop smoking,' I said, grinding out the cigarette. 'It just makes me puke.'

'That's good really,' said Ben. 'It'll save us a lot of money. I'll give up too. It's a foul unhealthy habit.' He paused. 'Let's burn the packet,' and he opened the stove doors and thrust the almost-full packet dramatically into the flames. I watched it burn, amazed and touched at my husband's strength of character, then decided that I must do something about food. I leapt up, barely stopping at the mirror to see if my bulge showed yet, and started cutting up onions and tomatoes to make a curry nightcap.

Chapter 28

Ben heard once a week from Nigel as to how *Personal* was faring. The Sunday papers had been mixed about the play; Hobson said it had great depth and perception and ought to be seen. Tynan was lukewarm. The bookings were building up steadily, but the theatre was not filled to anything near capacity. It would take several weeks before Abe would break even financially, and his other play which had now also opened in the West End was not doing well. Friends would enquire as to the welfare of the play, as though they were asking about an ailing relative who wasn't expected to survive the winter. Their voices would be hushed as they asked and their faces poised, ready to assume a mask of mourning at a moment's notice.

Neither of us succeeded in being discreet about the pregnancy. We had half-intended to keep it quiet for two or three months, but, as I had done with Zoe, Ben told the mothers immediately, unable to keep it to himself.

There were ecstatic phone calls from Cordelia, distant aunts, and even my brother Charlie was moved to pen a rare few lines from the Persian Gulf, where he was building a bridge.

Ben's mother made a family meal to celebrate and we went together with my mother. Mrs Mandel kept up a nervous litany to me, 'Put your feet up,' she would say, or 'Don't fall down those steps! Do be careful your chair doesn't tip. Are you warm enough? You feel well? Yes? Oh, touch wood it will last.' And she would sigh and put her hand to where here massive bosom and throat met, in the Jewish equivalent of crossing oneself.

Then, after the meal she and her sister took me into the bedroom.

'Sit, Kate,' said Mrs Mandel, pointing to a pink wicker chair. I sat down uneasily; sister Rachel remained standing, and Mrs Mandel sat heavily down on the pink candlewick bedcover and looked sternly at her daughter-in-law, and I realised uneasily that I was facing a committee.

'You can't possibly do your Diploma now Kate, can you?' said Mrs Mandel. 'You'll get far too tired, and it certainly wouldn't be good for the baby.'

'What do you mean?' I asked, staring at them in amazement. 'Of course I'll do my Diploma. That's why I'm pregnant now. We worked it out, to be the earliest practical date to have a baby.' I stood up.

'You sit down,' said Mrs Mandel, jabbing the air with her forefinger on every syllable. 'What are you doing to yourself?'

I sat down.

Rachel now joined in. 'There are risks, you know Kate,' she said.

'I know you love Ben,' said Mrs Mandel, 'At least I hope so. Whatever you want of life, I wish it for you too. But at this moment Kate, there are more important things.'

I gazed at the two pairs of dark accusing eyes.

180

Mrs Mandel tapped my knee, again in rhythm to her speech.

'You are having a baby,' she explained loudly and slowly, a though to a foreigner.

'I know that,' I said. I was trembling inside. 'But of course I've got to finish my Diploma. I feel terribly well. After all, it's a perfectly natural process.'

Mrs Mandel turned quite pale and panic-stricken, sucked in a great gulp of air, and supported herself by clutching at the bedpost till her knuckles were white.

'Well, that's your decision,' said Rachel, dead-faced.

'Is your painting more important to you than Ben?' said Mrs Mandel.

I didn't answer. It was quite a difficult question.

'Kate,' said Mrs Mandel, 'I am not trying to tell you how to run your life. Believe you me,' she said. 'All I want is for you and Ben to be happy. What more could I wish for you than that?'

I stood up. 'I need to go to the bathroom,' I said with quiet dignity. They let me go.

'Kate,' called Mrs Mandel as I reached the doorway, my mind jangling, 'If it's a boy. You'll have him circumcised!' It was a rhetorical statement. I walked along the corridor, and Mrs Mandel's voice followed me. 'For health reasons!'

I pushed the bathroom door shut, and sat down weakly. They really meant what they were saying. They genuinely thought that I ought to stop doing anything for myself, and to think only of my husband and baby-to-be. Bloody hell. Then I saw the gorilla crouched on the bath; she was frowning, and breathing heavily. 'Don't worry,' she assured me. 'I'll help. We'll do it. We'll do it all. Art. Kids. Plays. The lot. We'll manage. You've got to keep on painting. The more you do, the better you'll get.'

181

At least she made me feel better. I got up and cooled my face with water, and returned to eat too many cakes and drink tea with my in-laws in an uneasy silence.

At College people were very kind to myself and the more obviously pregnant Teeny Mary, who swelled apace. They would fetch our coffee for us, and Michael Phoenix fetched me a stool when he painted on my still-life. Mrs Mandel never pressed me again directly about my work, she sighed instead. She also became aggravatingly over-solicitous, and would warn me not to fall down a step I went up and down a dozen times a day, or she would push a chair to rights, when I'd been ensconced in it for ages. She did obviously worry about me and her unborn grandchild, but I found it suffocating, and a waste of energy. I didn't want to hurt the old lady by being brusque, but did so inadvertently, all too often.

'She's very kind, really,' I explained to Cordelia on the phone, 'Her knitting needles flash sparks almost, and will soon be worn to blunt stumps. It's more than you can say for my mother.'

Instead of vests, however, my mother made prognostications. She tied one of my long hairs onto her wedding ring and held it above my still entirely flat stomach. The ring hung and quivered for a moment, then, with my mother's hand poised immobile above it, it started to move firmly round and round in rhythmic circles. Ben and I stared hypnotised at the ring, which, like a dowsing-stick, seemed to have a will of its own.

'You see,' said Ma smiling round, 'It's a girl for sure.'

'Ha,' I patted my tum. 'Can't be. This is my son Leo, or Aaron, or Caspar, or David.

I worried about having a girl, because my daughter might turn out to be like I'd been – wild and dirty and noisy, always leading a desperate gang of filthy kids

182

along garden walls to steal crab-apples, or to gather up all the dead birds we could find, in order to give them dramatic Shakespearian funerals (with myself as orator). I didn't fancy living with a girl like that. And she might want to play Ludo and Snap all day; I shuddered. I wanted a boy. As we went to bed I asked Ben about circumcision.

'I don't know,' he said.

'Has your mother talked to you about it?'

'Yes.'

In the ensuing silence I realised that it was not a simple problem. He was still a Jew, even if he hadn't been in a Synagogue for twenty years.

'It goes back,' he said at last, 'three thousand years. I'll wait and see.' And I knew I must leave him free to make the decision.

As I drifted into sleep, wedged against Ben's naked back, I thought longingly of onion pickles and curried vegetables.

'We'll have to call him Chapati Popadum Mandel,' he snorted.

'It's just like thinking up titles, isn't it?'

'I'll send you a telegram,' he grunted.

The next day being Sunday, we sprawled in our toast-crumbed bed and read the papers. Abe had put in larger and more flamboyant ads for the play. Ben looked worried. 'That means it's failing. If this doesn't work and build up the audiences, it'll be off in a couple of weeks. He lay propped glumly on his pillows, and I wished that I could comfort him.

Chapter 29

On Monday I went to see Dr Wilts and discussed the confinement.

'I'd like to have it at home.' I said.

The doctor didn't approve of that at all. 'No, no,' he said briskly, scratching his athletic calf under his trousers where his cavalry boot met his shin. 'Not a good idea. First babies can be problematic. You need to be in a hospital, where they've got all the incubators and operating theatres, if you need them.'

I gulped. 'I'm very keen to do natural childbirth,' I said nervously. 'I've read quite a lot about it, and it seems to make sense to me, with its attitudes.'

'Oh well,' said the doctor cheerfully. 'Very modern, what?' He was humouring me.

I then suggested a small nursing home which older friends had described to me. I thought it sounded attractive because it had small wards – only two or three women sharing a room, and most of all it appealed to me because I had heard that the husbands were instructed by the old Highland Sister who ran it, to take their wives out to dinner, the night before they were sent home.

'I'll phone now and ask if they have any vacancies,' said the doctor, reaching athletically across for the telephone.

He dialled, spoke briefly, then put down the receiver and shook his head.

'I'm afraid we're not in luck there,' he said. Newly pregnant is a month too late, ha ha. Next time, my dear, you should phone them up about eleven months before you intend to lay your egg. I think you should go to the Royal Maternity Hospital. It's the largest and best-equipped in the city. They'll deal splendidly with you,' and he ripped off a sheet of notepaper and dashed off an illegible letter of introduction to the hospital.

During Antique class the following week, I went up to Mr Angelo. 'I have a medical appointment this afternoon, Mr Angelo,' I said. 'Please will you excuse me. I'll come back as soon as I can.'

Mr Angelo's tiny eyes drew even closer to register his disbelief. 'Where do you have to go Mrs Mandel?' he asked, and I felt that he emphasised the Mrs more than was necessary.

'I have to go to the Infirmary,' I said stiffly.

'Well I can't stop you,' he said, and looked at my drawing. 'You haven't explained that trapezius, and there's a lot more work to do in drawing those feet and hands.' I went, quickly, glad to escape the dreary re-rendering of the re-rendered plaster toes and fingers.

I walked through the hospital grounds, and then lost myself inside one of the old turreted buildings. I went along a cream-painted corridor, which had heaps of discarded crutches, deserted trolleys and dozens of thick pipes lagged with blankets running along its grimy walls, until I came outside again and at last found the maternity wing.

I presented my doctor's letter, which was by now a trifle paint-stained and had a small pencil drawing of an old lady on a bicycle on the envelope. A busy little woman with crimped hair and glasses struggled to decipher the letter, and checked my details with me. Then she said, 'Right dear, that's all fine. You'll be in Ward 87, with Sister Macalpine. Go straight through that corridor ahead there and they'll weigh you in and give you your card.'

I wondered what the woman meant by 'weighing in', but obediently walked along the indicated corridor until I found myself in a large airy room, with about sixty chairs laid out in half-a-dozen rows with a busily knitting pregnant woman in almost every one. The women all turned and stared at me as I entered.

There was a desk with a nurse sitting at it and beside her was what must be the biggest weighing-machine in the world. It was about six feet tall and was like a lamp-post with a great round dial, like a Town Hall clock, and at the bottom was a large square footplate, which groaned when the person being weighed stood on it.

I handed my card to the nurse at the desk, who asked me to sit down, then she produced a large double sheet of paper with a few words printed on it.

She asked me coldly if I had fits, diabetes or blackouts, and what my parents and grandparents had died of, if deceased. She asked my age and religion and looked disapproving when I said 'none', then she asked Ben's age, occupation and state of health and what injections or illnesses I had ever had. Then, when the two pages were nearly filled with writing, she said:

'Will you please take your coat and shoes off and climb on the weighing-machine now please.'

I took off my duffle coat and started to remove my cardigan, desperate to remove any surplus weight, because I dreaded the machine's pronouncement.

I then ascended the footplate, like a victim to the scaffold, and all the knitting women turned again to watch the sinister red pointer clang round the dial. I wondered if they knitted a purl for every pound over the ten stone.

The nurse watched and wrote down the total. 'You're

186

going to have to watch your weight, dear', she said. 'Put your things on, then come over here and I'll tell you about your diet'.

I was depressed, because I had already realised that you don't need to eat for two when pregnant: in my case it seemed necessary to eat for three at least.

The nurse guided me to a glass-fronted cupboard which was filled with hideous, dusty, painted plaster models of food. There were pretend wedges of cheese and be-cobwebbed steak, a china egg and a mock-up of tomatoes and apples and a lump of lettuce and what I guessed must be a piece of fish. There was also a glass of pretend milk, which was decidedly sooty.

'These things you must have every day,' said the nurse, 'because they will give you and your baby good vitamins. But these,' and she indicated more dusty models, this time of ice-creams, bread, jam, potatoes and cornflakes, cakes and sugar, 'you must only eat in moderation, and if possible avoid. You are only supposed to gain a few ounces a week. We will take note of your weight carefully whenever you come in for your monthly check-up.'

'Monthly check-up?' I thought in a panic, 'And on a Monday? Old Angelo will do his nut.'

After this I was told to sit beside the other women on the seats. Every three minutes or so, as each woman's turn came, the one nearest the door to the next room rose, and as she vacated her seat, each one of the sixty pregnant women, weary with waiting, would rise and simultaneously heave their bulks into the newly-vacated neighbouring chair. It was bureaucratic madness. Two hours later, every bottom, including Queen Kong's, had sat in every chair. Queen Kong, imprisoned, foamed with rage and rattled her bars as she listened to our neighbours. Many of the women had come from miles away and gone to considerable trouble to leave their other children being looked after, and they had

187

all, like myself, been given specific times like 3.55. In future, I determined, I would come with a drawing pad.

The next room was the place for urine samples. I had not expected to be asked for a urine sample and had gone to the lavatory whilst I waited, asking my tired neighbour to shift my belongings for me, so when I was handed my sample beaker, I was nonplussed.

'I can't, I said. 'I've just been.'

'Well you must dear', said a plump little black nurse. She added, with a briskly cajoling manner, like a toddler's exasperated mother, 'Just you try, like a good girl.'

I went into the small white toilet and tried, but had no success. At last, agonised, I went back to the little nurse.

'Oh dear', said the nurse, clucking and shaking her head. 'I'll fetch you a glass of water. You must give us a sample.' She bustled off, and brought back a beaker of water, which I drank, watched by several tittering nurses and a couple of mothers-to-be.

'Now, just sit on the chair and wait. I'll do your blood test meanwhile'.

I sat, clutching my empty sample-bottle guiltily. The young nurse pricked me in the thumb, then leant over with a thin see-through tube and sucked up several inches of blood from the prick. She gave me a piece of cotton wool and I rubbed the injury and felt vulnerable.

The nurse then took my blood pressure and smiled like a Black Mammy.

'Off you go now dear, and do your doings.'

I locked myself in and turned the tap on to encourage my diffident bladder into action. It was quite hard to aim tidily and successfully, but at last I produced a tiny trickle so that there was maybe a quarter-inch in the bottom of the beaker.

I dressed, washed and presented my tiny trophy to the nurse, who said I was a good girl, and took it across to a table where a young girl in a white uniform sat. This person now

188

dipped a long stick into the beaker and held up a colour chart which she compared with the resulting colour from her test. Then she wrote down something on my chart.

'Looks pee green to me,' whispered Queen Kong.

After these trials, I stood in the middle of the room, feeling lost. The small black nurse bustled up. 'Off you go now, dear, along that corridor and go into a dressing-room and remove your pants and stockings.' I did this and emerged from the tiny dressing-cubicle feeling exposed in every sense of the word. I sat on a long bench with about six other women, all of whom had white naked legs, with their feet sitting oddly in their outdoor shoes. Some wore stockings which they had rolled down to their ankles.

I leaned across to a red-faced girl who sat heavy-eyed beside me. 'What happens next?' I hissed.

The girl looked dully at this innocent. 'It's your internal,' she said obscurely. 'It's horrible.'

I was called into a curtained-off room and told to hoist my skirt and climb onto a trolley. There was a young doctor in a face-mask and he snapped on a pair of thin plastic gloves, lubricated his index finger and, after asking me to turn my naked lower half onto my side, he did what he had to do. I lay quietly (deep breathing seemed to be the secret) and tried to concentrate on the floral pattern of the screening round me. Privacy and modesty were now things of the past.

'That's all O.K. Mrs Mandel,' said the young doctor. 'Everything in the right place.'

I smoothed down my skirt and slipped on my shoes and resumed breathing normally. 'Off you go to the Breast Sister now,' said the doctor. I wondered if I had heard correctly.

'Who?' I asked nervously.

'The Breast Sister. The nurse here will take you.'

I was taken along yet another long corridor, and told to sit outside a screened-off cubicle. I looked round at the nega-

189

tive cream walls and became aware of a deep bass voice saying 'You'll need to work on your nipples and roll them between your fingers.'

I was beginning to feel that I had had enough for one day, if not for one lifetime. I wondered what to tell Mr Angelo. I couldn't very well give him the details of the afternoon. Anyway, I looked at my watch, the class had finished twenty minutes ago, and I was going to miss the start of Lithography too, if the Breast Sister didn't get a move on.

A thin, tearful girl stumbled out from behind the curtained screen. She looked at me with swimming eyes, shook her head and blindly felt her way back down the corridor.

'Next please,' boomed the voice.

The Breast Sister was formidable. She was thick-set and muscular, grey-haired under the white cap, aged about fifty and bulged like a wrestler in her dazzling white-and-blue uniform. I looked at her, noticed that she had a bristly chin, and gulped.

'Now dear, what's your name?'

I told her.

'I want you to take off your top and bra please, so we can have a look at your bosoms and see if your nipples are all right to feed your baby. You want to feed your baby yourself now, don't you?' and she looked piercingly at me, from under her beetling brows. I did very much want to breast-feed my child, but I couldn't imagine anybody ever having the courage to deny to the Breast Sister that they wished to do so.

I shakily unbuttoned my blouse and cardigan and removed my bra, which I was relieved to remember was clean, and stood, pink and nubile, naked to the waist, blushing from hairline to hairline.

The Breast Sister leaned over and stared critically at my embarrassed breasts, then, flexing her shoulders, she

190

spread out her brogued feet and clutched at one side of my bosom, which she fiercely pummelled and pulled, as though she was making dough. She snorted, then turned her attentions to the other breast, and gave it the same vicious treatment; then she dropped her grip and stood, arms akimbo and gave her verdict.

'You have a splendid pair. Perfect for breast feeding. All you need to do is rub them with lanolin at night and roll the nipples like this' – and she leant forward with huge thumb and forefinger, but I whipped aside my already tingling titty, like a child playing tig with a tiger.

Then I was permitted to dress and leave – on condition that I made an appointment at the entrance hall for my next check-up. I felt like a wrung-out floorcloth and barely made it to the desk, where the same crimped-haired receptionist wrote an appointment on my card, again with a specific time, which made Queen Kong snarl 'Hypocrite!' as we pushed our way through the glass doors into the foggy dusk.

At the hospital gates I met Hector.

'Hi, Hector, where have you been?'

'I've just taken Myfanwy in again,' he answered, 'She's not well at all, and they're giving her more X-ray treatment and things.

Myfanwy had been very poorly during the last weeks; she had no energy, and no longer even did her yoga. Big Hector had walked with her encircled in his great striped arm, and helped her with canvas-stretching and priming. He was very low, and full of fears about Myfanwy's illness. 'She's lost nearly two stone,' he said. 'She's got nothing on her at all.'

I pulled my coat tightly around myself, and we walked wordlessly together towards College. Life was becoming altogether too grim and earnest.

Chapter 30

I clattered into the Lithography class half-an-hour late, but had time to run off some of the second colour prints of the old lady busker, in between eating – crisps and rolls which Zoe had thoughtfully saved for me from the tea-break. Some of the crisp crumbs fell into the oily blue paint which I was rolling onto the lithographic stone, where they enhanced the textural qualities and made the old lady's gymshoes look atmospherically ragged.

At home Ben hugged me and asked how I had got on at the hospital and I burst into tears of rage and indignation. He was appalled when I re-enacted the afternoon for him. He comforted me with a bunch of small yellow chrysanthemums which he had bought. We ate our simple meal of soup and toasted cheese, then Ben locked himself up with his play, which was still not going well, and I rushed back to College to finish tiredly my uncompleted Antique drawing. That, I thought, would at least stop old Angelo from nagging me.

On the way home I met Zoe, with an oddly bulging pocket. 'What have you got?' I asked. Zoe looked guilty and beckoned me into a dark corner just outside the building and pulled out a Victorian crystal gerundel – a sort of elaborate glass candlestick, delicately painted and hung with prisms. It had come from one of the Still-Life cupboards, which were filled with delicious treasures, to which Diploma students had access.

'Hey!' I said, shocked, 'Michael Phoenix will murder you if he ever knows you've taken that.'

'But he never will, will he?' said Zoe. 'After all I'm just borrowing it so I can paint it at home. And Kate,' she added, I'm sure nobody will miss it and just imagine how divine it will look on the piano.'

I nodded. Undeniably it would look incredible on the inlaid piano in her digs, and, come to think of it, that light blue one with the hyacinths painted on it would look magnificent on my own mantelpiece, against the ochre wall. Surely Mr Phoenix wouldn't really mind as long as we were being visually stimulated by the objects. After all, that was what College was about; and it would be nice to get something positive from the place.

Personal ended its London run after only six weeks. Abe explained to Ben that some managements were rich enough to keep a company going for three to five months, until audiences did at last build up properly, and busloads of ladies poured in from the provinces to fill the empty seats, because its name had been advertised for so long that it appeared to be a success. But Abe couldn't afford this risk, so he reluctantly took both plays off. Ben was disappointed, but he'd realised the end was in sight, and anyway he'd had a West End production. The French and Dutch rights had been bought, it was due to be published and the BBC might well take it for Television. We were flush for once.

Theo, Larry and Hazel wrote beautiful letters. Larry's writing was large and exuberant, and he said

193

that he wanted to put it in writing that Ben had what it takes. Larry had done well from the play, and was booked to make a film in New York. Abe's predictions were proving right.

Abe's option was for the play Ben was still struggling with nightly, and the one after that. But Abe had, as he succinctly put it, all but lost his balls with his two flops, so he didn't intend to be an impresario for some time to come.

He phoned once when Ben was out and spoke to me.

'Ethnic sculptures are more secure than theatre management,' he said, and remembered my mask.

'I'm keeping it,' I said. 'If you bought it you'd do too well out of it.'

Abe was amiable, and said, 'Sure, darling, but any time you do want to get a fair price for it, send it to Sotheby's with a reserve of two hundred pounds on it.'

I thanked him and said, 'If we're short, I'll keep it in mind.'

'And anyway,' I explained later to Ben', 'It's mine, and I'm holding onto it, and it goes so well with the ger-undel.'

I was determined to find somebody who would teach me relaxation and natural childbirth. There was no actual organisation in the city where I could go, but my mother found someone, through her Jungian connec-tions. Mrs Hindelbaum was a very tall German lady with starey blue eyes and bird's nest of wispy faded blond hair. She wore purple woollen stockings and hand-woven clothes, and had five children. For my first lesson she came into the sitting-room, dropping par-cels, gloves and bags, and puffing slightly, because she had bicycled.

'Goot afternoon,' she said, disentangling a parcel string from her glove-finger and extending a large red

194

hand. 'I am happy I can help you is it not wonderful to be heffing a baby? And you are so young, and so artistisch.'

I smiled vaguely and tried to help as Mrs Hindelbaum's knitted hat fell to the ground and a button pinged off her huge hairy tweed cloak, which had a long kind of scarf-cum-hood with which Mrs Hindelbaum had difficulty, as she unwound it from her thick throat. At last she was unfolded and stood in her thick-soled brown hiking shoes, ready to work. 'We need a rack,' she declared, after looking carefully around the room.

I paused uneasily 'A rack?'

'A voollen trafling rack to lie on zé floor.'

'Ah,' relieved, I fetched a tartan travelling rug and stretched it on the floor.

When she actually got to work, Mrs Hindelbaum was good. She made me do several exercises, using all of the body, and then she asked me to sit on the rack, whilst Mrs Hindelbaum briefly told me about the stages of labour, and how I must deal with them all by gentle deep breathing. 'Except,' she added, 'for ze last stage. Here you are about to burst into flower like a rosebud vich vill open into its full splendour and vonder, so here you must push and push and hold your bress, zen your baby vill komm out into ze vorld and be born at last.'

I took her word for it, but the whole thing still seemed rather unreal to me. Mrs Hindelbaum then rolled up the sleeves of her shaggy jersey, catching her wrist in her dung-coloured pottery beads with a clank of copper bracelet as she did so. She knelt beside me to show me how to lie down on my side and relax completely; then she heaved herself up and put out the roof-light and put her drooping hat on the standard lamp to dim its glare.

195

'Now, breeze very deep. In . . . two-sree-four-five, and out . . . two-sree-four-five . . .'

I lay feeling very sleepy; Mrs Hindelbaum then told me to relax in turn my toes, feet, legs, then knees, until my entire body flopped heavily on the woolly rug.

Mrs Hindelbaum lifted up my flaccid hand and dropped it down, then she tested my leg.

'It's goot,' she said, pleased. 'You are very relaxed.' I heard her stand up, and bump into the table. Then her voice came soothingly. 'Imagine zat it is summer and you are lying on ze beach, in hot sun. You can hear ze sea and feel ze varmth.'

I did, and it was pleasant, until Mrs Hindelbaum suddenly brought in religion and chanted the next bit like a priestess.

'Feel ze spirit flow into you. Feel ze gootness and God's eternal peace and vonder flow and harmonise in you.'

I was half-annoyed. I opened one relaxed eyelid until I could see Mrs Hindelbaum's popping blue eyes staring raptly at some unseen Power and found it hard not to giggle.

Mrs Hindelbaum quietened after a minute and crooned, 'Just lie and be peaceful and breeze very deep,' and I lay doing that until I was almost asleep. When, after ten or fifteen minutes, I was gently roused by my beaming teacher, I felt refreshed and strangely grateful to the odd Teutonic lady.

As I was showing Mrs Hindelbaum to the door, the German woman sniffed at the aroma of my oxtail stew, which was bubbling away in the kitchen.

'You like to cook?' she asked. I nodded.

'Ah, you must have a haybox!' cried Mrs Hindelbaum, her parcels and cloak jerking excitedly, 'All you need is a big box filled with hay and you put in your pot of anything. Porridge, stew, soup, and ze hay will keep it varm and cook it for you all ze day ven you are at vork. It is vonderful and it cannot burn ze food. You must, you must haff a haybox!' She was intense and the haybox seemed to affect her with almost as much fervour as invoking the Deity had done.

I said goodnight, and went back to practice my deep breezing for a little. I fell asleep. Dreamt I was in a haybox, and was awaked by the smell of burning stew.

Chapter 31

During the Christmas holidays, which seemed to have come upon us all of a sudden, I first felt my child quicken. I was peacefully painting in the sitting-room one evening. Ben was at work in his small room – and at last he thought he was on a final draft.

There was snow outside; the little stove was roaring and I enjoyed looking at the blue and orange flames. I was drinking bitter-lemon and dipped my brush into it instead of the turpentine; I only noticed that I had done this because I heard the bubbles fizz in response to the brush. I was painting a small girl I had drawn in the street. There were chalk marks on the wall behind the child and a thrilling design of bell-pulls, and the child wore a very bright dress with little blue-and-yellow animals on a red ground. I was utterly absorbed, mixing a rich, cool grey and spreading it across the background to make the brilliant colours sing out, when suddenly I felt within my very centre a flutter, faint but sure, like a butterfly imprisoned. I held my breath and brush motionless for some moments and there was the flutter once more, then nothing.

Weak with emotion, I sat down. It was real, this child, it was an entity of its own, living inside me. I was

198

almost unbearably moved by the importance of the happening. I stared at our belongings in the room and the fire as though seeing them for the first time; I knew, all of a sudden, that my life would be different now that the knowledge of the baby was an actuality for me.

When Ben came through I told him and he hugged me and laid his palm on my tummy, filled with love and wonder.

'This is the most creative thing you've ever done,' he told me. But I resented that view, and never felt it to be true. It was a miracle, but it had nothing to do with my creative self. It had happened to me, but it was as autonomous as a cat in a sack, this growing, moving creature inside my body. But I longed with all my heart for when it would free itself from me and choose to be born.

We had a splendid Christmas. We were sure of Ben's golden future, and felt briefly rich, and spent a lot of money on flamboyant presents and food. Ma cooked us a meal on Christmas Eve – which is the Swedish time to celebrate. Mrs Mandel was there too, and my brother, several relatives, and Cordelia and Tony. There was paper all over the floor, candlelight, tinkling Swedish angel-chimes, cream, turkey and fulfilment.

Almost immediately after Christmas came the January sales. I put on my wellingtons, big black coat and fur hat and braved the melting slush. We needed some new mugs because I had used several for turpentine and oil-paints, and I had also broken most of the others in my impulsive and disorganised washings-up. I found some brown ones, which I liked, then I somehow found myself gazing into a large nursery shop. I felt that it would be tempting fate to stock up on nappies and baby-gowns when I was not yet four months pregnant, but my gaze fell on a ravishing golden-brown teddy bear. I could have sworn that he winked; he was plump with a black embroidered woollen nose, and kindly brown glass eyes, and was quite big. As inspired as I had been by the first sight of the mask, I knew I must have him. 'How much is he?' I asked an elderly black-clad assistant. 'He's very cheap, because he's a bit grubby and he's lost his squeak,' said the woman. 'He's reduced from four pounds to one pound.'

'Who wants a squeak anyway?' I asked myself. 'It would probably drive us dotty and even if it is a little grubby, it will get grubbier later.' I handed the woman a wrinkled, ink-stained pound note, pleased that the teddy was also a bargain. The woman wrapped the teddy up in a big bag and handed it to me.

I sat exultant on the bus and pulled open the bag just enough to gaze at him and dreamed of how my child would love him. Queen Kong, however, was sceptical. 'You say you want it for your baby? Humph. Time you emerged from your childhood, girl, or yours and your child's might clash.'

When we next had a meal with Mrs Mandel, the old lady asked if I had bought anything for the baby yet.

'Yes,' I said enthusiastically, 'I got a beautiful teddy,' and Mrs Mandel's eyes rolled towards the ceiling in dismay at the *mishegaassen* of her daughter-in-law, and as for her son, with that awful beard and those dreadful shirts, and that long face, he looked like God-alone-knows-what.

College started again and it was a term of real hard work. I drew, painted and attended lectures pretty regularly and amassed as much work as I could. I had to work especially hard now, in case there were problems with the pregnancy, or the baby came early. My motherhood books had pages about troubles like toxaemia and enclampsia but I felt well and buoyant. As my bulge became more obvious in the spring, I realised that it was in fact quite an asset if ever I felt exhausted and destitute of helpers – and sometimes I did. 'You should pad your tum,' I reminded Cordelia, who was complaining of tiredness from running after her little daughter all day. 'People will give you seats whether they are old or young and you'll be half-lifted on and off buses and given understanding smiles.'

Cordelia smiled hollowly. 'You take advantage of it, dearie,' she said, 'Because if you don't, in a few months you will regret the footstools and the pillows that were plumped and the cups of tea that were poured and the soothing words that were whispered. Believe me, it's tiring, this motherhood bit and I certainly don't want another one yet.'

Teeny Mary caused great drama at College by producing twins on Christmas Day. She breast-fed them, one on either side, and Zoe and I would draw her, fascinated.

Cordelia's daughter, now walking, had dark curls and sea-green eyes. The child was very small and startlingly beautiful. 'I'll paint her sitting on the floor in those brown clothes, with the sewing-machine behind her.' I determined, and Cordelia brought the baby several times so that I could draw her. The painting was done with only a few colours – ochre, umber, prussian, cobalt and white, and was successful and right in its own terms. I was even pleased enough to put this one on our wall. At College Willie Winkie twinkled at me after we had had a long discussion on how best to make chicken liver paté and had said, 'That wee painting of yours is very nearly a very nice painting. You're coming on.' I was thrilled. It was great praise.

Myfanwy came back a little after the term had started. She looked radiantly beautiful, with a burning, wild-eyed, yet desperately thin loveliness. She danced into class in a red woollen dress and we gazed at her. She had been in hospital for three weeks and had been given more radiotherapy because she had some lymphatic disorder. I spoke to her in the canteen and admired her dress and vivid looks.

'I've lost so much weight,' said Myfanwy, 'but I feel marvellously full of energy now. I got this dress in the children's department. I've got so thing that I fit a child's size. It makes my clothes very cheap.'

Pete became gentle and protective towards me, as my tummy grew larger. He was fascinated when I told him that my navel was sticking out like a little thumb. We arranged to draw each other one Saturday and Pete came to the flat for a whole day and he drew me looking intense and fecund in my smock, and I drew him gazing at me through his dark-rimmed glasses, with his long fingers on his cheek. He had sore gums, and I realised with a shock that he was as thin as Myfanwy.

'I'm scared to go to the doctor,' he confessed.

'What do you live on?' asked Ben.

'Buns, beer, chips and tea,' said Pete. He told us his father earned just over the limit for him to have a full student grant, yet refused to give him a supplementary allowance.

'I'm a chemist, Pete,' said Ben, 'and I think you're suffering from malnutrition. You must promise to go and see a doctor.'

The doctor told Pete that he had scurvy and the shocked Pete ate dozens of oranges until his gums mended. I knew it was Pete's birthday, and asked Ben if we could give him a sweater, as he was so ragged and cold. We were still being a little mad with money. Ben said of course we must, but that the spending spree must end, because he had bought a hundred pound washing-machine for Christmas (for the nappies), 'And darling,' he said seriously, 'We're going to have to move, you know. This house won't do us for more than the first few months of the baby.'

I was shocked by the realisation of it. The play, baby, the flat and my Diploma, occupied my mind almost entirely, but Ben was right. I would need a proper studio when I left College and the baby would need a room.

A house with two more rooms – but Ben needed a proper study – three more rooms. But when would Ben's next play be on to pay for it? When would it even be finished? Would I ever paint well enough to sell my work? I shrugged off these flashes of grim earnest reality and went to buy Pete a dark blue polo-neck. He was almost speechless with pleasure (and wore it daily to Graduation Day). He looked quite handsome in it and I was touched to see as he drew Alberto Rotondo that every so often he would gaze down at his sweater and wonderingly stroke the front.

At last Ben finished the play and sent it to Nigel. It had taken so long in the writing and had been so painful that I found it hard to be objective when I read it. I so wanted it to be good, but it seemed to me a grey play. The main character was a man of sixty-five who could be a star part for a leading actor like Guinness or Olivier, but I was afraid to become too enthusiastic after the disappointments of *Personal*.

But there was an immediate response. Nigel wrote a hurried, elegantly dashed-off note-written in a transatlantic airliner. 'You are a *marvellous* writer. More anon. Nigel.' It augured well.

We heard no more till he came back from America a month later. There was the tenseness of a constant hope that the telephone would ring, and a life-changing letter come through the door. At last Nigel wrote. In the nicest possible way, he said that he didn't like the play, and couldn't handle it in its present form.

'The bastard!' I shrieked, 'After that schmalzy note in delicious purple ink about your marvellous writing, and a four week wait. How dare he!'

Ben reacted in the only way he knew. He marched into the study, slammed the door, and started a new play. I went after him. 'Please,' I said, 'Ease up for a while.' But he wouldn't.

Then Marcus came to supper, and asked how things were. 'I hate the act of writing,' Ben spat out with awful bitterness. I listened, shocked and frightened. It seemed terrible to me that anyone coulsd so hate their art. I could see that he hated it because he did a full day's work, then came home, prepared lessons, did homework, did things about the house, and then had to go off and write into the small hours of the night.

It was not an easy life, and I longed for him to be free to be only a writer. I wondered about the future. 'I'll send you out to work,' Ben said several times; I didn't find that funny. What about Art? What about Art and the baby? And cleaning, shopping and cooking? It seemed more than enough for one life, even if Queen Kong had promised to help.

I grew larger and larger, and Ben found me beautiful. At the hospital I was prodded and listened to by several students, who pressed my mounded belly with little old-fashioned ear-trumpets and pitter-pattered the rhythm of the baby's heartbeats to me. The doctor let me use his stethoscope to listen to myself and I could hear my own steady blood-beat and the rapid tiny tickings of the embryo heart.

The baby used to roll around inside me and kick Ben in the back as we lay in bed. 'I'll be flying out of the bed in a few weeks at this rate,' he said. I loved to try to fol-

204

low the movements of the limbs as they pressed and slid away and prodded outwards as I imagined the child stretching or exercising.

At Easter we had our last holiday together before the child was due. We chose Iona. We crossed by an old steamer, filled with sheep and cows from the western mainland, to the small green island, set in turquoise sea. We picked flowers and searched for greenstones and found a strange succulent bog-plant with sticky leaves which ate flies, and we wandered hand in hand over the hills, enchanted by the sight of each other in woollen scarves and wellington boots. It was a blissful time, of reading, watching seagulls soar, climbing small hills, and exploring caves. We met an archaeologist, a woman, who fascinated us with tales of bones and brochts and picts and standing-stones and showed us as ancient fort where we found shards of ancient salt-glaze pots, but no adzes or arrow-heads, to my disappointment. I did a few drawings of rocks and sea. The ancient Abbey of the island was stone-built, beautiful and simple, with strong carved pillars topped with sculpted figures and leaves. We attended a couple of candle-lit services which were strangely peaceful and satisfying and we listened after-wards to a man who played heart-tearing gales of storms of music on a piano, oblivious to his silent listeners in the shadowy church. Ben argued with the Moderator of the Church of Scotland, who finally said God was a horizontal blur, so Ben stopped arguing.

On a sunset hill we dreamed.

'I'd like to give up teaching one day,' said Ben, 'This writing at night is a killer, and once the baby's here it will be even harder.' He sighed. 'And what are we going to do about space? The baby will need a room, and if we put it in the study where will I write? We'll have to move. We'll have to start house-hunting.'

Worriedly, I imagined Ben, hunched over a typewriter, balanced on a Moses basket filled with shrieking baby, and myself, surrounded by wet canvasses and dirty brushes heaped up in our small sitting-room.

'But houses cost so much. We'd need a studio as well as a study – and maybe help with the baby? An au-pair?'

He nodded. 'And we'll need a lodger to pay for the au-pair. We need quite a big house. We might be able to get a mortgage – we've still got a fair chunk of money from the London run, and you'll start earning when you leave College.'

I wished that I felt certain of that, I tried not to look at the gorilla's sceptical face. I couldn't see how what we had in the bank could ever buy a house – at least not the big house we both wanted.

Ben stood up and gazed towards the group of blue-and-purple islands to the north, with an orange-and-purple sky beyond. He pulled me onto my feet.

'Let's go and look at the *Scotsman* property columns.'

I hugged my bump and realised that there were four weeks to go before the Diploma exams started. I needed to mount and frame all my best work; there was a lot to think about.

Chapter 32

Two weeks before the exams started, Myfanwy disappeared. Zoe came in and said 'Have you heard?'

'No, what?'

'She's ill again, and you're only allowed so much of that X-ray stuff, Hector's in a dreadful state. Her mother is travelling up from Wales.'

I was aghast. 'How serious do you mean?'

'Nobody says, but it sounds awful. I mean to say, they don't give you X-ray therapy for ulcers or appendicitis, do they?'

I remembered how careful the radiologist had been to stand behind her lead shield when she X-rayed my tummy at the hospital a few days ago. It really must be serious.

The Saturday before the exams started my mother took me out, and bought lots of baby things – nappies, nighties, a bath, and a rush-woven Moses basket. We took them back to the flat, and Ben looked at them dazed. 'I'll have to make a box to hold them all,' he decided. He spent the whole afternoon designing its construction and went to buy the wood. He sawed and screwed and sanded and finally sealed, and we stood the box of plain yellow wood in the bedroom, and we put the nappies, sheets and covers inside. Mrs Mandel had quite a heap of little jerseys knitted and she gave them to me and they also went into the box. The teddy presided smugly on the shut lid.

The Diploma Life-painting pose was a nice one. We had a blonde girl with a hip-bath and a mirror, and we set up our primed and stretched canvases and started to draw in our designs.

Hector was in an agony of worry about Myfanwy, who was to be sent home by ambulance to Wales because the hospital could do no more for the moment. He said that she had asked for Zoe and me to visit her before she went. The day's Diploma work ended at four.

It was sunny, but rainy too. My black coat flapped and Zoe's brown hair whipped out of its stern bun and stranded across her face. We walked through the gardens under the grim dark grey castle, which crowned its sheer black rock, and stared across the city from its vantage point. Zoe had an umbrella and I was thrilled by the railings, and the incredible zig-zags their reflection made in the wet. It was fantastic, and Zoe with that umbrella! And everything twinkling like diamonds; what a world!

Even Zoe thought it was a magnificent afternoon and she pointed through the glittering trees, across the grey city roofs to the brilliant blue sea, where we could see far off a ship and the hills on the other side of the big sea-river. We were hungry, so near the bus-stop we bought a vast sticky bun each, with big square sugar crystals on their shiny orange domes. I held the paper-bag with the buns and looked around at the nearby shops.

'What can we take Myfanwy?' We saw a flower and vegetable shop and bought grapes and a bunch of blue flowers, which Zoe held tightly as we climbed on the bus. We sat in the front top seats so that we could look at the laburnums and copper beeches of the suburban gardens the bus would drive past.

Zoe looked worried and examined her posy. 'They're forget-me-nots. That's not being too obvious, is it?' she asked. Then she laughed an anguished, nervous laugh.

I opened the paper-bag. 'Have a bun,' I said. 'The flowers are beautiful, Myfanwy will love them.'

Zoe nodded and silently we ate the buns, powdering our chins and coats with sugar, and wondered what the visit would be like. Neither of us felt at all brave.

Myfanwy was almost translucent, her face a pale ivory against the startle of her black hair. She looked ethereal and still had an extraordinary, delicate and haunting beauty. Her arms were thin and bare, and her fingers ceaselessly plucked at her hospital sheets; she wore a thin, blue lacey nightie.

'It's lovely to see you,' she whispered. 'It will be awful for me to re-sit the Dip. next year, without any of you there.'

'Don't worry dearie,' said Zoe heartily. 'Probably most of us will be re-sitting anyway – and Kate here will need to use Mr Angelo as a babysitter during Antique.'

Myfanwy smiled. 'How are you Kate? You look blooming.'

'I feel marvellous,' I said. 'And the baby kicks and punches me all day long. I'm sure it'll be a boxer or footballer.'

Myfanwy loved her blue flowers. 'They're almost exactly the colour of the dress that my sister is making me for the Graduation Ball.' she said.

Zoe and I were aware of not catching each other's eyes. 'My mother is taking me home for a little,' said

Myfanwy, 'to recover from all this therapy – it makes me exhausted – but I'll come back for Hector's Graduation. Maybe I could wear flowers on the neck of the dress, it would look super.'

She was tired, after talking, and shut her eyes, her fingers still nervously pulled at the bed-linen. I walked quietly to the huge window, which looked back to the castle and dozens of towers and church spires. It was a splendid skyline, with hills all round behind the buildings. Across the small ward was another bed with an old woman in it, yellow-faced, with bird-like eyes. She grinned and nodded, then scrabbled in her locker and offered us each a boiled sweet to suck.

'She gets awful tired.' The old woman indicated Myfanwy, who still had closed eyes.

'We'd better be going,' hissed Zoe. I nodded, but a large woman with very dark curls and a sweet but anxious face came into the room, and walked towards Myfanwy, whose eyes opened and then she smiled.

'Hello Mum,' she said quietly. 'Meet Kate and Zoe. 'Ive told you about them.'

Myfanwy's mother had a musical Welsh voice and great gentleness of manner. She shook hands with us and sat down beside her frail daughter with much dignity.

We stayed as briefly as was polite, and Myfanwy's mother asked about College and the baby, then looked from me to her daughter. I wished that I could shrink, and pulled the big black coat across myself, as though to hide the ironic and inopportune reality of my bulge.

We touched Myfanwy's bony fingertips – which she still kept immaculately manicured and varnished pearly pink. 'Goodbye,' said Myfanwy. 'I'll see you at the Graduation – wheeling a pram, I hope.'

We walked silently through the polished corridors,

210

past big glass windows and into the open air and wet grass. We said nothing, and sat on the bus and instead of our reflections, saw only Myfanwy's plucking hands and desperate eyes.

At last I asked, 'Do you think she knows?'

Zoe shook her head. 'She won't allow herself to.' Then she said brusquely, 'Come on, let's get our men.'

She was right. Sex, food and oblivion were what we wanted. For once, Ben allowed me to drag him from the study, and later as we made love I tried to shut out my constantly-recurring images of Myfanwy's wasted body and of her hands holding the forget-me-nots.

Chapter 33

At College the students were dazed with work. We drew, painted, cut mounts and sawed frames. Pete met me one morning when I was staggering along the corridor with great bundles of boards and long pieces of wood. I was tired and heavy.

'Here, fellie,' said Pete gently, 'I'll take them. You go and have a sit.'

I nearly wept as I watched him lumber out of the studio, clutching an enormous painting of Saggy Jim, naked, in a bowler hat.

I was beginning to be nervous. The baby was due in exactly a week and although I knew that babies never came on time, I was convinced that mine would come on the appointed day. Mrs Hindelbaum looked in one night, wearing a frightening dress of violent yellow tartan, with hairy legs and feet in what looked like orthopaedic sandals.

'I vant to vish you luck,' she said, 'and vonce more to remind you of ze breezing.'

I was glad to see her and felt relaxed and confident again after she had gone. My own mother was a strength to me, when we talked about birth. 'It's a hard job of work,' she said. 'But you're used to hard work, and you just jolly well get on with it.' Mrs Mandel was no help. 'Don't you worry,' she said. 'Takki, God willing, everything will be all right.' Cordelia phoned almost every day to say, 'Haven't you had it yet?' and I tried to ferret out more details of her birth, remembering how shattered she had been after Catherine was born, but Cordelia was encouraging. 'Don't worry, Kate,' she said. 'It was hellish for me but it isn't for everyone and anyway, you've been practising breathing and doing all those exercises, it'll probably pop out like a piece of toast. If I ever have another baby I am going to make sure that I am pissed out of my mind, and am carried in singing.'

Ben was determined to be with me and see his child born; I was glad, I was aware of the empty Moses basket staring back at me from the top of the box, with its immaculate white pillow and soft blankets. It seemed impossible that it was up to me to fill it with a baby within the next few days.

My Dip. painting had a black cat in it, and I felt very daring and gave it a bright yellow anus – I needed that accent of colour just there. It also had a horse pulling a red milk-cart, and a couple of workmen reading a paper and a small girl with a bunch of flowers. I was conscious with every brush-stroke that it was my Dip. painting. Michael Phoenix flashed past me one day and saw that I was depressed. 'Use a warm neutral,' he said out of the corner of his mouth. I mixed greys with reds, purples and oranges, and tried them all in turn on the background, and became even more lost. I was sure some basic fact of painting hadn't percolated to me.

At last all the Dip. work was finished. The students drew lots to decide which wall they should hang their show on, and we hung up all the best of the year's work.

213

It was a hard day's work to hang a show, with the help of the staff, flitting from wall to wall, and aligning the bottoms of the paintings. I was exhausted, and certainly not happy with mine, and when I was finished I went to the pub with Pete and Zoe to drown my sorrows. We found Hector at the bar, kilted, and almost speechless from whisky.

'Are ye hung?' asked Pete. Hector looked at us dully.

Zoe came with our lagers.

'Are you all right, Hector?'

And to our horror, Hector, the great Highland teddy bear in his comical striped jersey, suddenly shut his eyes and burst into great rendering sobs.

'My God . . .' Our eyes met.

'Hector, is it Myfanwy?'

The sobs tore from him, and his shaggy head was buried in his great arms on the bar.

Tentatively I touched his heavy striped back.

'Tell us. Please.'

'She died this morning. She was in a coma. Seven o'clock.'

We were aghast. Death was not something any of us knew well.

'I'm going on a trawler,' said Hector. 'To Iceland. I'm going away.' He had stopped crying, and looked at us with unhappy injured eyes.

We didn't know what to say. We drank our lagers and cried, and I went to fetch my gear from College. I met Willie Winkie on the stairs.

'Shows all hung?' he asked.

I nodded miserably.

'And you think they're all terrible?' he asked, and I caught his smile. He took me by the arm.

'You know, Kate, you can only really begin when you leave College.'

I knew he meant to cheer, but it sounded hard to me. I

214

went home to Ben, but he was deeply engrossed with his note-book, and I couldn't even tell him about Myfanwy.

On the day the baby was due, I stood in the small bedroom looking at my great tummy; Ben and I were punctual people, so our child ought to be as well, oughtn't it?

I went to College and ate a picnic lunch with Pete and Zoe. Everyone was lying on the grass drinking coffee or beer. We went to look at the Diploma exhibitions of the various departments. Hector's was the best, we thought.

I wasn't happy about my show at all, and was eyeing it mournfully when a tall man in a suit came into the big studio and looked carefully at the paintings on the wall. He then went to my folio which lay on a table in front of my wall, and started looking through my drawings and lithographs, he was very absorbed, and I tried to feign disinterest by scrutinising the neighbouring exhibition – of porridge-grey canvases painted by a Little Knitter.

The man was looking at a self-portrait I'd done of myself in a smock. He smiled.

'Are these yours by any chance?'

'Yes.'

'I like your drawings very much. Especially the ones of children. I see that you've done a bit of illustration.' (There were some Christmas cards and a cookery book in the folio.)

'I'm an educational publisher, and we're always on the hunt for new artists. Can I give you my card? Maybe we can get together sometime?'

I gave him my name and address and took his, and wafted off to find Zoe. The baby was kicking furiously.

When suppertime came there was still no sign of my

waters breaking, or contractions starting. I supposed it would start after I had gone to bed. I went early to bed and slept like a cat, and was surprised to find the sun streaming into the room when I woke. Several days passed like this, and hourly I awaited a sign that the birth would commence. I felt laden like a rucksack, and longed for it to happen.

Ben shook off his gloom and took to reading property columns, and we went to view several wrecks of houses. We were depressed by the slums we saw, until we found an old two-storey house with eight rooms, including a huge flag-stoned kitchen, in a block of tenements. We fell in love with it; Ben was enthusiastic. It would give us a work-room each, family space, and a room we could let to pay for the au pair we had realised we would need for me to continue working. We decided it was the house for us. The owner, an old lady, was keen for us to have it, she didn't want it to become offices. Ben enquired about a mortgage, but they wouldn't look at him because the house was old and had subsidence. (From 1840, but subsidence nevertheless.) That information, in surveyor's fees, cost us a week's salary from school. Even if we borrowed some money from a relative, we were still seven hundred pounds short. It was impossible, even though it was incredibly cheap for all that space, being unmodernised.

When the baby was a week overdue, we were eating supper in my mother's kitchen, and I was blackly glum – convinced that either I had a phantom pregnancy or was going to remain in a perpetually suspended state of gestation.

My back ached, I was idly chasing baby legs and arms, when my tummy hardened rigidly all over, as though my muscles were clenching of their own accord. I said nothing, and my tummy relaxed. We all drank coffee. I watched the blue-flowered Swedish clock and noticed that my tummy was tensing up again and again, regularly, every few minutes. 'Hey,' I told Ben and my mother, 'My tummy's going funny every so often.'

The three of us tried to act unconcerned, and be cool and self-controlled, but watched the clock like hawks. Whenever there was a lull, Ben would ask, 'Hasn't it come yet?' Then after an hour or so of tummy-tightenings, Queen Kong appeared at the door, holding my ready-packed suitcase. 'Shall I call a taxi?' she asked.

'I think we'd better go,' said Ben.

The hospital was dark but for a lone weak bulb in the entrance hall. We waited and wondered, but nobody came. At last a nurse came and took me to a lift, where she pressed all the buttons in turn, but none worked; we went to a second lift and went up in it and I was led along a half-lit corridor to a cubicle where the nurse told me to strip, and handed me what looked like a knee-length flour-bag with square sleeves tacked onto it. I noticed, as I stood unglamorous and foolish, that the tummy tensing had stopped. 'I'll take your clothes to your husband, dear,' said the nurse, and disappeared with my belongings bulging in a huge sack.

A student nurse now entered and sinisterly fitted a sterile blade into a razor.

'We need to shave you now, dear; up on the trolley please.'

I hadn't been warned about the entire removal of my pubic hair. The student nurse was not experienced and it took her a long time, and I felt ridiculously exposed and immodest as the young girl breathed and puffed and scraped. When she was done, the nurse screeched through to the next cubicle, 'Come and see if I've done it right, Isa!' and Isa screeched back, 'Aye, and you come and see mine!'

I was then given an enema and vast amounts of water

217

were siphoned into me. I tried to count spots on the roof, not that there were any, but it was better than grinning idiotically at the nurse while she went about her business. Anyway, you can't smile with your nether lips.

When all this was over, including the dramatic aftermath of the enema, I was laid on a trolley, panting, and wheeled madly through long blackened corridors, hanging onto the iron head-rail for dear life.

The ward was dark and bare, with gaunt iron scaffolding for curtains silhouetted against several white heaps of pregnant women. I noticed that I had a bald neighbour with glaring eyes, and smiled feebly at her. The woman grunted and glared in return; then I was given a sleeping pill, which I accepted because I was exhausted. There was a clock on the wall which heaved and wheezed like an unhinged garden gate and there were loud thumps and crashes, wheel squeaks and the frequent hurried clattering of nurses' feet. I needed to pee and wished that I was at home and rang the bell beside my bed, which the nurse had shown me was there if I needed anything.

There was a violent electric alarm scream, and flashing lights. My neighbour heaved with rage and stared at me with smouldering eyes. A bedpan was eventually brought and I noticed that beds were wheeled in and out during the night. At 5.30 I woke, dizzy from my sleeping pill to the cheerful shout of 'Good morning girls! Coffee or tea?' which sounded like a holiday camp summons.

I drank my unwanted tea, had my temperature taken and went back to sleep, and was shattered awake by a stentorian voice saying, 'Get up and wash now girls!' I walked a mile to the familiar room where I had lost my pubic hair, then staggered back to sleep. With a clang,

218

batter and thud, breakfast was thrust upon me. Melancholically, I chewed a barely-buttered roll, and asked the red-haired breakfast lady if I might have sugar on my cereal; she raised her eyebrows. I grovelled and explained sycophantically that 'I didn't have sugar in my tea.' The woman sprinkled a few grains on the cornflakes and I chewed thinking miserably, 'Well there's no baby this breakfast.'

During the morning many people prodded my tummy, and took my temperature and asked accusingly, 'Have your waters broken? Any show? Any contractions?' I shook my head in answer to them all, and wanted to hide under my rubber sheet in shame.

My neighbour wasn't in fact, bald, but had half-a-pound of kirby grips stabbing her sulphur locks. I tried to chat, but the woman was indignant with frustration. She had been in the ward for two nights watching lucky labouring women being trundled in and out, but like myself, her contractions had stopped. I was told to get up and walk around. I did this with frequent visits to the lavatory, which, I discovered, was also used by the new mothers. They seemed victorious and self-confident, sported fresh lipstick and newly-curled hair and spoke proudly of 'ma wean' or 'mai little boy'. 'Nine pounds faive.' 'Six pounds two.' I wilted and hugged my bump, my face haggard, my hair lank.

Back in the ward, I lay reading, until a cheerful thirty-seven-year-old woman was wheeled in, blooming with expectation. She was thrilled to be having her first child after thirteen years of marriage, and was having strong contractions every three minutes. We chatted for a time between contractions till she realised that she too had gone off the boil, so I had company. The gorilla seemed to have gone on holiday.

The women in the ward were chatty. 'Did you have

an anenema?' I had a vision of sea-growths and flowers. 'It's like a sword slitting ye.' 'There ought to be a law against this.' I was becoming depressed and angry with the bald woman who was constantly moaning and complaining, which demoralised the other people in the ward.

One of the nurses asked brightly as she patted the bald woman's pillows, 'What does that man of yours want?' There was a silence and the glaring eyes filled with tears. She didn't have a man.

A girl across the ward was sick.

'Any contractions dear?'

'Have your waters broken yet?'

'I've had a fine show.'

'Five minutes.'

'Oh, my God!'

'Three minutes.'

'Nurse!'

Maybe a bookie would do well in this place, I mused. The hospital should lay on a maternity tipster.

'Mrs Mactaggert had a wee girl, yes, a wee girl and Mrs Robertson's still in there.'

I wondered if I would be pregnant in a month's time. I got out of bed again and sat with the other women who were allowed up, beside the silent, cold telly, and read old raggedy magazines. They gooed over pictures of babies; everybody except me seemed to have decided on a name and I listened avidly in case somebody suggested the name which I would suddenly recognise as the right one for my baby.

'It would be nice if it came before the visiting hour.'

'Aye, it would an' all.'

'I'm a month late.'

'I'm two weeks early.' Some of the women smoked furtively. There was a small, frightened girl, with a face dark with freckles. She was terrified because she and her sister had had a double wedding and both fallen pregnant simultaneously and all had been a delight, until the sister had lost her baby the week before. I was devouring a Superman comic when I was ordered to go to get my tummy prodded. The prodding made me need to go to the bathroom and by the time I had walked the long walk there and back, I needed to go again.

The doctor who prodded me talked across me and said to the nurse. 'Mrs Mandel is just thinking about it.'

Hospital cooking, it seemed to me, consisted of three stages. Stew, boil and chew, so that all the ingredients are reduced to clay.

'Ma Goad!' shouted Baldie, 'The lettuce is smothered in slugs!'

I longed to be home. The curly-haired girl now seemed to be in great pain, so I rubbed her back for her, until she was whisked away. I was now the sole survivor of the night, everybody else in the ward had gone into proper labour, even Baldie.

Suddenly to my great surprise, an old schoolfriend of mine was wheeled in. She was a girl called Jane and I hadn't seen her for at least three years and had no idea that she was married or even pregnant. We greeted each other, but Jane was too busy with her contractions to be more sociable. Supper came, which was also clay, green and runny.

I noticed that Jane looked white, and waited for the visiting hour when I would see Ben. He was the last to arrive, with a huge bunch of red-and-pink flowers and we shared a feast of cherries whilst I stroked his chest with the back of my hand. Jane was wheeled out half-way through the visiting hour. When the husbands had to leave, I walked along the corridor with Ben, and

221

we saw two new babies being carried out of the labour room; one of them was wearing a little green hat. Ben held me tightly, and I went to wash and put the flowers in a beaker, hoping that I would see them in the mother's ward in the morning. The women in the ward were again all thermometered, prodded, drugged and given cocoa, when to my great surprise, Jane was wheeled back in.

She looked utterly lovely and seemed to glow. She patted her flat tummy and said, 'I've got a son now. I had him in half-an-hour.'

I was amazed and pleased for her. 'I saw him come,' said Jane. 'It was marvellous. I feel great.'

I couldn't take my eyes off her. The thirty-seven-year-old woman was now wheeled off to the labour ward, and another demoted, off-the-boil woman, with whom my sympathies lay, was wheeled in. A little blonde girl and another couple of women were having hard contractions, and the demotee and I were full of envy.

In the morning, thinking that I could beat the system, I got up at 5.30 to go and wash, in order to be able to sleep for two hours. I was deep in a sunlit morning doze after this, when there was a clatter, bash and shout.

'You're all to get up and bath girls!'

Weary, bleary, squinting and sick, I bathed again, put on a new hospital flour-sack, embroidered in red with LW for Labour Ward, on the neck, and the hospital's name where I hoped the baby's bottom was.

There was marmalade for breakfast, which was bliss. I phoned Ben, who was a nervous wreck and hadn't slept, then I walked corridors all morning.

'Have your waters broken?'

'Any show?'

'Any contractions?'

'Yes, she had a wee boy, Victor.' – that was the thirty-seven-year-old first-timer.

'She had twins.'

'Hers isn't quite here yet.'

The demotee was sent home. I asked the Ward Sister if I could go home. 'No,' she said. I fought for sleep. There were more proddings and trumpets put on my tum. 'Please God, don't let me widdle,' I prayed. And I still had no sign of a contraction.

New women were wheeled in – all on the point of producing offspring. I supposed that I might now be present but still pregnant at the Graduation ceremony in two days time. What, I wondered, if the baby decided to stay put? Could anybody be pregnant for ten or eleven months? – after all, the curly-haired girl said that she was four weeks overdue and indeed I could have judged her to be six or eight weeks overdue from her size, unless she was having triplets.

After lunch I was told that I could go home. They must have met me pacing the corridor too often, or heard all my phone calls, I thought. I nagged them for my suitcase. They looked relieved when I left.

'See you soon dear,' said the little blonde nurse, flourishing an enema. I wondered if I would be shaved again when I came back.

Then I was home to the bliss of my own bed and soft toilet-paper. Mrs Mandel came with more baby clothes; I was past believing in my state, it was all unreal. I phoned Cordelia and made her roar with laughter at tales of the hospital – and say comfortingly, 'Oh yes I knew a woman who was in for a week like you.'

'Why does it have to happen to me?' I wondered and resigned myself to a week or two of good books, until the reluctant child decided to make itself known to its parents. I went to bed, relieved to feel the comfort of Ben beside me, but filled with slight unease. Surely the later the baby, the harder the pain. It would be bigger, wouldn't it? And that would hurt more.

Chapter 34

After a lazy day spent doing very little I started counting contractions again. They were slight – nothing to make one weep or drink sherry, and came every five minutes. Ben and I had supper and clock-watched assiduously, again pretending not to be neurotic. I didn't want another false alarm, so we waited until they came every three minutes before calling a taxi.

There was once more the long dark wait under the bronchial clock, while the hospital night-staff searched for my card. The rows of empty chairs in the reception room stood starkly in neat straight rows, supervised by the silent, forbidding presence of the weighing-machine, which always made me feel guilty. Ben paced about and looked at the dried-up models of the Ideal Diet, and we measured our heights against the wall-ruler, and watched the clock pace its way through the night.

I was taken away at last, torn from Ben.

'They've promised to phone me whenever the baby is really almost there,' he comforted me.

Again I was given a list of questions. 'You *are* Kate Mandel? You *are* twenty-two years of age?' and yet again, 'Have your waters broken? How often are your contractions?' My almost bald pudenda was again shaven, and I was bathed and dealt with as before, heaved onto a bed, then wildly wheeled past flashing lights and hurrying nurses.

This time the ward was a labour ward proper with no off-the-boilers. There were three white heaps of women and all of them grunting and heaving. The fourth one I would never forget. She lay and snored ceaselessly, making a noise that I would not have believed possible to emerge from a woman – or, for that matter, a man. Rhinoceroses running a race, several broken tractors or a couple of steam engines could hardly have competed with her. She was having her seventh child, another woman stopped to inform me at dawn. A brittle, falsely gay nurse tripped in with four huge pills nestling in a spoon. I hated taking drugs and asked if it wouldn't spoil my chances of being awake and alert for the birth; the nurse gave a Draculine laugh, 'Don't you worry, dear, you'll need more than that when your pains start in earnest! This is merely the *hors d'oeuvres*,' with which chilling information she shovelled the pills down my astounded gullet.

The contractions were fast – three minutes for an hour – then they slowed to every five minutes for the rest of the night, so there was no sleep, despite the pills. I relaxed and did my deep breathing as best I could and thought it helped a little, but during the actual pain-spasms I didn't find the breathing of much use. I rubbed my own sacrum, and that was a comfort, and I longed for Ben or somebody to be with me, it would have helped so much. Sadly, Queen Kong had deserted me. At her first sight of the labour ward she'd said 'I'm off,' and lurched off down the corridor as fast as she could lurch. I felt very alone. Between contractions I watched the other women groaning, walking

226

restlessly about, or muttering indignantly at the pain, in the darkened room. It was interesting to see how differently people reacted to pain; some became aggressive, defensive, feeling that they were being got at, and others made as much row as possible, the noise seemed to be a release for them. But mostly they quietly and bravely got on with the job.

Dawn came and found most of the women awake, although it was only five a.m. I couldn't eat, but gratefully drank iced orange juice. Early in the morning, I was wheeled into a room of my own with a large window full of sky and was left to get on with it. The nurses this time were kind and friendly and made me feel cared for. I was shocked by the soreness of the contractions and by the slowness of the first stage. I had been certain that my labour would be quick and easy, and the unexpected reality of the pain was bewildering.

The hours passed, I was dopey from an injection, but each pain was sharp, like a rusty curved Samurai sword carving slowly through me and splitting me gradually in two. I was enormously relieved whenever the pain stopped, and I could catch up with myself. At least they were rhythmic, these contractions, not erratic and unpredictable.

I wanted Ben. My back was raw and chafed from where I had rubbed myself, through the hospital nightie.

In the afternoon I lay alone in the streaming summer sun and cried with the pain; I knew I was clutching at the bars of the bed, and howling, when I heard a nurse's voice say:

'None of that now, dear; only Elizabeth Taylor is allowed to do that in films.'

Bereft of help or hope, I raged within myself at the nurse's silly ignorance and cruelty. I was sure that

227

something was wrong, and was certain that the child was grinding away, unsuccessfully trying to get out. This feeling was borne out by the arrival of a woman doctor who came and broke my waters with a painless snip. She showed me a steel dish of the watery-yellow liquid when I asked to see it, and was gentle and comforting and, after feeling my tummy she said that the baby was a whopper and must be at least nine pounds. I heard the doctor and nurse whispering and looking worried. 'What does O.P. mean? I asked, repeating the term they had just used.

'Oh, its just a private term we use, dear,' soothed the doctor.

'Oh, aye,' I thought. 'I believe that,' but just then the nurse leaned over to say that Ben was coming soon, so I must be making progress after all.

The woman doctor told me that I was four fingers dilated and to be careful not to push until I was told.

'You have a beautiful pelvis, dear,' she said. 'A perfect pelvis, don't worry. You're built for this job.'

I was given a mask on a tube which reminded me of childhood wartime gas-masks. I had intended to reject all drugs, but grabbed at the mask and sucked the gas greedily. It didn't make me unconscious, but took the edge off the pain a little. Ben at last appeared, looking funny in a white mask, hat and gown. I, woozy from trilene, gazed lovingly at him and asked, 'Did you reach the Valley of the Kings?'

He sat quietly and held my hand and I gulped trilene.

I heard the nurse say, 'The head is showing,' I surfaced and surged with excitement. 'Can you see it? What's it like?' I kept asking Ben. I felt the head popping in and out, and tried to sit up and see it, but was firmly pushed back into my supine position.

'The hair is black,' said Ben. 'It's marvellous!'

'Push harder dear, push harder,' said the nurse.

I imagined that I was going to turn myself inside out. It was like being constipated to infinity. I was certain that the baby was about to come out. The nurse listened with her trumpet for the foetal heartbeat and there was a sudden pause and terrible seriousness.

'Forceps,' somebody whispered briskly.

'Please! No! Please!' I shrieked, desperate. 'Don't hurt my baby!' And Ben was made to leave. And I was rapidly wheeled into the delivery-room, terrified, and utterly alone.

I was slid onto a bed with steel struts jutting up like bedposts on either side of its end. There were white slings attached to these, and a young doctor was there, in little white gumboots and cap, with serious brown eyes above his mask. My feet were fitted into the slings so that my legs hung in front of me, like a prisoner in the stocks, and a large green waterproof sheet was put across my knees so that I could see nothing but green sheeting and the doctor's face. I sucked in the trilene whenever it was offered, greedily inhaling all I could, and I pushed, and pushed, possessed and ravished by the autocratic and tidal demands of my body. There was half-a-minute of searing agony and I let out a great yell, then the pain stopped suddenly and I felt a warm squirm on my thigh. I knew it was the baby, but there was no cry and no more movement. And I asked and asked again.

'Is it all right? What is it?'

At last a voice told me quietly, 'It's a girl,' and, 'The baby is born, dear,' but I could see nothing but the serious eyes of the young doctor cutting the huge and shining purple corkscrew of the baby's umbilical cord.

I knew that the baby had been removed; I hadn't seen her at all, or been allowed to touch my daughter. I lay filled with terror for the child and watched with dull half-interest as the doctor caught and eased out the afterbirth, which was also pushed out from my body, in the same way as the baby. It was, I recognised, exactly like a plate of liver – only it had scalloped edges. 'Is the baby all right?' I asked. 'Is the baby all right?'

A nurse sat with me quietly holding my hand, and told me that the baby's heart had got a little slow, and they were giving her oxygen. There was still no yell. I wondered if the child was dead. If she were how utterly empty Ben and I would feel.

I looked across to my left and saw three of four gowned and capped medical backs. They were still and serious and were standing intently round a small leaden-coloured head with tubes and machine things leading to it. They looked like people at a graveside. One of the masked people saw that I was watching, and whisked a big green curtain across to hide them.

There was a whimper. I lay, with the nurse holding my hand. Then at last there was a howl. The nurse said, 'That's your baby.' I lay in a daze. Ages and ages passed, then they brought my new daughter to me, wrapped in a pink towel, her head slightly bloody and damp, wisps of dark hair and a definite little nose – with a smattering of small white pores across it. Lovely, clean, unbruised skin, a tight concentrated crease be- tween her brows and eyes firmly closed. She looked tired out and her expression said 'Leave me alone.'

I looked at the child and realised that I felt almost shy of this unknown person. The baby was such a definite creature. I was utterly exhausted and lay numbed in mind and body, whilst the doctor worked with great concentration, sewing up my torn skin. My feet were still in the stocks and I watched his serious eyes. 'Immodest,' I thought, then turned to the baby and

230

said, 'Hello.' The baby was whisked away. Hot tea and toast was brought. No drink ever tasted so beautiful; I sipped it blissfully, then at last Ben was allowed in to see me. He had had the most awful hour of his life, and had thought that both the baby and I were dead.

'The baby is lovely,' he said, 'Tremendously determined, she looks.' He wasn't allowed to stay long, but he promised to come back in the evening at visiting-time.

I was wheeled along the familiar corridor again. It looked quite different from my new vantage point, across a flat stomach. The labour ward nurses of the last few days recognised me, grinned and asked what the baby was.

The ward was a big one: I recognised a couple of the women from downstairs. We compared sexes, sizes and baby's names, but I didn't know. Then there were bed-pans, cups of milk, and supper, which I started on but sicked up at once. I had never felt so tired in my life: I had conversations with people as though through a glass partition. The other women's babies were then all brought in to be fed, and I watched emptily for mine, but she wasn't brought – I had a half-memory of the labour room nurse saying that I might not see the baby for twenty-four hours, because of her heart weakness. Ben arrived and I promptly wept on him.

He was wearing a red jersey, beaming and carrying a large bunch of purple irises. Nobody had told either of us what the baby weighed.

All the fathers looked cocky and had bags filled with magazines and presents. For visiting-hour the women's hair suddenly reared into careful waves and curls, lipstick flashed onto rosy faces and eyes sparkled above bright fluffy bed-jackets. Then the fathers trooped through to look at their offspring. Ben came back and said he'd waited in a queue to see the babies held up at the glass window. As each turn came, the fathers gawped at their tiny doubles. Our baby, he said, was beautiful, but her eyes were still tightly closed and she was asleep.

My baby was brought through to me the next morning. She was wrapped in a white blanket this time, and had a plastic identity bracelet on her wrist which read 'Baby Mandel'. I unwrapped her entirely from all her swaddlings and gazed in wonder at the sweet perfection of the solid little body. The gorilla had come back on the scene now; I was glad. She sat beside me on the bed and counted the baby's tiny toes and fingers with her great paws.

'She's wonderful,' she said, and I saw her surreptitiously wipe her eye with the back of her paw, and sniff.

The baby's eyes were open, and very dark, and she had tiny folds, almost like corners on the top of her ears, which were downy with dark hairs – like baby rabbit-ears.

Her solid little back was downy too. Her tiny nails reminded me of the minute pink shells I used to find on a dawn-washed holiday beach; her fingers were long and she was unbelievably beautiful, rosy and perfect, and, today seemed at peace with the world. The birth had been difficult because she had been lying on her tummy instead of her back.

'Very distinguished entrance,' said Ben. 'She is her father's child. She wanted to see where she was going.'

O.P. meant face to pubis. It was just bad luck that she was round that way, the doctor said. And Zoe wrote a note saying that Richard the Lionheart had been born that way, and it was supposed to indicate a determined and unusual personality.

The night before, when I lay childless, I had glared at

the women who'd had sons, but now that I saw and held my daughter, I was enchanted, and thought how silly I had been to think a boy could possibly be better.

Next day I was positively shell-shocked. My marvellous natural childbirth and gateway to golden motherhood had gone for a Burton, and I wondered to myself how many women turned into neurotic wrecks after the shock of a difficult birth. I had the 'blues' and wept, filled with frightened thoughts about coping with the massive new responsibilities, and wondering if I would ever be a decent painter.

The bully of a Sister – middle-aged since she was eleven – stopped at my bed and gazed steelily at me.

'Tidy your hair, Mrs Mandel,' she ordered coldly. 'You look like an artist.'

I glared back at her.

'I am an artist,' I said aloofly, and watched with quiet enjoyment as Queen Kong lifted the thrawn spinster up with an easy gesture, and hurled her down the length of the ward like a shot-putter's weight; she landed on her head, cupped on her white cockatoo of a hat, on a trolley, which in turn waltzed her out through the glass double doors to the huge spiral staircase, where it lurched and spiralled down and around until she was deposited in a gibbering crumpled heap on the marble floor of the main hospital entrance. A joyful sight. I turned over and tried to sleep before the next feed.

The hospital regime for new mothers was amazing. The patients would be advised by bright and understanding nurses to 'Take a lot of rest, dear, relax, and sleep all you can', and then they would be subjected to the same seventeen-hour shift of almost ceaseless incident. From five a.m. reveille till cocoa time at night I blearily surveyed the world through a clattering of bedpans, and violent crashes of dropped steel containers,

233

and slammed doors. It was as though the hospital kept a butter-fingered maniac in permanent residence, whose job it was to mark out the day by dropping or clattering every enamelled or steel object he or she could find.

For four days the new mothers were kept firmly in bed and I was grateful for this, because I had a constant sawing pain like toothache in my stitched parts. For a few days I could hardly turn, sit or lie. Feeding the baby would have been delightful, but I was reduced to the shakes from the strain of protecting the punished area and also from leaning on an elbow, trying to stop the baby's head from rolling off the bed onto the floor.

After about two days 'The milk came in', which was deeply dramatic. I woke to discover that my breasts were swollen as large and hard as half-melons, all blue-veined and bulging. The baby, who had wired onto the nipple during the first two days, with no problem at all, likewise plugged onto this new huge breast and sucked passionately, so that the breast deflated like a balloon with a leak. As the child sucked, I could feel in my own body how the shrunken uterus, which had held the baby, quivered within my newly-flat stomach in response to the baby's sucking.

Early morning was a time for bedpans and tail-swabbing – which last varied in awfulness according to which nurse did it. There was one huge, sweaty nurse, who bustled in with a heaving of bosom and hip, and always managed to slam into my bed with her mighty buttock, almost collapsing the bed as she did so, making me gasp in agony as my stitches seared – and at the same time sending the medical chart smashing to the ground from the bedrail. She would then proceed to swab my afflicted private parts, turning red and hot as she did so, breathing through great flared nostrils with a touching

234

dedicated intensity, as she searched for the tenderest parts and scraped them with her emery-block of cotton-wool and red hot Dettol. This done, she would pull back the curtains with such energy that they flew round the rail and landed in a bunched-up mass at one corner of the bed, leaving me naked and perched on the bed-pan, revealed to all who passed, before she puffed off busily towards her next victim.

Every morning at six a.m. the babies were brought in – they were always laid out in a row, wrapped in tight little white parcels, in lots of about ten, on a trolley topped with a plain, white tray, with sides about five inches deep. If they weren't all making an orgiastic symphony of wails, bleats and rattling whimpers, they would lie, blissfully unaware of anything but the sensual delights of sucking energetically at the bald head of the neighbouring baby. I remembered the previous New Year Mrs Mandel had given me a box of sweets which were little candy babies in pink and blue, laid out in two neatly matched rows – and these trolleys of babies looked just like that. When they had been fed, the nurses would cover the white box – heads, toes and all – with a big white sheet, and wheel the resulting anonymous white linen box, sighing, burping, sniffing and whimpering on its way.

Big Jeanie opposite me, had called for a bedpan in the night, and had been fair worried in case she'd wakened the rest of the women, because her two wee bullets had clattered round the pan like cannonballs.

'How's yer bust dear?'

'Fine, dear, still a bit hard, but it's got thousands of wee red spots on it.'

'Ma bust's all flabby again.'

'Oh, mine's dripped a' ower the bed.'

235

'Has yer bowels worked yet?'

'Naw, I'm waiting till I get back tae ma castor oil. I ken fine thae anenamas hae made me constipated.'

By the sixth day the stitches-pain had subsided, and my memory was already dulled. I had to make a conscious effort to remember the hell of it, and even my own vow – sitting enthroned as on knives on a forgotten bedpan – that I wouldn't go through this again for anything, was distant.

It was a great joy to have a flat tummy again. I felt it every day, greeting my newly-emerged contours with delight. The baby was an indescribable pleasure to me.

'She's so funny,' I told Ben. 'Nobody ever told me how funny babies could be. She cries madly if she loses hold of the nipple, and then I plug her back on and she sucks and gulps until she sounds like a full hot-water-bottle when you lift her up. I'm sure she's terribly intelligent.'

'Of course,' said Ben smugly, 'She sounds almost human.'

He had brought me news from College. I had gained my Diploma, but the Post-Dips had gone to nobody that I ever thought would be a painter, except for Big Hector who had been awarded a year's scholarship. I hoped that he would come back from the fishing-boat at the end of the summer, with his heart less broken. The Little Knitter's boring, diligent and incessant work had won them both post-graduate scholarships and that really hurt, although I knew that my Diploma show wasn't very good. My work was original maybe, but competent it was not, as yet. Zoe had never expected one, but Pete, like myself, was all set to be a famous painter, so it hurt him too that his talents hadn't been officially recognised. Zoe told Ben that she and Pete had clapped madly when my name was read out at the

Graduation ceremony, but I supposed they had clapped alone. I felt very sorry for myself, and wondered what on earth it would be like living and trying to work with this autocratic but enchanting little person, whose very hunger-cries made my breasts ache, and fill with milk. It was all frightening and I hated the hospital and wanted to go home.

In the morning Big Jeanie talked of wearing ordinary clothes and said of her huge elasticated maternity knickers:

'I'm economic. I'll cut oot the gusset and make a wee coatee.'

The restless mothers laughed (and wept) till their beds rattled. The cleaning-lady, Bella was a wonder of cheerful couthiness.

'Aye,' she'd say as she polished the vast expanse of green linoleum, 'They go up easier than they come down, thae weans,' and, 'You're all the same, you lassies. Ye cannae wait tae get in here, and then the minute ye're in, ye're screaming tae get out.'

And Jeanie said of me, whom she saw had made Ben bring me pickles and salad-dressing to relieve the hospital food, 'I can see ye wi' your wee fancies, dearie, and I seen ye snogging away wi' yon beardie o' yours. I'm telling ye, ye'll be back in here before next summer.'

'No fear,' snorted Queen Kong, and swung off through the jungle, intent on making herself impregnable.

Ben had announced the birth in the *Scotsman,* and this resulted in a mountain of advertising literature being sent to me. I was inundated with advice on contraception and powdered milk.

'You take heed,' urged Queen Kong. 'You're not going through that again, not if I can help it.'

I was boredly leafing through the mail, when I came

237

across a letter addressed to me in my maiden, or what I hoped would be my professional name. I was surprised to see that it was from the man in the suit who had admired my drawings in the Dip. show. I had forgotten all about him. He was offering me a job, illustrating work-cards for schools. Primary schools. He wanted pictures of children weighing things, counting beans, and pouring sand. He needed a lot. Hundreds. And he needed them by Christmas.

I told Ben almost before he'd sat down at visiting-time. He looked even cockier today. I noted fondly.

'It's a helluva lot of work,' I said dubiously.

'It would need to be a lot of money.'

'But when could I do it?'

'Between feeds. We'll get an au pair.'

'But we've no room.'

Ben was grinning. 'Oh, yes, we have.'

'Huh?'

My husband was being obscurely gleeful.

'Darling, what is going on?'

He took a deep breath, and sat back in his chair.

'We've got the house.'

I thought he was joking, 'What do you mean?'

'I mean we've got the house.'

'The lovely one? The big one?'

He nodded. 'Our offer was accepted an hour ago. The old lady saw the announcement in the *Scotsman,* and because it was a girl she decided to let us have it for two hundred pounds less.'

'But we still didn't have enough. We were seven hundred pounds short.'

He beamed wider. 'Something else happened.'

'What, for God's sake?' I shrieked.

'*Personal*'s been sold to the telly. Five hundred quid!'

238

I gawped and grinned as wide as Ben, and he held my hand.

'So we're householders.'

I couldn't believe it. Queen Kong was already in the house, carrying our sofa on her head, and she swung from picture-rail to picture-rail, yodelling with joy. I saw her hang the mask up on the wall, and next she was on the doorstep, complete with paint-tin and brush, feverishly painting the front door a brilliant red.

'When can we get in?'

'In about a month.'

'How will we move our stuff?'

'We don't have very much. Tony says he'll move us in his van. And Cordelia.'

I was bemused. 'And what about this illustrating job. How can I do it?'

'Go and see him in a couple of weeks, when you're on your feet. I'll phone him and say yes, in principle, if you like, if you can agree the money and time. And I'll say you could start after we've moved.'

'I'll have a studio. And you'll have a lovely study . . .'

'Yes. And we'll get a lodger when the new term starts, and Mrs Hindelbaum has a niece who could come and be our au pair.'

It was almost too much to take in. Ben left me, and I fed the baby in a state of dazed euphoria, and imagined all the lovely junk I'd have to buy to furnish the enormous house. I could hardly wait.

Chapter 35

At last I was allowed to go home. It was extraordinary to dress in normal clothes again; the skirt did up with difficulty, and I felt oddly wobbly. At home there were presents for the baby and flowers all over the place. I proudly laid Natasha, as we had agreed to call our daughter, in the Moses basket in the corner of the room. The mothers came and argued as to whether the baby was a Lawrence or a Mandel. We presumed that they were both right.

At the hospital I had been advised by my serious young obstetrician 'not to resume marital relations' until my check-up six weeks after the birth. This sounded pretty interminable, but at least we were back in bed together. The snag was, that being a nursing mother made by breasts untouchable to Ben, for they filled with milk at the slightest caress, as well as at the baby's cry.

The joy of the child was enormous. The little girl smiled ridiculously early, and seemed to know what was going on. She was rounded, beady-eyed, and had a warm grin that melted our innards. I watched Ben as he bathed her and sang to her and soaped her solid little body. But there were also broken nights, and the sitting-room got clogged with nappies and paints, as well as tea-chests which we packed with belongings, ready for our removal to the new house.

Tony moved us in his van with a large cow painted on the side (advertising animal feedstuffs). It took four trips across the city, as we were moving to the older part. Cordelia helped us to hump our few pieces of furniture, and our one-and-a-half carpets.

'It's a huge house,' said Tony. 'Are you going to keep breeding to fill the empty spaces?'

I lay in bed and cried on our first night in our new, bare and dusty bedroom. It seemed a huge and cheerless task suddenly, and Natasha was always wanting to be fed. If she cried, I cried, and my breasts leaked in sympathy.

But the next morning things seemed better, the house was golden with late summer sun, and we hung up some pictures and put the mask on the sitting-room wall. It looked wonderful with more space to offset it. Ben was delighted to have a decent-sized study, and I set my easel up in the room that was to be my studio. The old lady whose house it had been had left a simple table that I intended to do my primary school work-cards on.

We had been in the house for a couple of weeks when Mrs Mandel decided to visit us unexpectedly. It was a Sunday, and Ben was typing out his play, in his new study. My heart sank when I saw my mother-in-law. I was busy drawing Natasha (I needed to draw a baby being weighted for my educational cards), and it was going well. Neither Ben nor I wanted to be disturbed.

Mrs Mandel swept in with a basket bulging with parcels. 'I was just passing,' she said, 'I was at the Yiddishe shops, and I thought you might like a few things. And I'd love a cup of tea.'

'You can't stop your drawing in the middle!' yelled Queen Kong in outrage.

241

'Don't worry,' I said. Mrs Mandel pushed past me into the sitting-room, and gasped when she caught sight of her grand-daughter, naked and gurgling, on a rug set on bare floor-boards in front of the gas-fire.

'Oh! Dear! Isn't she cold? Are you bathing her?' The older woman set her parcels down on the sofa, and held out her arms, waiting for me to give her the child.

'I'm sorry,' I said firmly. 'You'll need to sit for a few minutes. I'm just drawing her. I must finish it.'

I was annoyed to be disturbed, but was cussedly pleased at the same time, to be seen to be at work. Maybe one day she would realise that I was now a professional artist.

'Can't I hold her?' asked Mrs Mandel in disbelief.

'No. I need her down there.' I picked up my block and pencil and tried to concentrate.

'Mrs Mandel sighed noisily and shook her head, and sank unhappily onto the sofa, still wearing her hat and coat.

'Where is Ben?' she asked at last. I drew the baby's back with one swift curve, I was getting places.

'He's writing. Typing out the latest play.'

'Is that the one for the television?'

She never quite understood. 'No. That was the one that went to London.'

'I see,' she said, but I knew she didn't. She shook her head sadly at Natasha. 'Wee soul,' she said, 'She must be freezing.'

Natasha cooed blissfully.

I redoubled my concentration and started a new drawing, trying to capture the solidity and softness of the round little body.

'Shall I make a cup of tea?' asked Ben's mother at last.

'Ooh, that would be lovely,' I said, dreading what my

242

mother-in-law would or wouldn't find in the shambles of the barely extant kitchen, but desperately wanting some peace to finish my work.

Mrs Mandel went through and there were some clatters and bangs and then she came back, looking dazed. 'Its funny,' (she fibbed) 'but I can't find any tea at all, or coffee, or even milk.'

'I'm sorry, there isn't any,' I said calmly, drawing the baby's starfish hand, 'We didn't shop yesterday.' Mrs Mandel winced visibly at the 'we'. Fancy her son shopping. 'We've really only got some soup and a couple of eggs in the house,' I continued matter-of-factly, 'and Government orange juice.'

'Well, is there not a shop open so you can go and buy some milk and tea?'

'The nearest one that's open on a Sunday is miles away,' I said. 'I'm sorry, but we decided just to do without until tomorrow. We were both frightfully busy.'

'It's lucky I brought something,' said Mrs Mandel.

'I'm grateful,' I said absently turning my sheet of paper over, and starting another drawing. The last one really looked like Natasha's legs, I thought approvingly.

Mrs Mandel went to her basket and started to unpack the parcels. 'Now Kate,' she said, 'Here are the things I brought you.'

'Ooh, lovely,' I murmured, biting my lip as I concentrated on the structure of the baby's head. I was delighted that Ben's mother had brought the food, but wanted to get my drawing done.

Natasha cried a little, then stopped. 'Oh, it's wonderful cream cheese,' said Mrs Mandel, inhaling from a white paper-bag. 'And the bread, it's so fresh, aah . . . feel it Kate, taste it.' She crooned and thrust a loaf of rye bread towards me. It did smell delicious, but I had a fantasy of chanting 'It's lovely, it's lovely, it's wonderful, it's wonderful, it's marvellous,' over and over like an automaton.

Natasha cried again, this time in earnest. Reluctantly I slammed my book shut, and fetched a nappy and clean nightie. Mrs Mandel watched me beadily, then she grasped her clucking grand-daughter. 'Oh,' she gasped, almost vacuum-cleaning the baby's cheek with a kiss. 'I could eat her!' Queen Kong and I watched her uneasily, hating that cannibalistic gesture. Mrs Mandel rocked the child and sang a lullaby to her, but the baby yelled louder, and I had to put her in her pram.

I sat on the floor and felt ashamed of my new but already filthy kitchen and empty larder. I hoped that Mrs Mandel wouldn't have cause to go into our messy bedroom with unmade bed, unpacked boxes, and clothes scattered everywhere on the carpetless floor. I knew that she had been hurt by my behaviour, and felt guilty, but at the same time I felt angry that she had disturbed me. We eyed each other; she looked stern.

'Now Kate,' she said, and fleetingly I was reminded of Mr Angelo's most accusing look. 'I want to talk to you, Kate.' With deliberation she removed her hat, gloves and scarf, and laid them beside the food parcels.

'It is time,' said Mrs Mandel, 'that the pair of you stopped this *mishegaasen*. You have a baby now; not just yourselves to think about.'

She stared at me and shook her hatless head in pain and perplexity. 'You must tell Ben to get a proper job. This teaching in an off-beat private school that pays a pittance is not good enough. He must go back into industry. I don't know why he ever left. He could have been on the Board by now. You need proper money. You need to get yourselves a nicer house.'

'But we have . . .'

'You're going to need a garden. You need money for carpets and furniture. You could have a car if he went back to a proper job.'

A decent income, I thought, with Ben in suits and ties, driving a Jaguar, and a house with spacious green lawns and Natasha playing on the grass.

'It might be sensible,' I granted dubiously. 'But it's not possible. He's a writer. He needs to write, I need to paint. That's us.'

Mrs Mandel brushed me aside like a fly.

'If he must write, let him write in his spare time. As a hobby. At least he's got a room now. But you. You're a mother now. A married woman, and now that you've proved yourself and got your Diploma, can't you see that it's time to stop painting and devote yourself properly to your husband and baby? They need you, Kate. And you need to see to your house. It's *meshuga*, the way you live.'

Queen Kong saw a keeper with a net coming through the jungle to put her in a cage.

I looked seriously at my mother-in-law. 'I can't stop. I don't want to stop. Nor does Ben. We want to live this way. And anyway I have a hundred cards to draw by Christmas, and I hope to have an exhibition next summer.'

Mrs Mandel gave a quick flash towards heaven with her eyes, momentarily touched her throat and muttered *Oh veh* to her Maker. I remained silent.

Queen Kong was ruffled momentarily. She wondered uneasily if life might well not be better in a cage as opposed to freedom in the jungle. Especially if Ben had a Jaguar . . .

'I can do without a cup of tea,' said Mrs Mandel, martyred. Silently she got up to go and gathered together her basket, gloves, scarf, hat and umbrella. She paused outside Ben's door and said very loudly:

245

'No, don't disturb him if he's too busy to see me.'

And, as she clattered towards the front door, the phone rang, and we heard Ben answer it.

'Abe! Hello!'

Mrs Mandel and I were transfixed.

After a moment Ben emerged. He greeted his mother with his hand and said, 'Darling, it's Abe. He wants to speak to you.' He was puzzled.

I went to the phone and saw Ben and his mother listen to the ensuing conversation with intense curiosity.

'Hello,' I said.

'Is that you, Kate, darling?'

'Abe! It's great to hear you!' I listened, and shook my head. 'No. It was a girl. We didn't call her Abe.'

Ben bright with hope, was trying to hear what Abe had to say. I nodded at Abe's voice, and felt my eyes grow round in wonderment.

'Seven hundred!' I said dazedly.

'Seven hundred,' Abe confirmed. 'A certain sale. It fills a gap in a Melanesian collection.'

He had found a buyer for the mask.

'He wants to buy the mask for seven hundred . . .' I whispered to Ben, hand over the mouthpiece of the phone. Mrs Mandel said 'Takki,' and made as though to faint. Ben's eyes were popping, so were the gorilla's.

I could see the mask across the hall, hanging on the sitting-room wall. What was Life for? What was Love for? What was Art for? And the mask was full of wormholes anyway. I gulped.

'Tell me again Abe.' He talked fast and persuasively. I looked from Ben to the mask to the baby in the pram. I wanted them all.

'Go on,' urged Mrs Mandel, her hat nodding feverishly. 'Tell him yes, of course.' My mind was made up.

'Abe,' I said, 'I'm not selling it. I want to keep it.'

'O.K., darling,' he said easily. 'I understand. You may be sorry. But I do understand.'

'Maybe I will be sorry,' I granted. We talked a little more, and I put down the receiver, and turned to my stunned husband and aghast mother-in-law. Her eyes were round with horror. She searched behind her for a chair, and sank down shakily.

'Do you mean to tell me that you just said no to seven hundred pounds?'

Ben was looking at me quizzically.

'Yes. I said no.' I wanted to giggle.

'But you need money,' said Mrs Mandel. 'You need carpets, you have none. You need furniture . . . a car . . .'

'It is an awful lot of money, darling,' said Ben. His voice was mild, and I caught the ghost of a smile.

'It's a beautiful mask,' I said. 'We like it.'

Ben looked across at it. 'Yes, we do.' He nodded benignly.

Mrs Mandel fanned herself with her gloves.

'I do not understand you. Either of you,' she said weakly.

'You don't have to,' said Ben gently.

'You're *meshuga,* the pair of you.'

She rose dazedly to go, clutching basket, umbrella, gloves and handbag, and exited, clucking and shaking her head painedly. Tasha woke up and cried and I stood on the doorstep with her in my arms, watching Ben walk his mother to the bus. He was gesticulating dramatically.

Queen Kong suddenly appeared at my side. She had taken the mask down from the wall, and was wearing it on her head. She looked spectacular, with her hairy body, topped by the great carved face, with its dignity of wooden feathers.

247

'For God's sake!' I hissed, 'Put it back! That's worth a lot of money!'

She danced on the doorstep in circles, humming. Teasingly.

'Go!' I hissed again. 'Ben's coming.'

She wiggled the head at me, and glided balletically backwards into the house as Ben reached our railings.

'Well?' he said.

'Well?' I challenged.

'I don't think she'll ever get over that one.'

'And you?'

'It's nice to know that we've got something worth so much money on the wall. We might need it one day; and anyway, it'll be worth more next year.'

'Are we mad?'

He nodded vehemently. 'No doubt about it.' He took the baby from me and nuzzled her.

We smiled at each other, and went into the sitting-room and looked at the mask on the wall; we danced a strange sort of mutual Highland Fling together, and ate some of Mrs Mandel's cream cheese. I took out my book to draw him with his dazed, hopeful smile, as he sprawled on the sofa-cushions with our gurgling baby. And he said the drawings of Natasha were fabulous, and his play was almost finished, and it was going to be good. And I saw Queen Kong stretched luxuriously out along the marble mantelpiece, her head resting on one paw, whilst with the other she toasted us all with a small bottle of Government orange juice.

'*Lechaim,*' she said. 'Or as some say, *Skål.*'

248

If you have enjoyed this book and would like to receive
details of other Piatkus publications please write to

Judy Piatkus (Publishers) Limited
Loughton
Essex

HINST.